Deeper Than Secrets

Deeper Than Love, Book 3

...

I0553948

EMMA ASHE

This is a work of fiction. Similarities to real people, places,
or events are entirely coincidental.

...

DEEPER THAN SECRETS
First edition. February 21, 2019.

Written by Emma Ashe
www.emmaashe.com/books[1]

ALSO BY EMMA ASHE

Deeper Than Love
Deeper Than Desire, Prequel[1]
Deeper Than Destiny, Book 1[2]
Deeper Than Lies, Book 2[3]
Deeper Than Secrets, Book 3[4]
Deeper Than Temptation, Book 4[5]

An Indecent Apposal
Something Real, Prequel[6]
Show Me Your Secrets, Book 1[7]
Claiming The Secretary, Book 2[8]
Second Chance Romance, Book 3[9]
All For Her, Book 4[10]
Better With You, Book 5[11]
Anyone But You, Book 6[12]
...

1. http://www.emmaashe.com/books/deeper

2. http://www.emmaashe.com/books/deeper

3. http://www.emmaashe.com/books/deeper

4. http://www.emmaashe.com/books/deeper

5. http://www.emmaashe.com/books/deeper

6. http://www.emmaashe.com/books/apposal

7. http://www.emmaashe.com/books/apposal

8. http://www.emmaashe.com/books/apposal

9. http://www.emmaashe.com/books/apposal

10. http://www.emmaashe.com/books/apposal

11. http://www.emmaashe.com/books/apposal

12. http://www.emmaashe.com/books/apposal

An Indecent Apposal Volume 1, Books 1-3[13]
An Indecent Apposal Volume 2, Books 4-6[14]
...
An Indecent Apposal Collection 1, Books 1-6[15]

Get notified of new releases & free reads:
www.emmaashe.com/signup[16]

---

13. http://www.emmaashe.com/books/apposal-set

14. http://www.emmaashe.com/books/apposal-set

15. http://www.emmaashe.com/books/apposal-set

16. http://www.emmaashe.com/signup

ACKNOWLEDGMENTS

As always, I wouldn't be anywhere without some of the greatest writers I know. Thank you Skylar Hill and CiCi Coughlin.

DEDICATION

For Tony

CHAPTER 1 | Holly

I think part of me knew Beau was up to no good even before our newest groom came running to get me. I was sitting on the bleachers, watching for our sales horse to be led in for auction and doing Beau's emails while I waited. In fact, I was almost done when I heard boots pounding down the aisle. I looked up and spotted Maisy heading straight for me, eyes nearly bugging out of her head.

"Holly," she gasps when she reaches me. "He's at it again."

I frown. 'It' is drinking, and technically, Beau hasn't stopped long enough to be at it *again*. He's more like...at it *still*.

And as his personal assistant, it's my job to stop him. Or try. Honestly, over the past two months, I haven't been that successful, but I give Maisy my best "I got this" smile and slip Beau's smart phone into my bag. "Where is he?"

She swallows. "The bar."

Of course he is, I think, trying to keep from grimacing. Appearances are important and I can feel about a dozen sets of eyes following me as I stride through the bleacher seating and take the stairs to the top walkway.

Of all the flipping places for him to have a meltdown, I think, *did it have to be here?*

Here being Atlanta's inaugural Southeast Sporthorse Auction. It's being put on by my best friend's boyfriend, Caleb Reese. He's the manager/owner/brainchild behind Jacks or Better Farm. It's also being endorsed by Adele Mar, the billionaire heiress who happens to be my boss *and* Beau's boss.

Not that Beau ever acts like he remembers it.

I spot Beau trailing through the crowd, a drink in each hand. Somehow I doubt this was what Caleb had in mind when he organized the auction's themed out food and drink menus. Then again, I wouldn't necessarily put it past him. Caleb's girlfriend is *also* employed by Adele Mar and if Caleb thought he could move Beau out of the way so Ellie could take the top rider spot, he'd do it.

Honestly, I don't think there's much Caleb wouldn't do for Ellie and if I didn't love her so much, I would be jealous as hell.

"How can you walk in those things?" Maisy whispers as we work our way through the crowd.

"These?" I peer down at my shoes. They're vintage red platform sandals and I love them. Love. Them. I'm a firm believer they go with everything, but Maisy doesn't look like she agrees. "Oh, walking in heels just takes practice. I wore them a lot for my last job. Heels, mini-skirts, I wore this see through top once that everyone loved—it was considered normal."

Maisy pales and I realize how that must sound. "I worked for a fashion designer in New York," I explain.

"Oh. I thought you'd always worked for Mrs. Mar."

"Nah, just for the last few months. I'm...rebuilding."

Which is a tactful way of saying I'm figuring out my life since the design company I worked for went under.

"Rebuilding?" Maisy looks at me in confusion again, but before I can explain the crowd thins and I spot Beau by the railing behind the bleachers. He's staring down into the auction paddock, consumed with the horses and oblivious to the stir he's creating all around him—wives sliding him sideways glances, husbands getting annoyed at their sideways glances, and excited fans struggling to get the courage to come talk to him.

I stifle a sigh. I get it. Even if he weren't a two-time showjumping gold medalist, Beau Kent is easy on the eyes. Over six feet with a lean build and panty-dropping smile, he looks like trouble.

Mostly because he is.

"Can you go get my car?" I ask Maisy, one hand deep in my purse as I search for my keys. "It's parked in the A lot. First row."

Maisy pales. "I can't drive stick."

I stifle another sigh. "Remind me to teach you. Why don't you go check on Mrs. Mar, see if she needs anything?"

The poor girl whirls away, more than happy to leave me to wrangle Beau alone. I don't really blame her. When Maisy signed on as a Twelve Oaks groom and exercise rider, she was expecting to learn from the once-upon-a-time Number One rider in the world. I should specify she expected to learn riding, not whether he's about to black out.

Ahead of me, Beau weaves further on, studying the horse being led in a circle below. The auction has been going on for two hours now, horses selling at a steady and pricey clip. The four-year-old being presented now is approaching fifty thousand and the bids are still climbing. I've been around the horse world my whole life and it still blows my mind that some people have that kind of money.

I sidle up to Beau, bracing one hip against the railing so I can lean close to him. He smells like whisky, and his skin has a clammy sheen. "We're leaving."

Unsurprisingly, he ignores me.

"Hey," I say, thumping his arm hard. It makes his drink shake and I pause. I've never seen him this bad before. Beau is usually a friendly drunk, the kind you meet at late night parties. This is...different. Worse. "We're leaving," I repeat. "Dump the whisky."

"Don't talk to me like that. I'm your boss."

"Nooooo," I tell him. "Mrs. Mar is my boss. *You* are my project. You're like a spreadsheet that has to be updated."

Slowly, Beau turns to me, brown eyes narrowed to slits. "Spreadsheet?"

"Would you rather be a pie chart?" I pretend to think. "A PowerPoint presentation?"

He scowls, the Beau Kent equivalent of a Care Bear stare. It causes most women to fall all over themselves. Thankfully, I am not most women.

"You know that doesn't work on me," I say.

A deeper scowl, but when I don't start taking my clothes off or try to take his clothes off, he turns back to the horses, passing one shaky hand over his mouth and drawing my attention to his lean, bare forearms.

Usually, Beau always wears long sleeves. They hide the tattooed scripts that run up his forearms and (rumor has it) across his chest. Other guys go for barbed wire or naked women. Beau went for the names of his greatest horses and the dates of his greatest wins. They wind like veins across his skin and whenever I see them, I have the urge to trace each line with my fingertips.

Or maybe my tongue.

Like I said, Beau Kent is trouble.

"I'm not leaving," he tells me at last, eyes still tracking the horses below us even as he takes another swallow of whisky. "I have something I need to do."

Suspicion makes me tense. "Like *what?*"

I follow his gaze, and my stomach curdles. He isn't watching the sale at all. He's watching Dell Landers. The thickset businessman is sitting in the stands with a small group of people, enjoying lunch and the horses.

"Beau..." I trail off. I have no idea what to do with this. Dell owned one of Beau's horses, Arch, an up and coming Grand Prix showjumper who dropped dead a year ago.

While Beau was *riding* him.

He'd been pinned underneath the poor animal, suffering a head injury, cracked ribs, and a broken back. Everyone called it a horrific accident, but Beau's been muttering that it was intentional for *months*. He thinks Dell's groom, George Parish, killed the horse so Dell could collect the insurance money.

And as I watch, a wiry, dark-haired man joins Dell's party. Yep, that's Parish. This is going from bad to worse. I try to edge around Beau to get his attention. "Beau? What do you think you need to do?"

He drops his drink onto the concrete and hurls himself forward, striding straight down the steps for Dell.

Oh shit, I think, tearing after him. *He's going to start a fight!*

"Beau?" I catch up and grab his shirt with both hands. "No! Stop it!"

He shakes me off, and I stumble. "Beau!"

Too late. Two more steps and he's right in Dell's face, Beau jams a finger into the other man's meaty shoulder. "Buying something else to kill?"

"Excuse me?" Dell's face flushes bright red. "What did you say to me?"

"You heard me."

Dell's friends begin to shuffle around. No one knows what to do—including me. How do I play this off?

You can't, I think, planting myself firmly in between the two men. Heat radiates off Beau. I can feel it right through the back of my T-shirt. "Sorry, Mr. Landers. He's...not well."

"The fuck I'm not."

Dell jerks his jacket back into place, and behind him, Parish smirks. "Get him away from me now," Dell snaps. "If he can't speak respectfully, he can leave."

"Of course." I back up a step, trying to force Beau to move. He doesn't. "We were just leaving."

"I know what you had Parish do," Beau says to Dell, moving around me. I yank on his arm, but it makes zero difference. Beau leans into Dell like he wants to kill him, and the older man's eyes widen when he sees it. "Beau! *Please!*"

He jerks. "This doesn't concern you," he says, cutting me a dark glance.

I give him another yank. "If you can't think about yourself then think about Mrs. Mar," I whisper and to my utter relief *that* actually does it.

Beau steps back, his arm brushing my shoulder. He's shaking and for a second I think it's from the exertion and the booze, but then I see his clenched jaw. He's not sick.

He's furious.

I swallow, tugging him toward me. "I'm sorry, Mr. Landers," I say. "It won't happen again."

"You better see that it doesn't." Dell tugs at his jacket again, face almost purple with fear and fury. "And don't think I won't talk to Adele about this."

I wouldn't expect any less, I think, steering Beau up the stairs. He's moving funny, disjointed almost. All the booze must've finally caught up with him. Briefly, pity tugs at me and then I notice a couple of reporters whispering to each other. So not good. This will end up on one of the gossip sites for sure.

Beau stumbles, curses, and stalks on. He's oblivious. Wish I could say I was the same. Forget the snatched glances and subtle looks from earlier, *everyone's* staring now. My skin crawls as we leave. I'm really not sure how much more of this I can take.

CHAPTER 2 | Beau

I lean against Holly's ancient Bronco while she rummages around inside, sneaking glances at me through the window. She thinks I'm drunk. Hell, between the swaying and the uneven walk, I look drunk. But I'm not. It's the pain.

It's been a year since the accident. I'm supposed to be getting better, and I'm not. My hands are almost always numb. My back almost always feels like it's on fire. I can't ride. I can't sleep—or I can't unless I drink.

In fact, if I drink enough, I don't see Arch anymore. I don't feel that sickening impact when his body hit the ground and I followed.

Freak accident, everyone said. Undiagnosed heart condition, everyone said. But all that matters is he was my horse, and he died under me.

And I know his owner had something to do with it.

I roll both hands into fists, remembering how Dell's face had looked when I yanked him close. He was scared—and not just of me. His eyes kept skittering around, looking at anyone who might be listening. He had Parish kill Arch for the insurance money. He knows it. I know it.

Now I just have to prove it before he destroys another defenseless animal.

"Hi, Beau!" The voice is lilting and unmistakably southern. I turn, spotting one of my former clients walking through the parking lot, heading for the auction.

I lift one hand, nod. Once, she would've stopped to talk. She would've wanted to be seen with me. Kind of sucks to be reminded again that I'm well past worth being seen with, but whatever.

More people are coming in for the afternoon sales listings. I recognize a fair number of them too. Riders, trainers, some very wealthy owners. This is my world.

Was my world?

My cell rings and I pat my pockets for a couple seconds before I remember Holly has my phone. I hold out a hand for it, and she rolls her eyes.

"As *if*," she hisses at me, answering it herself. "This is Holly...no, he can't come to the phone. Can I take a message?"

Holly bends down to grab a stack of fabric from her passenger seat, and I can't take my eyes off her ass. God, she annoys me. She's uptight, rides *my* ass like she stole it, and I have never wanted to fuck a woman more in my life.

Which, honestly, annoys me even more.

Holly says something about 'no problem' and 'we'll get back to you,' and stands up, motioning for me to get into the Bronco. With those heels on, we're almost eye level. If I ever do get a chance to fuck her, I'm going to leave the heels on and revel in it every time they dig into my back.

"What?" Holly brushes a fringe of blonde hair out of her eyes. "What are you thinking about?"

"You don't want to know."

"If you're going to be sick, do it out here. I don't get hazard pay."

"What if I can't help it?" I give her my laziest grin. "What if I get sick *on* you? Accidents happen, sweet."

"I'm not your 'sweet,' and if you puke on me, I will punch you in the ear. Got it?"

She'd do it too. I look her up and down, deliberately taking my time to garner maximum annoyance. Unfortunately, it only makes me even more aware of how those curvy hips look in her skirt, how perfect her breasts look in that T-shirt.

Holly's always coming up with something interesting to wear. Gotta admit, I don't really get the whole worn T-shirt with the formal pencil skirt and sky-high heels thing, but I like the effect. She gravitates toward fabrics I want to touch.

I ease into the Bronco's passenger seat while Holly stalks around to the other side. She cranks the engine, blasting us with hot air as the retro-fitted AC begins to work. She shifts into reverse and then stops, both hands on the wheel and eyes focused on the windshield. "Beau?"

"Yeah?"

"Do you really think Dell Landers had something to do with your horse's death?"

"I know he did." I pause, another wave of pain washing over me. I moved too fast on those steps and it's catching up with me. "I just can't prove it."

Yet.

"That isn't something you can just go around saying," she whispers. "I mean, that's a serious allegation and he's your boss's childhood friend. They owned that horse together. If you're saying Dell did something like that, you're basically saying she would've known, and after everything Mrs. Mar has done...I mean..."

She trails off unable to say, *After everything Mrs. Mar has done for you.* Or maybe even *After all the money Mrs. Mar has spent on you.* Either—both—would be accurate. Not many broken down riders get kept on by their sponsors, but after twenty some years of working together, Adele and I are practically family. She's let me recover, kept me on the payroll, and hasn't even brought up riding.

Probably because, like everyone else in the horse world, she thinks as soon as I'm healed, I'm headed straight for the top again.

Holly pauses, waiting for me to say something and when I don't, she gives up, steering the Bronco out of the parking space. I stare out the window, flexing my hands over and over again in the exercises the doctors taught me. The joints catch, shooting pain up my forearms. By the time we've hit the main road, I stop. There's no point—not with the exercises, not with pretending I'll eventually get better. Arch is gone. I'm not healing. I'm not going to ride anymore.

Actually, that's not accurate: I won't be able to ride at the level I did and international showjumping? Being number one in the world? It's everything I've ever wanted, everything I've worked for.

If I lose that, what will be left of me?

CHAPTER 3 | Holly

We get back to Twelve Oaks in time to see Ellie finish exercising Beckon. The pretty, dark mare gallops around the arena like the huge jumps are nothing and Ellie's grin is practically wrapped around her head.

"They look good," I say to Beau.

He doesn't respond, and I can't tell if it's because he isn't speaking to me or if he's worried because they *do* look good. Ellie won her first Grand Prix two months ago. The mare jumped like she had wings, and people are already whispering about how the pair will win championships and Olympic gold—all the things they used to whisper about Beau.

Thanks to his accident, he's been stuck on the sideline for a year now. He hasn't been able to ride, hasn't been able to compete. It flamed his international standing. He was number one in the world. I think he's around the sixty-something mark now and with every passing competition, he falls further and further down.

I angle the Bronco into a parking spot between two of the Twelve Oaks work trucks and Beau gets out, walking off toward the paddocks. Part of me wonders if I should follow him. He's not right. I don't think he's totally wasted, but he isn't himself either.

The rest of me remembers that I have a metric ton of work now, thanks to him. That last call I took for him was from the farm vet. He didn't process her invoices and now we're behind. Plus, Beau was supposed to review the client schedules today, but I clearly that's not happening—which means I'll have to do it.

My cell buzzes, and I glance at the screen, part of me hoping it's my other best friend, Parker, *finally* calling me back, but it isn't. It's Scott. Again. We've been arguing for months now about whether I'm going to return to New York to find another job. I say I can't return until I have something firm lined up. He says I should just come anyway because everything will work out. We've been arguing about it ever since.

Scott was my *first* nightmare boss. Thrust onto the international fashion scene after being discovered in a reality television show, he burned up runways, reviews, and assistants. Scott would describe himself as exacting. Everyone else describes him as a pain in the ass. Technically, both descriptions are correct.

After design school, I went to work for him, learning everything I could about the fashion industry. I wanted to start my own dress line—I still do—but life had other plans and the company we worked for went bankrupt. Scott had savings to fall back on, but I had to come home.

I send him to voicemail and hop out of the Bronco, my heels sinking into the finely ground gravel. A smarter move would've been to wear boots, but I was running late this morning and forgot my change of clothes.

"Holly?" a voice calls. "Can we talk?"

I freeze. Mrs. Mar. She doesn't sound angry, but I'm sure Dell Landers has already called. I shoulder my bag and plaster on a smile. "Sure thing!"

She's waiting for me just inside the arched stable entrance. It might be October, but we're in the south and that means temps are still hovering in the low eighties. I'm actually a little sweaty, but Mrs. Mar looks pristine in her white collared shirt and dove gray breeches.

"Office?" she asks, tilting her head. Sunlight catches on her high cheekbones and almost black hair, and briefly, I see a glimpse of the beautiful young woman she must've been behind the stately woman she is now.

"Sure," I say, following her past rows of stained wood and brass horse stalls. The Twelve Oaks office is just off the tack room, a sunny, whitewashed space that always smells like high end leather and Chanel perfume since Mrs. Mar spends so much time in here. She reviews the farm's accounting herself, and often takes work calls here, watching her horses play in their paddocks through the huge picture window.

As I close the door, Mrs. Mar takes a seat at the antique desk, glancing over some paperwork while I get settled. I drop into the closest armchair—a fluffy, overstuffed thing by the window—and curl my legs under me.

"How's Beau doing?" Mrs. Mar asks.

I take a moment to consider my response. There's a lot I could say here: He's not doing well at all. He's drunk. He's an ass. Honestly, any of those answers would be accurate, but I hold back. "He's having another bad day," I say finally.

She nods, biting her lower lip and looking out the office window. A breeze brushes through the flowers and they wave, tapping the glass. "I heard. Emily called."

I swallow. Emily is the head of Etoile Saddlery, one of the premiere saddleries in the world. Beau's been one of their sponsored riders for years. He's photographed all the time with their saddles and bridles—or he used to be.

"She's not going to renew his contract," Mrs. Mar continues. "She doesn't approve of his behavior outside the show ring. That will make the third sponsor he's lost this year. At the rate he's going..." She trails off, refusing to say what we both know: at the rate Beau's going, Mrs. Mar is going to be the only person still by his side. "I don't know what to do," she says.

That makes two of us, I think. I don't know what to say so I decide to go for bracing honesty: "He believes Mr. Landers killed Arch. "He admits he doesn't have proof, but he still believes it happened."

Mrs. Mar swallows and glances away again. I don't blame her. Mr. Landers and Mrs. Mar grew up together. Although Mr. Landers found Arch in the beginning, Mrs. Mar was also a part owner with him and, of course, it was *her* rider, Beau, who competed the horse.

I can't imagine what she thinks of the allegations. When Arch died, they both collected insurance money, which means Beau's accusations reflect on her as well.

She sighs. "I've told him again and again Dell had nothing to do with it. Parish works for Dell. He just happened to be walking by when Arch started thrashing, and he went into the stall to check on him. It's what any good horseman would do—but that's not to say I haven't heard the rumors. Everyone has. Dell's been in financial difficulties for some time. Then again, that doesn't make him an animal torturer."

I nod. I totally agree and she's completely right, but worry still clouds her expression and for a half a heartbeat, I wonder if she knows something more than she's saying.

"I'm going to have to keep them apart for a while longer, I guess," Mrs. Mar says.

"Probably for the best." The way Beau looked at Dell...I shudder. I don't want to think about what would've happened if I hadn't been there. Maisy and I thought Beau was just drinking and blowing off steam, but he wasn't. He was lying in wait for the other man.

"Well," Mrs. Mar says brightly, bringing both hands together. It makes her gold bracelets wink in the sunlight. "I think we need to focus on what we can do. How are we going to fix this?"

I blink. "Mrs. Mar...no one can fix him because he doesn't want to be fixed." I pause. "Maybe he needs rehab. Maybe he just needs a wake-up call, but you need to find another rider. I know how this ends."

"Really?" She arches a manicured brow. "I thought this was going rather well. You've lasted longer than any of his other assistants."

I try for a non-committal nod. I bet none of his other assistants ever talked to him like I do either. Beau has pretty much been an equestrian phenom since he was seventeen or eighteen, and he's ridden for Mrs. Mar since he was fourteen because she spotted his talent so early. From what I understand, Beau's taste in personal assistants ran to starry-eyed fangirls.

Which I am certainly not.

"Holly," she begins, leaning a little forward. "I know you're not seeing Beau in his best light, but I promise you he's going to come through this."

I give her another non-committal nod. Mrs. Mar's commitment to Beau borders on fanatic. She's said in several interviews he's like a son to her, but I think it runs deeper than that—they share a passion for horses and show jumping. Mrs. Mar will never ride like Beau rides, but by sponsoring him, she can experience it through him.

"Furthermore," Mrs. Mar continues, "I need him to keep it together until my company's board meeting. My new charity organizations are on the line, and I need them approved."

I wince. That's not good. One of those charities happens to be an equestrian outreach program. It's designed to bring in kids from impoverished areas and let them experience horses and the outdoors. I'd hate to see it get torpedoed because Beau can't get his crap together.

Mrs. Mar levels me a grim look. "I need you to make it happen."

I consider her for a moment, comments like "And people in hell want ice water" flitting through my head.

She smiles like she knows exactly what I'm thinking. "I know it's easy to think this is simply a hobby for me, but it's more complicated than that. I run my farms like businesses. They may be a labor of love, but they're still *businesses*—and moreover, they reflect my family's real business. I can't have Beau melting down in public. It's bad for him and it's bad for the farm's image—my family's image."

I nod. I get it. In fact, I've seen the articles on Noelle Floyd's website and in the *Chronicle of the Horse* magazine. It wasn't pretty before I came on and it hasn't been much better since. Beau's imploding and it feels like the whole world is watching and *judging*.

She studies me. "Moreover, the company's board won't approve additional charity funding if they don't think I'm on top of things. We need to look in control. We need to *be* in control." She pauses. "So what do you recommend?"

"He's not going to get better until he decides to get better. You should find another rider."

"You mean I should fire him."

I squirm. It's exactly what I mean, but saying it out loud is awful.

Mrs. Mar skims one hand over her smooth chignon. "I have another idea. If you can get him through the board meeting and the charity program announcements, I'll bonus you twenty thousand dollars."

My heart double thumps. That would be enough to start my dress line.

That would be enough to start my *life*.

"What do you think?"

"I think you have a deal."

CHAPTER 4 | Beau

I meet Charlie down by the lower barn. Usually, we keep newly-arrived horses here for quarantine or client horses if there isn't room at the main barn. Today, Charlie's down there with Adele's retired gelding, Ace. They both look up as I slide the heavy doors open, casting a wide wedge of sunlight across the brick floor.

Charlie glances at his watch. "You're early. Weren't you supposed to stay at the auction until later?"

"Something came up."

Charlie nods like this makes perfect sense. For him, it probably does. Lanky and dark-haired, Charlie mostly survives on coffee and beef jerky. He takes a weekend off *maybe* once a quarter, but when he does, he comes back four days later smelling like perfume and beer. If you ask him what happened, he'll just shrug and say, "Life, man."

"Hey, Ace," I say. The dark brown gelding nickers at me, and sniffs my pockets for treats. I unwrap a peppermint and give it to him. "Did you bring his tack?"

"Yeah. Over there." Charlie nods toward a saddle and bridle tucked into a corner, waiting for me. "Explain to me again why we can't do this up at the arena."

I pick up a saddle pad and smooth it across the gelding's back. "Because everyone at the farm will effing show up to watch, and I'm pretty sure I know how this is going to go, and I don't want witnesses."

"But you'll let me. I'm honored."

"Don't be. You'll get to call nine-one-one if it goes worse than I think."

Charlie curses a blue streak under his breath. "It's an honor and privilege working for you, you know that?"

I grin at him. Charlie's an ass, but since I have also been called an ass from time to time, we get along. Plus, he's an amazing groom. I hired him a few years before the accident. He was with me at my last Olympics. Other people might not like him, but my horses do and that's always been good enough for me.

I place the saddle on Ace's back and tighten his girth, ignoring the twinges in my hands. They don't mean anything. They *don't*. I can always get help saddling and un-saddling. It's the riding that's the important part.

"So what's the deal?" Charlie asks as we walk Ace to the other end of the barn so I can get on. There's a grass arena just beyond the paddocks. It's shady and private. "When did the doc clear you for riding?"

"She didn't." I check the girth one more time before pulling my stirrups down to mount.

Charlie watches me, still scowling. "You fall off Ace I'm telling everyone."

"I'm not actually worried about falling off." Even with the pain and numbness, I know I can stay on a dead quiet horse. It's how I *feel* sitting on that dead quiet horse that worries me.

I lift my left foot to the stirrup, find my grip, and swing into the saddle, landing softer than I thought I would.

Okay, I think. *Not bad so far.* Ace flicks one ear back, patiently waiting for me to get my act together. I gather up the reins, threading them clumsily through my numb fingers as my other foot finds its stirrup.

"Ready?" Charlie asks.

I nod, squeezing my calves into Ace's sides. He obediently moves off, ears pricked, heading toward the arena like we do this every day. Gotta love a horse that knows his job. I concentrate on moving with his stride as we walk under the stretch of oaks lining the fence line.

It almost feels...normal. I've been riding since I was three, competing since I was six, and have probably logged tens of thousands of hours on horseback. Sitting up on Ace is like coming home.

It's also aggravating my hip. I ignore the flashes of pain, and as we turn into the grass arena, I ease Ace into a trot. The flashes turn to sickening pangs and I grit my teeth.

If I can't manage this on Ace, I'm in serious trouble, I think and immediately shove the thought away, concentrating on circling back and forth around the arena. After a few minutes, the pain subsides into twinges again and I decide to push it.

I ask for a canter. Ace's shoulders lift as his hind legs come under, lifting us into the canter. The energy rides right up my spine with lightning. Briefly, my vision wobbles.

Most horses have a twelve foot canter stride—meaning they can move twelve feet forward with one step. Some horses are larger, some are smaller, but most jump courses are created with that twelve foot stride in mind.

The extravagant movers are wonderful to watch and even more fun to ride, but they're hard on you too. You have to absorb all that swing and power through your core. And at the moment, I have no core. I have no back. I can't feel his mouth. I can't...I just can't.

I pull up under a patch of shade and rub my right hand until black spots flash before my eyes. It isn't supposed to do that anymore. The numbness should be gone by now. The pain should be a memory.

My mouth goes sour like I might be sick. I can't ride like this. I need my hands, my legs, my back. Riding is all about communication. It's weight and pressure and *feel* and right now, I don't feel much of anything.

I walk back to Charlie and swing down from Ace. I pat his shoulder, and he bumps me with his nose, reminding me that pats are fine, but peppermints are better.

"Yeah, yeah," I say, fumbling as I unwrap another and give it to him. Charlie watches us without saying a word. Then again, he doesn't need to. We both know how that just went, and we untack Ace in silence.

"I'll turn him out," Charlie says at last, taking the gelding's lead rope from me. "Can you take his stuff back?"

"Yeah."

"Hey, Beau?" Charlie hesitates, mouth pressing into a pale line. "I asked around about Landers."

Everything in me stills. "And?"

"You were right: he didn't pay off his debts until after cashing Arch's insurance check. And you're also not the only person who saw Parish coming out of Arch's stall."

"Who else saw?"

Another hesitation. Charlie looks at me like I'm some sort of stranger.

"Who else *saw*?"

"Kat Bowman. She works for the Fisher family. They were stabled just up the row from us."

Blood thumps in my ears. "And she didn't say anything? What the hell?"

"What's she supposed to say? You're the only one who thinks something went down with Arch."

I hoist the saddle up, balancing it on one arm. "I'll talk to her."

"She won't tell you anything more. I tried. She likes her job. What you're digging for...it's serious shit, Beau."

"No kidding. An animal *died* because Dell Landers killed him for the money. I was riding him and now my career's—you know, what? Forget it." I give Ace one last pat before turning away, walking straight through the lower barn and back into the sunlight. It should make me feel better, but my chest won't loosen.

At the top of the hill, Ellie leads another one of our young horses to the mounting block and hops on. She points him toward the jump arena and he jigs underneath her. I rebalance Ace's saddle in one arm and sling his bridle over my other shoulder, watching them. The young horse is a half-brother of Arch, fully owned by Adele. They look like bookends, almost identical down to the flashy white stockings and rich chestnut coats, and for a second, I feel like someone's punched me in the gut.

It's like looking at everything I lost and for another second, I hate her. Unreasonable? Yeah. Asshole-y? Definitely. I like Ellie. She's a great rider and she's only going to get better with time and experience, but right now? Right now, she can still ride and jealousy nearly drops me.

And rage. I *knew* Dell needed that check to pay off his barn bills—and if he couldn't afford his hobby, I'm damn sure he couldn't afford some of his business ventures. I bet those were paid off with blood money as well and I'm going to prove it. Just because this Kat woman can look the other way doesn't mean I will. I need to track her down, talk to her, and—

"Beau!"

My back teeth click together. Holly. She sounds pissed too. I look up, spotting her coming around the side of the barn, loose blond hair streaming behind her.

"What?" I ask.

She stomps closer, eyes skittering over the saddle and bridle and then swinging to my face. She's curious what I'm up to. If she asks, I'm going to tell her I need them for my date tonight.

I brush past her, heading inside the barn to hang up the saddle and bridle. The grooms scatter as we walk down the aisle. Clearly, my little episode at the auction has already reached them and they figure Holly's about to finish chewing me out.

"Can I have a word?" she asks when we reach the tack room.

"Do I have a choice?" I hang the saddle on Ace's rack and give Holly my laziest smile, the one that usually annoys her the most.

She smirks, and there's something about it that runs chills down my spine. She's up to something, and I don't think I'm going to like it.

"I have great news for you," she says.

"Oh yeah?" She's close enough I can smell her perfume—the lightest mix of flowers—and catch myself taking a deep breath of it. "What's the great news?"

"I'm moving in with you."

CHAPTER 5 | Holly

Beau's mouth opens, closes then opens again. Nothing comes out and I nearly laugh. I like the Speechless Look on him.

And knowing I gave it to him? Even better.

"What the hell?" he finally manages. A groom walks by the tack room, glancing in at us, and Beau slams the door in his face. "What are you talking about?" he asks me.

"I'm moving in with you," I repeat, stepping closer. He backs up, eyes wide. I have him pinned against the door now. "You can't be trusted to behave yourself until the company's board meeting so I'm going to stick around and make sure you do."

"By moving in with me?"

"It's the only solution. You aren't going to make it otherwise."

More mouth gaping. Without taking his eyes off me, Beau stomps around me and hangs up a bridle on Ace's hook.

What's he doing with that anyway? I wonder and squash the urge to ask. Odds are very good I don't want to know.

"Are you *nuts?*"

"Very possibly. But this is happening, Beau. We need you sober and focused for the next two weeks. Since we can't trust you to do it yourself, I'll have to make sure you do. No booze. No outbursts. No groupies."

He straightens. "You move in, it's going to be nothing *but* groupies."

"No way. You bring girls home, I'll kick them out."

"You can't kick people out of my house!"

"Sure I can. All I have to do is walk into your bedroom and go, 'Honey? Who's she?'" I drop my voice so it's breathy and look up at him with wide eyes. It was meant to underscore my point, but now we're sharing the same air. My skin prickles.

"Then," I add, "she'll look at me and I'll look at her and the games will begin."

He actually goes a bit pale under his tan. "You're not kidding. You'd really do it."

"In. A. Heartbeat." This close, I can feel the heat of him. His eyes drop to my mouth, and I swallow. I can't help it.

"Interesting," he breathes.

"Not really." I pull away. "Living with you for the next two weeks is not my idea of a good time."

That sort of comment usually gets a rise out of him, but Beau's notably silent. He stares at me. I stare at him.

Then someone knocks on the door. "Holly?"

We both jerk. The tack room door edges open and Ellie sticks her head inside. "Sorry. I forgot my whip." She pauses, gaze swinging from Beau to me and back again. "Everything okay?"

"Peachy," I manage through gritted teeth.

Beau blurts out an impressive string of swear words and flings the door wide, stomping off. I glare at his back, most of me wishing I could kick him, and the rest of me noticing he still isn't moving as fluidly as he should. There's the slightest hitch in his stride.

He should be past that, shouldn't he?

Ellie bounces up to me, her riding boots heavy against the polished wooden floor. "What was that about?"

"I'm moving in with him." And I'm still so busy glaring at Beau's back, it takes me a full minute to realize Ellie's gone completely still and silent. "What?" I ask.

"'What?'" Her dark brows climb another inch higher. "What do you mean 'what'? Have you lost your mind?"

Very possibly, I think, forcing my shoulders to loosen. Being that close to Beau was...disconcerting. I need to avoid letting it happen again. When I move in, I'll have to keep space between us. Lots of space.

And not shave my legs, because if anything will keep from jumping Beau Kent, unshaved legs are *it*.

Not that I'm thinking about jumping him.

"Mrs. Mar offered me a bonus," I explain at last. "But in order to get the bonus, I have to get him on the other side of the company's board meeting without any more scandals."

Ellie picks up her whip from one of the tack trunks, and jams the leather handle into her breeches' back pocket. "Is that even possible?"

"We're about to find out."

We both go silent. "What about your mom?" Ellie asks.

I frown. Thanks to a nasty bout of flu, she hasn't been feeling well and I'm not comfortable leaving her alone. Honestly, even when she's well, I'm kind of not comfortable leaving her alone. I didn't realize until I got back from New York how frail she seems to have gotten.

"It's okay," I say at last. "I'll call Dane and tell him he has to come down." My brother won't be happy about it, but I rarely ask for favors. "I'll make it work," I add.

"I don't know about this, Holls. You can't stop someone from destroying themselves."

I nod. It's so true, and yet somehow, I'm going to have to manage it. "You can survive anything for two weeks."

Ellie blows out a long sigh. "If Parker were here, she'd tell you how crazy this sounds."

Parker would be right, I think. But she *isn't* here. In fact, even though Ellie and I have been best friends with Parks since high school, it's been months and months since she's talked to either of us. She's someone else I worry about.

I shrug. "I think my idea is brilliant."

"It's something alright." Ellie hesitates. "You really need the money, don't you?"

"Yeah." I take a steadying breath, closing my eyes and picturing everything I've dreamed of: my own dress line, my own shop, a future all my own making. "It's a ton of money. It will change *everything* for me—and if I have to make it happen by locking Beau Kent in his room and only letting him out for supervised engagements so be it."

CHAPTER 6 | Beau

I walk all the way back to my place, a mistake because my hip is now throbbing and my hands are shaking.

Too bad it's not enough to distract me from how Holly swallowed when I looked at her mouth. She'd been close enough to kiss and I couldn't help noticing. It's that damn mouth of hers. It's generous and always twitching into a little smirk, or spreading into a smile, or holding back a laugh. I catch myself staring all the damn time.

Of course, I catch myself staring at her ass too.

And her breasts.

And, well, all of her. I walk faster, pain shooting up my leg. Moving in with me is not a good idea. I won't be able to focus for shit.

Another spike of pain hits me and I have to stop. I study the horizon until the urge to vomit passes.

Focus, I tell myself. *The next step is running down Kat Bowman and getting real answers about Parish.*

Parish was one of Dell's grooms. He didn't work specifically with Twelve Oaks horses, but he was seen coming out of Arch's stall an hour before I showed up to ride. He shouldn't have been in there and I've never gotten a clear answer on why he was.

Of course, asking questions like this pretty much goes directly against what Adele wants and now that Holly will be around to babysit me, it'll be even more difficult to get away.

I take a deep breath and start moving again, my hip not protesting as much. Everything in me wants to stomp forward, *run* forward, but I force myself to slow, babying myself for the last twenty yards or so until I reach my porch steps.

It helps. My head clears a bit, but that only brings me back around to Holly moving in. I won't get jackshit done, which I'm sure is the point. I'll have to distract her, but how?

And that's when it hits me: she *might* know I'm affected by her, but I *definitely* know she's affected by me. The way she swallowed. The way her eyes widened.

Mmmm, I think, and in spite of my hip, my dick begins to stir. I scowl. What is my deal with this woman? I'm not exactly a "hit it and quit it" guy, but I don't exactly linger either. There are far too many women who would enjoy being with me for me to see the point in chasing after Holly.

I ease up the porch steps and unlock the stained wood door, letting myself inside. Twelve Oaks has several small staff cottages dotted around the farm and I've been in this one since I joined Adele's staff at eighteen. It's only about twelve hundred square feet, but all the windows and the wraparound porch make it feel larger. If you open everything up, it's like the farm comes inside.

I'm pretty much directly across from the main barn, only separated by the paddocks. It's not as quiet as some of the other cottages, but I like being able to see my horses.

Well, not *my* horses. They're Adele's horses, and sometimes, other clients' horses, but when you spend as much time with them as I do, they start to feel like yours. I don't bond with all of them, but Arch was special. We just...clicked.

Not seeing him galloping around in his paddock, acting like an idiot, still punches me in the chest. It's like I lose all my air. Every time.

I shake it off—or try to—by focusing on my new roommate's arrival. I weave through the living room to the two bedrooms on the other side. Since the cottage was originally designed to house more people, they're separated by an adjoining bathroom, but it's only my stuff in there. I've never had roommates.

Guess that means Holly's crashing in here, I think, opening the door to the unused bedroom. Adele decorated it in soft grays and yellows. It's demure as hell and doesn't fit mini-skirts-and-high-heels-Holly at all.

I lean against the doorframe, rubbing my numb right hand and picturing Holly sleeping in that bed.

Or getting up to come yell at me while I'm in my bed.

I grin and shuffle to the kitchen, helping myself to my meds and coffee spiked with bourbon. Dinner of champions? Not hardly, but it's what passes for meals around here.

I lean against the countertop, staring at the horses grazing in their paddocks and my thoughts keep returning to Holly.

And that damn bed.

Maybe...maybe if I had her, I would finally lose my fascination. The idea turns around and around in my head. Or better yet maybe I could get her on my side?

I have a knack for that—especially after I sleep with a woman. Not sure if it's my dick or their hormones, but it's amazing what women will do for me after we fuck. I don't stick around to test it, mind you, but maybe for Holly, I could make an exception.

A flash of movement up at the barn catches my eye. It's Holly's Bronco. She guns it into reverse and then powers forward. I expect for her to turn toward the property road that leads to my place, but she continues up the driveway, heading for the main highway.

I guess that means I have a little bit of time to get my act together.

Step One: track down Kat Bowman.

Step Two: distract Holly from the fact that I'm tracking down Kat Bowman.

And in spite of the shitstorm that is currently my life, I catch myself smiling.

CHAPTER 7 | Holly

Of course, in order to pull off this whole "staying with Beau thing," I'll need to bring in my brother to check on our mom, and honestly, I'm really dreading the conversation. Dane lives in midtown Atlanta, not so far away as to be another country, but with all the traffic and hours he works, it might as well be. Mom and I are lucky if we see him every few months.

Sometimes I feel like this is my fault. I should reach out more. I should plan more things for us to do. But the last few years have felt awkward, and I keep letting it slip. I think part of me keeps hoping he'll notice, and when he doesn't, my feelings get hurt. Stupid, yes, but I can't seem to stop. Our dad left when we were little. Dane and my mom are all I have.

I swing the Bronco into my driveway and park, staying inside to make the call. If we're going to argue, I don't want Mom to overhear. It would make feel like a chore and she isn't. She's our mom.

But that doesn't stop the whole situation from being hard.

The phone rings once and Dane picks up, the sounds of keyboard typing coming through even before I hear his voice.

"Holls!"

I grin. He actually sounds pleased to see me, and for a second, I feel like we're back to the way we were as kids. Dane is three years older than me. Growing up, I idolized him and he let me tag along everywhere he went. It's some of my favorite memories.

"Hey," I say, tugging loose strands of hair behind my ear. "Did I catch you at a bad time?"

"Sort of. I have to go into a meeting in a few. What's up?"

"I have a work thing going on. Can you come stay with mom for a few days?"

"No. Sorry." His typing speeds up and I can picture him glaring at his computer. We look a lot alike: same blond hair, same eyes, and according to Ellie, we have the same crazed, focused expression when we're in the middle of something. "Work is nuts right now."

I switch the phone to my other ear and pray for patience. "Dane, please. I need the help."

"And I can't give it to you." He gives me the exasperated sigh that always makes me want to reach through the phone and shake him. "I'm working. I can't get away."

I pinch the bridge of my nose, reminding myself to breathe. The thing is, I get it. I get being pulled in so many different directions. I get how hard it is to admit you need to take care of your mind, instead of your mom taking care of you. But I don't usually ask for his help. In fact, I try not to ever bother him and maybe that was a mistake. Now he's far enough removed he can pretend she isn't struggling.

"Listen," I say finally. There's something very close to tears snaking underneath my voice and I can't seem to stop it and it makes me *furious*. I'm not the kind of woman who falls apart. Except with Dane, I guess I am. "I don't ask you for much, but I'm asking you for this: come stay with her. She's still getting over the flu. She needs help and I *need* this job."

"Where are they sending you anyway?" The clackety-clack of his keyboard speeds up again. "I don't understand why a horse groom needs to travel."

"I'm not a groom. I'm an assistant."

"I still don't see why you need to travel."

I frown, looking through my windshield at the graceful water oaks that shade my yard. I am *so* not explaining to my brother what I'm really about to do. "It doesn't matter if you understand, you just need to be here for us."

The clacking slows and relief pours through me. I have him. He'll help me. I had to practically strong arm him to do it, but Mom won't have to be alone and I won't have to worry.

A curtain peels back and a furious cloud of white hair appears. It's my mom. With knobby knees and a penchant for blindingly bright caftans, she's a promise of what I'll eventually be and I kind of love it.

"Do you *want* Mom driving herself to the doctor this week?" I ask. It's my last threat. If he doesn't go for this, I'm screwed. "Because that's what'll happen if I'm not here. Remember the gas station."

Mom's always been an aggressive driver. Jumping curbs and speeding were to be expected, but when she confused the gas and the brake and backed over a gas pump earlier this year, the police got her license revoked.

"God, no!" Dane splutters. "Fine. Just *fine*. I can work remotely from her house, but you have to give me more notice next time."

"Sure. Thanks for doing this," I add, and then wonder why I did. I'm making it sound like he's doing me a favor instead of doing his part to care for our mom.

"I'll talk to you later," Dane says and hangs up. I toss my phone in my purse, waiting to feel happy I've worked everything out...and I don't. Instead, I just feel horribly, *horribly* alone. When you call your brother for help and he agrees, you should feel relieved, but with Dane I just feel worse.

I hop out of the Bronco and slam the door hard enough to make the SUV shake. Mom meets me at the front door, one white brow raised. "Bad day at work?"

"Totally."

"Time for wine," she says, turning unsteadily to lead me into the kitchen. Her electric pink silk caftan swirls around her bony bare legs. Never a curvy woman, she lost even more weight fighting the flu.

"The doctor said no drinking while you're on antibiotics," I remind her.

"Darling, that child doctor can get over it. I endured a week of labor without painkillers. I can have some wine with my meds."

I grin. "It wasn't a week."

"Collectively it was. You *and* your brother. Plus, his head was huge." She grabs the box of wine we keep on the counter—we call it our Cardboardeux—and pours both of us a healthy glass. "Now. Tell me about your day."

I give her the highlights eventually finishing on Mrs. Mar's bonus offer. "It would give me enough to start my dress line. It could jump start...everything." I sneak a glance at her, trying to gauge her reaction. As soon as I do, I wish I hadn't. She's grinning like this is the best thing ever, but her eyes are sad. The hand holding her wine shakes the tiniest bit.

"I think it's a fantastic opportunity," she says. "If anyone can keep him in line, you can."

"Doubtful, but I'm going to try." I pause. "Dane's going to come down and stay for a bit. He can take you to your doctors' appointments, the grocery store, that stuff."

It shouldn't be possible, but her grin actually widens. "How lovely. I'm hosting Bunko this week. I'm going to have a lingerie party—the *nicest* young lady is going to come by with samples we can purchase. Dane can help with snacks."

I wince. I'd forgotten about that. Mom's Bunko club doesn't actually play Bunko. They go to each other's houses, drink, and party. Sometimes this involves Magic Mike-type of movies. Sometimes it involves poker. Last month, Mrs. Harding had hosted some sort of sex toy party, and now Mom had to top it.

"Lingerie," she'd told me after I picked her up. "It'll be the perfect follow up. Plus, you use lingerie way more than you'll ever use half that other stuff. Did you know how many things you can put up your bajingo these days?"

I hadn't, but she'd been happy to tell me.

I watch her over the rim of my wine glass. "Will you be okay while I'm gone?"

She brightens. "Of course, darling, I'm *always* okay."

She sounds completely truthful too, like she's looking forward to it, but I know my mom—I *am* my mom—we always sound truthful, especially when we lie.

***

A few hours later, I sling my overnight bag onto my shoulder and shut the Bronco's door. The afternoon light turns everything pink and gold, and the air smells like fresh cut grass. I take a deep breath, and in spite of everything, feel my shoulders unknot.

Beau's cottage is neatly maintained: close-cropped lawn, squared off box hedges. Since I'm going to be staying here for the next two weeks, I'd like to think it's because he's not a total slob, but I'm sure it's one of the Twelve Oaks' staff who keeps up with the weeds.

The stable sits on the bluff above, the paddocks spreading down and around until they sweep up next to the cottage. A few horses are still outside, playing and grazing. Honestly? The company is going to suck, but the view is beyond lovely.

I walk around Beau's truck, heading for the front path when I spot the horse and man down by the fence line. They're half in and out of shadow, but I can still tell it's Beau. He faces the chestnut, scratching the gelding's shoulder back and forth. After a moment, he stops and the horse sighs. They stand in happy silence.

I stare longer than I should. It's a private moment and I should let him have it, but I can't reconcile the jerk who mows through people with the man standing quietly with this horse now. I've been in the horse industry since I was eight. My mom hired Ellie's dad to teach me and I grew up on the backs of various ponies. I loved them all. Riding was my happy place and even though I rarely hop in the saddle anymore, I still enjoy being around horses.

But I knew at a young age, I was never meant to go professional. My horses were my friends. For professionals, they're a means to an end: a competition win, a paycheck, a livelihood. It isn't cruelty—although it can be—it's reality. But looking at Beau with his horse now, I wonder if there's more to him than I thought.

Like he feels me watching, Beau turns and I'm so busted. He sees me standing by the porch and right before my eyes, he morphs into Beau Kent Olympian Playboy. Everything soft and loose in his body tightens and he gives me a smile that's damn near indecent.

I shiver. I can't help it.

He pats the chestnut on the neck and saunters toward me. "Hey there, roomie," he says, coming close and taking my overnight bag from me like he's some sort of gentleman. His fingertips graze my bare shoulder.

"Welcome home," he whispers, and the whisper walks across my cheek, trailing heat with it.

I swallow suddenly realizing moving in with him might be my worst idea yet.

CHAPTER 8 | Beau

Holly looks up at me through lowered lashes and it makes my mouth go hot. She wants me. I've been stupid about a lot of things in my life, but I'm not imagining this. Ideas about all the ways I'm going to take her whirl through my mind, landing on this: Holly spreading her legs for me. Holly arching her back.

Holly, who has relentlessly ridden my ass for two months, under me.

Screaming my name.

"Stop grinning like that," she says, voice wavering.

I don't. I can't. I actually grin wider—and lean closer. "Why? You seem to like it."

She brushes past me, but not before I see her swallow. It hits me low and I take a moment to watch that gorgeous ass of hers as she climbs my porch steps and lets herself inside.

"Nice," she says, surveying my living room with her hands on her hips. "It's cleaner than I expected."

"You sound surprised." I shut the door and stride ahead of her, ignoring a twinge of pain in my hip. "What did you expect? Beer cans and pizza boxes?"

"And used condoms and passed out heiresses."

"Oh please. Like I'd let them stay the night." I carry her bag to the spare bedroom and toss it on the white painted bench at the foot of her bed. When I come back out, she's hovering by the couch, tugging at the hem of her drapey tank top. She's still wearing that short skirt from earlier and my brain instantly goes to how good it would feel to pull it up and bare her to me. "You're in there," I tell her. "Bathroom's connected."

"And you're...?" Her eyes are already resting on my closed bedroom door.

"In there. Want a tour?"

"No."

Too bad because you're getting one, I think. Then again, it might be even more fun to take her out here. My brain bounces from images of Holly bent over the arm of my couch to Holly sitting on my countertop, pretty legs held wide for me.

Or even better, Holly lying naked on my couch, head in my lap, looking up at me, while I play with her. I could keep her going for hours, keep her right on the edge until she begs me for it.

Shit. The idea makes me instantly hard, and I swallow. My throat clicks.

"So what now, roomie?" I ask, deliberately letting my arm brush hers as I sit down on the couch. "Chick flick? Pillow fight?"

"Cocktail party."

My stomach drops a couple inches. "What?"

"Mrs. Mar's cocktail party?" Holly turns to stand in front of me, hands on her hips. "Did you forget? I sent you an email."

"Never got it."

"I left you a Post-It in the tack room."

"Didn't see it."

"It was *on* your coffee mug."

I shrug. "I have other plans."

"Like what? Drinking spiked coffee by yourself?"

"Well, now that you mention it."

Holly shakes her head. "Not happening. Mrs. Mar *specifically* asked for you to be there. I get you don't care about me, but I *know* you care about her."

I scowl. She's got me there, and she knows it. I've never been able to say no to Adele—or at least not until Arch died.

Holly walks past the couch to check out the kitchen, taking a few minutes to go through my cupboards. For someone who just got here, she's remarkably at ease, going from drawers to shelves and muttering to herself. "Are all horse people this bad about keeping food around?" she asks at last.

I can only assume she means Ellie has my same penchant for cooking—as in, we don't.

Holly opens my fridge, sighs, and closes it. "I can pick up some groceries tomorrow. Anything you don't eat?"

"No." I pause. "Do you cook?"

She nods, looking through a spice rack Adele bought me when I moved in. She holds out a canister of something powdery and shakes it at me. "You do realize these things eventually expire, right?"

Annoyance prickles me. I lean back on the couch, draping my arms along the back. "So what's the deal? Why are you *really* here?

"Oh, gosh, Huckleberry," Holly drawls, expression dead pan. "I just want to see you become the man I always knew could be."

Another flash of annoyance. Normally, I love sarcasm—in women especially—but something about Holly's sarcasm works my last nerve.

Not that I'm going to let her know it.

So, instead, I smile, staring at her and saying nothing until a hint of pink darkens her cheeks.

She turns her attention to my spice rack. Sunlight streams through the kitchen window, edging her light. "Mrs. Mar made me a deal," she continues. "If I keep you sober and well-behaved until after the company's board meeting, I get a bonus."

My stomach goes icy. Has it really come to this? Who am I kidding? Of course, it has. Adele doesn't believe me. She thinks I'm a liability. Landers and Parish didn't just take my horse and my career. They took my family.

"So if you get a bonus, what do I get?" I make the question sound as suggestive as I can, and I know I hit pay dirt when that hint of pink spreads.

Holly clears her throat and faces me. "Oh, I don't know. Maybe you get to keep your job? I would think that's a pretty good outcome—especially since Emily from Etoile Saddlery called Mrs. Mar. She isn't going to renew your contract."

I try not to grind my teeth as we stare at each other. I've been endorsing Etoile saddles for *years* now. They're great to ride in, and have the nice added bonus of paying me well to say they're great to ride in. Losing the endorsement is a bad blow, not only financially, but for my reputation as well.

Whatever, then, I think. *If staying quiet about Arch means I keep sponsors, I'd rather be poor.* But by now, my silence has stretched on for too long and Holly's eyeing me like she's trying to decide if I'm listening.

"That makes what?" she asks, crossing her arms. "The third sponsor you've lost? You can't keep doing this."

I frown. As much as I hate to admit it, she has a point. I can't keep losing my temper. It distracts everyone from looking hard at Dell.

"Beau, you can't have another outburst tonight."

It's the closest thing I have ever heard to pleading coming from Holly. It's almost like she cares. I give her an unwilling nod, and her whole face brightens.

"Fine," I say.

"No, not fine. You have to *behave*," she says, and in spite of everything, that one little word lights me up, makes me hard.

I grin, and Holly swallows. "Make me."

CHAPTER 9 | Holly

"Is that a challenge?" My voice sounds great—not fluttery or strangled at all—but I can't stop staring at his mouth, and Beau definitely notices. A soft noise escapes him, and he steps closer.

"It's definitely a challenge," he breathes. "Make me behave, Holly."

I glare up at him. God. He makes my nipples tighten. I need to get control here, but there's something about Beau that makes me want to be under him.

Or bent over for him.

His hand slides under my chin, caressing the soft skin of my jaw. "Or maybe I should make *you* behave. Think I could?"

I force a smirk.

It makes him grin. "Oh, I think I could make you behave," he whispers, and dips his head to kiss me. His lips nudge mine apart, sending a sizzle down my spine. I've wanted this—and I didn't realize how much until now. All our fights. All our arguing.

It was like foreplay.

His hands explore me, one diving down to cup my ass and the other sliding up to mold my breasts. I gasp. It feels amazing. *He* feels amazing.

His chest is even harder than I imagined. His hips nudge against mine until I'm backing up. He pins me against the kitchen counter, and kisses me harder, his tongue sweeping my mouth and setting a toe-curling rhythm.

I let my hands explore: the firm skin of his chest to the tightness of his shoulders. My fingers curl when he pulls up my skirt, exposing my lacy thong. I'm already wet, and this only makes me wetter.

"You're so damn hot," he whispers, and grips my bare ass with one hand, and then two. I moan, pulling a hiss from him. He grinds into me, his hardness meeting the softness of my belly, and anticipation makes me shiver.

His fingers slide into my panties. He plays with my clit, and I go boneless. "Do you like this?" he whispers.

I nod, eyes sliding shut.

"Say it." There's a playful edge to his voice, but his fingers are far more insistent. He firmly rubs me once, taking me right to the edge, and stops.

"Yes," I pant, arching against him, desperate for more. "I like it."

"Me too. Come for me." He rubs and teases and...pinches, and I go over the edge, screaming into his shoulder as I bite down. Beau rides each aftershock, touching me with just enough pressure so I can drift down satisfied.

There's a moment of perfect stillness, and then: "Who's behaving now?"

The question is undeniably smug, and I know I should be embarrassed. I mean, he totally just made me come.

But he totally just made me come, and I smile. I look up, making sure to hold his gaze as I boldly cup his hard, huge shaft. His eyes go bright and he thrusts into my hand. He needs release, is desperate for it.

I cup him harder, smile wider, and say, "That was fun! Thanks!"

And then I walk away.

***

I get my own bedroom, but we have to share at bathroom, which means the entire time I'm getting ready for Mrs. Mar's party, I have to think about Beau being on the other side of that door.

Naked and *hard*.

My hand slips, jamming my toothbrush into my gums. I wince. He's probably not naked. He's definitely still hard though. I can't believe I'm even thinking about that. I can't believe I let my libido get the better of me.

Then again, that orgasm was fantastic.

Handling him via blue balls is not smart, I think. But it *was* fun. I spit into the sink, rinse toothpaste from my mouth, and tell my body to stand down. If Beau is naked or waiting to get naked, it's because I'm taking too long.

I hate how he's playing stupid with me about the whole behaving himself thing. Hate. It. Beau Kent is a lot of things, but stupid isn't one of them.

Childish? I lean close to the bathroom mirror, putting on my eyeliner. *Definitely.*

Ridiculous? I slip my dress over my head. *Completely.*

Delusional? Very, very *possible*. I shake my hair out, letting the curled ends fall over my bare shoulders. Too bare? I'm not sure.

I frown at my reflection. I've never been to one of Mrs. Mar's cocktail parties and I don't know how people will be dressed. I would ask Ellie, but Ellie will show up anywhere in riding clothes, and be oblivious that people are trying to avoid her Eau de Sweaty Horse. I love her, but she kills me sometimes.

In the past, when I didn't know dress codes, I just dressed for myself, and it always worked out. I mean, at least *I* was happy with how I looked.

But I'd like to fit in.

You will, I tell myself, turning in the mirror so I can double-check the hem. Done almost entirely in pale peach lace, the dress reaches demurely past my knees until I move, revealing a thigh high slit.

"Dress, don't fail me now," I mutter, tossing the last bits of my makeup back into its bag. Normally, I would leave my stuff on the counter, but Beau's bathroom is as suspiciously clean as the rest of the cottage. "Getting rid of the evidence," I tell myself.

Or maybe he's not as much of a pig as I thought.

"Bathroom's all yours," I yell, padding back into my bedroom through the adjoining bathroom door. I toss my toiletries onto the bed and grab my favorite boots and leather jacket from the closet. The combination of girly fabrics and tough leather has always been one of my favorite go-tos. Just putting on the outfit makes me feel better.

Which I think is really the point of fashion.

I scoop up my now empty overnight bag from the floor and take it to the closet, rummaging around for a spot to put it. There's a shelf at the top of the closet, but someone's crammed a brown packing box up there. I try to lift it and nearly buckle. It's way heavier than I expected.

What is he keeping *up here?* I wonder, hauling it down and swearing under my breath.

There's a clink of glass, and for a second, I'm absolutely positive I'm going to open the box up to find Beau's hidden booze stash, but I don't. The box isn't filled with liquor bottles. It's filled with pictures.

And trophies.

Something at the back of my brain whispers to put the box away—*now*—but my curiosity drowns it out. And as Beau turns on the shower in the bathroom, I kneel on the floor and carefully pick through everything.

Beau winning the Maclay at sixteen.

Beau winning his first Grand Prix at eighteen.

First gold medal.

Second gold medal.

A picture of him at Twelve Oaks with his first jumper stallion. I hold the frame in both hands. Beau has one arm hooked around his horse's neck and his grin makes him look lit from within. I've never seen him even *remotely* that happy and it tugs something inside me. Why would you hide away such wonderful memories?

The shower cuts off, pulling me back to the present moment. I tuck the picture back in its box, and feel like I'm snooping. I guess, technically, I am. But if he didn't want me to see these, he should've moved them before I came over.

My cell beeps, reminding I don't have time for this. We're going to be late if I don't get moving. I leave the box on a chair by my bed, promising myself I'll put it away later. If it doesn't matter to Beau, it doesn't matter to me.

Even so, the discovery feels like it's following me as I leave. It's a tickling at the back of my neck. I open the door, pausing with one hand against the frame as I adjust my left boot. There's a scuffling to my right as Beau appears, walking toward the kitchen.

Actually, 'walking' isn't accurate. He's *limping* and my breath catches.

What's going on? I think, and as if he heard my startled inhale, Beau rights himself, striding forward like nothing's the matter. I blink. Was it a trick of my eyes?

No. No way. He's hiding pain, and I don't know what to think about that. Is he worried I'll tell Mrs. Mar or something?

"You coming?" Beau asks without turning around.

"Yep." I breeze along behind him, voice so light we can both pretend I didn't see a thing. But my mind's whirling. The accident was a year ago. He's told everyone he's feeling better, is only waiting for the doctor to clear him to ride.

What if he's lying?

Beau's cell beeps and he pauses to check it, corners of his mouth turning down as he studies the screen. I try not to ogle, but...gotta admit he does the broody thing quite well.

Even if the rest of him needs serious work.

Before Beau was sidelined, he was known for polo shirts and breeches—the uniform of most male riders. Ever since I came to Twelve Oaks, thought, his style is more like...homeless fraternity boy. He wears ripped cargo shorts and paper thin T-shirts. Sometimes there's a dirty baseball cap thrown in the mix, but mostly he wears his hair a little too long and way too tangled.

Tonight's not any better. He's wearing a pair of khakis so worn the wallet outline is easily visible and his button-up shirt is untucked, hanging raggedly around his hips. If it were up to me, I would've made him wear some sort of dark pants with a thin weave sweater, something that would highlight the hard build of his chest.

But questionable fashion sense aside, he's still the kind of gorgeous that makes me go a bit stupid, the kind of gorgeous where you're not surprised his life is working out perfectly.

Except, is it? My brain flashes between Beau hiding his limping and those hidden-away trophies and pictures. *Why* would you hide away such wonderful memories?

Then it hits me: Because you're so miserable now you can't stand to look at them.

CHAPTER 10 | Beau

Holly sails pasts me, smelling faintly of flowers and leather. Briefly, it muddles my brain—or maybe that's the jerking off talking. I had to come twice before I could trust myself to walk straight. She left me so hard I was aching—she also just saw me limping. I know she did. Holly doesn't miss a beat. It's what makes her so annoyingly good at everything. Which means she's *pretending* she didn't see.

Heat climbs up my neck, and I can't decide if I'm pissed or embarrassed or pissed that I'm embarrassed. I scowl at her. "What are you wearing?"

"Clothes."

"You know what I mean. Why are you wearing...?" I wave one hand at her outfit, a mishmash of utilitarian leather and delicate lace. It's unexpected.

It's sexy as hell, I think, and now I'm even more aggravated.

"What? You don't like the way I look?" Holly does a little turn, gifting me with another glimpse of her ass.

"You look..." Perfect? Sexy? Like a woman I want to strip?

"Oh, well." Holly meets my eyes and puts one hand on her hip, cocking it. "Because I *do* like the way I look. Now c'mon."

She strides for the door, remarkably light on her feet considering she's wearing a pair of boots that could probably kick my shins in. Briefly, I consider running the other way, but with the way my hip feels, I wouldn't make it far.

I drag myself after her and try not to draw attention to how slow I'm moving when I climb into the Bronco. Thankfully, Holly doesn't look at me. She buckles up and throws us in reverse, rolling down the windows so crisp fall air can blow through the cab. The Bronco shifts moodily under her, but she handles the thing really well.

That's so sexy, I think and then scowl, shifting in my seat because my pants suddenly feel tighter. *What the hell is wrong with you?*

It's like everything she does is sexy. I've reverted to a fourteen-year-old.

A thoroughly played fourteen-year-old because she definitely got the upper hand on me earlier.

"You okay?" Holly asks, snatching a glance at me.

I can't tell if it's concern or suspicion making her eyes narrow, and I look away. "I'm fine."

We drive the rest of the way in silence. Adele's house sits on the farthest corner of the farm, a secluded patch of lawn plunked down in the middle of the woods. At night, it's pitch black except for the stars. During the day, it's so quiet, you can hear the deer moving around in the underbrush. The seclusion would drive me crazy, but Adele enjoys it. She spends half her time dealing with her family's corporation, and the rest of it, she spends here, recuperating.

Holly parks on the far end of the guests' cars, and briefly, stares up at the house. She's a little open-mouthed. I get it. Adele is old, *old* money. Her family has been wealthy since some time in the thirties, which is probably when they first started building. These days, the Mar mansion sprawls over twenty thousand square feet and rises up four stories.

It's beautiful, done up in a weathered, Cape Cod style that might not exactly fit with the deep south, but works great for adding on wings and extensions. Some of the growth might be haphazard, but Adele's tied it all together by paying special attention to swooping rooflines and heavy trim work.

"It's not as intimidating inside," I tell Holly, and then wonder why I'm trying to comfort her. Judging from her expression, she's wondering too.

"I've never been to one of these," she says at last.

"I know." Adele has a cocktail party every Thursday evening without fail. Most of us at the farm have standing invitations. Ellie goes when she can. Sam and Charlie never bother. The grooms almost always come, but they usually end up eating in the kitchen because they're hungry and don't care for small talk. And me? I came a lot before the accident.

Holly takes a deep breath like she's pushing away nerves, but bounces out of the Bronco like she isn't scared of anything.

I like that, I think, unbuckling my seatbelt. She's annoying as hell, too beautiful for my good, and brave. She might be nervous, but she won't show it.

Been there. Done that, I realize. For a second, I look at her, but I remember how I used to do the same thing before my first international shows. I was young, intimidated as hell, and determined no one would ever know I was intimidated as hell. I'm not sure that I like how we share that trait.

I slide out of the Bronco to join her, and we walk past the other cars. I concentrate on each step, doing great until I spot the silver Mercedes parked by the blue stone steps.

Chills coast up my arms. Dell. He's here.

Holly touches my elbow. "Beau? Everything okay?"

Nope. It's not okay at all. How that bastard thinks he can show up here after what he did? Holly grips my arm and I suddenly realize I'm shaking.

"Beau. What is it?"

"Nothing." I shrug her off, and hurl myself up the stairs toward the house. Almost thirty steps and I feel each of them throbbing in my hip by the time I reach the top.

Adele's housekeeper, Martie, opens the door as Holly and I come up the stone walkway. "Well, well, look what the cat dragged in!" A compact woman with loads of dark brown hair and a penchant for chunky gold necklaces, Martie always makes me think of sophisticated southern grandmothers or polished Food Network hosts.

She waves us inside with slightly less force than someone directing a 747 onto the tarmac. "I haven't seen you in ages, Beau!"

Martie pulls me in for a rib-busting hug. "Sorry," I tell her, hugging her back. "Work."

We pull apart, and she smiles like she believes me, but I can't see in her eyes that she doesn't. "Who's here tonight?" I ask, trying to keep my tone light.

"Oh, you know, the usual suspects." She turns her attention to Holly, assessing her with the laser focus usually reserved for fussy French recipes and sky high tablescapes. "Hello, there. Holly, right? I hoped you'd come. I'm Martie."

"Nice to meet you." Holly steps up and the two women shake hands. If Martie's fazed by Holly's outfit, it doesn't show. She links their arms together and steers us deeper inside the house. "We're in the sitting room tonight," she says.

I stifle a laugh. "Sitting room" always makes me think of pocket-sized couches and cozy fireplaces, but, in reality, it's a massive living space dotted with huge couches and an enormous fireplace that takes up almost a full wall.

Adele's in the middle of it all, talking to a woman whose hair rises like a cirrus cloud above her head. "Beau!" Adele cries, breaking off from the other woman. "You came, darling! Thank you!"

My neck heats at the gratification. If she wanted me to come, she should've just told me to be here. She is my boss, after all. Then again, after so many years, Adele and I kind of feel more like mother and son than boss and employee.

She hugs me, the curves of her heavy bracelets biting me through my shirt. "And Holly! You look lovely!" Adele releases me and peers closer at the dress. "Is that hand stitched?"

Holly nods. "I did it myself."

"May I?" Adele gestures one hand toward the skirt, intending to touch it. Holly nods and we both watch Adele gush over the fabric. Apparently, lace like this is hard to do.

Learn something new every day, I think, mildly annoyed they get along so well. That can't mean anything good for me.

My boss and my babysitter continue to chat for a few more minutes, bouncing lightly from Adele's last trip to New York to Holly's ambition to start her own clothing line. I didn't know about that. Then again, it isn't like Holly and I talk about real stuff.

"Have you met Boyd and Lucia Davis?" Adele asks her as a pretty couple approaches us. The man's wearing a tux, the woman a fussy, black dress. She can't take her eyes off Holly and briefly, I'm not seeing Holly The Pain in My Ass, but the Holly everyone else must see: smiling, blonde, and intensely herself.

The other women at the party are wearing variations of black and Holly stands out in her bright dress and battered black motorcycle jacket. She's the draw of every eye, and yet she did it effortlessly.

Or at least it looks effortless. Because I know Holly The Pain in My Ass so well, I also know almost nothing the woman does is without calculation, and sometimes, spreadsheets. At some point, she put serious thought into that outfit. If I'm honest, it's another way we're alike: I always tell people 'if it looks like riding, keep practicing.'

Real riding must be effortless. It needs to look like the horse is doing all the work and you're just sitting there.

And watching Holly work this crowd? It looks exactly like that, like she isn't even breaking a sweat, like she does this stuff all the time.

Lucia Davis laughs at something Holly said, and Holly's gaze meets mine, one side of her mouth tipping higher like we're in on the same joke. I actually catch myself smiling back.

I like her. In other circumstances, we might've actually had something. Too bad she's in my way.

CHAPTER 11 | Beau

The party goes way better than I anticipated. I can rest my hip by sitting when I need to, and excuse myself to talk to other guests, when I need to move. I don't look like I'm hurting. I look like I'm being sociable and every time I spot Adele, she grins at me like she's totally proud I'm playing nice.

It makes me cringe a bit. I want to be the person she believes I am, but I need to be someone I can live with too.

"Here." Holly appears at my side and passes me a vodka and tonic. I take a sip, frown. Not vodka. Sparkling water.

I hold it out to her. "I think this is yours."

"Definitely not. I can be trusted with *my* liquor." Holly glances down, brushing one hand over her dress. "Incoming," she murmurs.

I glance to our right. The woman with a head of hair like a cirrus cloud is heading toward me, intent in her eyes and cell phone at the ready. Wants a picture, I'm guessing. Okay, fine, I can do that.

I turn to Holly. "Can you hold my—"

A side door into the sitting room opens, and Dell slides through. His face is pink and sweaty and he keeps tugging at his ill-fitting jacket. With all that money he brags about, you'd think he could afford a better tailor, but I've never seen him wear clothes that can properly contain his stomach. It bulges out like a snake's after eating a rabbit.

Just the sight of him makes my shoulders tense, and I force myself to take a deep, *deep* breath.

"Beau?" Holly whispers.

Or at least, I think it's a whisper. She sounds incredibly faraway. I let the breath out slowly, and to my total relief, my chest actually loosens a bit. It's working.

Or it is until another guest joins him.

Tall and slender with a penchant for wool sweaters no matter the temperature, John Grant is a horse dealer from Great Britain—and judging from the way he's greeting Dell, I'm guessing he's doing a bit of dealing right now.

My stomach turns over. *He really is going to buy another one*, I realize. Being at the auction wasn't just for social reasons, he really is shopping—and the thing is, it shouldn't be a surprise. People like Dell always have several horses on their string. And they might very well end up just like Arch did.

"Beau Kent!" Cirrus Cloud Woman plucks at me and, briefly, I'm disoriented. I look down at her and she grins. "I was hoping I'd see you tonight! I told Charles I was going to get my picture taken with a two-time Olympic gold medalist and he—"

I brush past her, heading straight for Dell and John.

"Is he always so rude?" the woman asks.

There's a pause before Holly says, "Well, sometimes, he's asleep."

I grit my teeth, bearing down on Dell. The asshole accepts a drink from one of the waiters, swirling it as he watches me approach. "Well, hello there, old boy!" he booms. "You look well!"

It's like a punch to the throat. *He's* the reason I *usually* don't look well. He's the reason all of this even happened. For a second, the room narrows, going sleek and long.

"Beau," John says, noticing me for the first time and taking a startled step back. He pushes both hands into his trouser pockets. "Good to see you again."

"You too. Been a while."

"It has."

There's a pregnant pause while everyone decides where to take this. John stares at me while Landers sips his drink, one hand fiddling with the buttons on his jacket. I know what I want to say—*shout*—but I can also feel Adele's eyes boring into me.

Hell, I can feel Holly's too.

Do not let them down, a small voice in my head tells me. *Just...don't.*
I pull myself a little straighter and listen to Landers go on and on about how John hasn't found him anything he likes yet.

Yet. Tiny fucking word and it makes me grit my teeth. What happened to Arch and me doesn't matter to Landers. We were collateral damage, and he'll do it again.

And people like John will help him.

"Dell?" Dell's wife, a bony, little thing in a strapless dress joins us. She links her arm through Landers's and looks down her nose at me. It's quite a feat considering I have over six inches on her. "Is everything okay, honey?"

"Of course it is," he tells her, smirking at me. This is my cue to smile back like a good little trained monkey. I actually think about it too. If I do, I wouldn't let Adele or Holly down.

But I *would* let myself down.

"Excuse me," I say, brushing past the three of them and heading for the front door. I'm distantly aware of people smiling at me and how I smile back, Holly's hot on my heels, and Adele? She smiles at me like keeping my mouth shut has made her proud.

Too bad I feel like shit.

CHAPTER 12 | Holly

Beau didn't say a word while I drove us home last night, and as soon as we got back, he hit the whisky. I fell asleep around midnight, but he was still going strong: sitting on the deck, lost in his thoughts and looking over the darkened paddocks, swigging straight from the bottle.

Which doesn't exactly make it surprising when his bedroom door stays closed for most of the morning. It's fine by me if he wants to sleep off a hangover. My first day of babysitting him wasn't exactly thrilling, and I don't mind the break before starting day two with him.

Instead of arguing with him, I get to take the morning to work on my stuff. I talk to Dane first, Mom second, and after I'm sure she isn't plotting to lock him in the garage, I wrangle my oversized suitcase out of the Bronco and haul it inside.

When traveling just for me, I can fit everything into an overnight bag, but when I'm taking work along I usually use the huge suitcase. It can hold dozens of fabric swatches, my sketches, my notebooks, and if I ever needed to, a medium-sized child. Sucker really is ridiculously huge.

I heave it up the front steps and inside the cottage, pausing to see if my banging around has woken His Highness. It hasn't. Part of me is tempted to start slamming pots and pans around, but the rest of me would rather take advantage of the quiet to do something for me.

When I'm focused, work is relaxing. It's just about the colors and the cuts and what I want the outfit to say.

Unsurprisingly, everything I can think of at the moment is a bit hostile.

I settle on the couch and spread the fabrics around until I can see them properly. I send a "good morning" text to Ellie and Parker, and settle in to concentrate. Seconds later, my cell vibrates with an incoming call. Scott.

For a heartbeat, my whole world becomes New York, the smell of concrete and exhaust, and the early morning excitement before a show. For another second, I miss it with everything I am.

I take a shaky breath and click the Answer button. Scott screeches something on the other end. "Scott?"

"Have you seen the new Farrow and Ball wallpapers?" he asks. "I'm obsessed."

I reposition a swatch of intense blue silks so I can get a better look at them in the sunlight. "Hello to you too."

"What? Oh. Yeah. Hello. I think I'm going to do similar patterns in my spring show. I'm thinking ball gowns and punk rock colors. You need to come home and help me do it."

"I *am* home." Well, not exactly, but it's not worth explaining to Scott. I drop the silk into my lap and stare out the windows, watching the young horses play. "The combination sounds fantastic," I continue. "Send me your sketches?"

"Come *home* and I'll show them to you."

I try not grin and fail. "I can't. I need a job first."

"You're killing me, you know that?" Scott makes a huffing noise, nearly deafening me. "You're going to die old and unfashionable and cats are going to eat on your body for *days* before they find it."

"I don't have cats."

"You will by that time." He pauses, breathing hard. "You'll have *loads* of them."

"Get cat," I say slowly like I'm writing it down. "There. Now it's on my to-do list."

"Holly, look, as your friend—"

"Friend?" I can't keep the splutter of shock out of my voice. "You threw your phone at me!"

"And you threw it back." Scott sounds genuinely perplexed. He probably is. I was the only assistant to ever yell back at him during one of his man-trums. He probably thinks it's just the way we communicate. "I thought we were having a conversation."

"A conversation doesn't involve pitching electronics at people's heads."

"Whatever," he says, and I can picture him waving his hand in dismissal. "The point is, as your friend, I have to tell you: you're making a huge mistake. You were meant for bigger things. If you stay in Atlanta, you won't reach them."

I pick at the silk. He has a point. It's been next to impossible to get things going from down here, but I've also been preoccupied. There's a thump from Beau's bedroom as, presumably, one of my main preoccupations wakes up.

After last night, I have *serious* concerns about scoring my bonus.

"Look," Scott says, a long suffering sigh barreling down the line. "I know I wasn't the easiest to work with, but you were amazing. Truly. You have the talent and the discipline to go far in this industry. If you don't get up here and start looking for opportunities, you're going to regret it."

I open my mouth to tell him I won't, but nothing comes out. He's right. He's so right it makes my insides turn cold.

"What's really holding you back?" Scott asks.

"Money for rent—plus, I'm needed here. My mom's getting over the flu. It's not a good time for me to bug out on her."

It's half excuse, half-truth, and something else. I miss New York, but I didn't realize until I came home I missed being here too.

"That's tough. I'm sorry." He pauses. "But you need to remember: this is your career we're talking about, and you have to have something for yourself, honey."

"When did you become so enlightened?"

"Since I started dating my yoga instructor. He's amazing. Come meet him."

There's another thump from Beau's bedroom, and I glare at the door, willing it to stay shut. I don't want him listening in on my conversation with Scott. It's too personal. He'll ask questions that I won't want to answer.

Or, worse, *can't* answer.

"It's not like I've given up on my dreams completely," I tell Scott. "I still want to start my own line. I just need a little more cash to do it."

I frown. Or like a *lot* more cash to do it.

"So come home and look for investors with me," Scott says. "You can still live in the boondocks and get eaten by cats when you die, but if you don't at least *occasionally* come to New York, people won't take you seriously."

Maybe he's right. I pick at the hem of my skirt. It's another one I designed—a white silk drawstring edged in black. I usually pair it with a soft long sleeved tee and vintage-y high-heeled sandals, but today I've gone for a loose, patterned tank. It's comfy and effortless and totally overdone for sitting in stupid Beau Kent's living room.

"Does the offer to crash at your place still stand?" I ask at last.

"Of *course* just come back. I'm surrounded by idiots."

"I'll think about it."

CHAPTER 13 | Beau

She'll think about what? I wonder. I tug my polo over my head, listening for more explanation and...there's nothing. I think she hung up. Or maybe the other person is still talking?

I open my bedroom door and step out, the sudden sunlight making me squint. I rub my eyes hard enough to make stars burst behind the lids and stumble toward the living room. Holly's sitting on the couch—or at least, I think it's the couch. I can't see it anymore. It looks like Barbie's closet threw up in here. Fabric is everywhere.

"How do you feel?" she asks, not looking up from her cell phone.

Like my skull is trying to fracture into a million pieces, I think, limping two steps before I realize I'm doing it.

Holly stands up, bright blue fabric falling on the floor. "What's up with your leg?"

"Nothing." I grit my teeth and force myself to walk normally into the kitchen. I move from the cabinet to the coffee maker, and every step sends lightning bolts up my thigh and into my hip.

"Liar," she says, coming closer. "Is your leg bothering you again?"

More like *still*, but I don't want her to know that. I don't want anyone to know that. I dump water into the coffee maker and fiddle with the buttons. My fingers feel like sausages. It takes me three times before I get the setting right.

"I'm *fine*," I say.

"Good. You want to talk about last night?" She's right behind me now, and from the tone of her voice, probably has her arms crossed in that pissy way that always lifts her breasts a good two inches. If I turned around, I could see them.

I don't turn around. "Why would I want to do that?"

"Because I'm trying to give you the benefit of the doubt and presume there's a reason you blew out of Mrs. Mar's party and then hit the bottle."

"Should I have reacted differently after being forced to socialize with a man who tortures animals?"

"Beau." There's a warning in her voice that infuriates me.

"Holly," I mock.

"You need to stop." She tugs my arm and I turn to her. We're breathing the same air now. I can feel her heat. "They didn't find anything at the necropsy."

"Doesn't mean something wasn't there."

"You sound like a lunatic."

"I know." I look her up and down—a mistake because now all I want to do is touch that drapey tank top and play with her skirt's edge—and say, "But what if I'm right?"

Holly hesitates.

"Look," I tell her, "you've been in the industry long enough to know people are constantly finding ways to outsmart the bloodwork tests we have. What if Arch was injected with something new? Something we haven't seen?"

"Okay, so what if someone *did* use an untestable injection on him? How are you going to prove it? It's untestable."

"I...haven't figured that part out yet." Embarrassing, but true and I fully expect Holly to jump all over me, but she doesn't. For a few seconds, she goes completely quiet.

"Why do you think something happened?" she asks at last.

I blink. "What?"

"I know what everyone else says about Arch dying. Why do *you* think it was something else?"

I blink again. She's completely surprised me. "He wasn't right in the Grand Prix. It wasn't just the refusal. It was..." I drift off, remembering how Arch seemed hesitant moving forward. Not lame. Just unsure. Not himself. I'd chalked it up to nerves at the time, making excuses to myself that he was being fussy, having a bad day, being sensitive.

It sort of made sense. The show grounds were a madhouse of visitors and riders and horses. It was mass chaos.

But Arch was experienced. It shouldn't have bothered him and I *shouldn't* have brushed it off. After he stopped at the second fence in the Grand Prix, I knew something was wrong.

"Uh, Beau? Hello?" Holly waves at me. "You going to finish any time soon?"

I scowl at her, but I'm more irritated with myself. When I pick through those memories, it's like I get lost. "He was off before our class," I explain, "but not in any way I could articulate. I don't know why he refused that jump. He'd never refused before. It was weird.

"Later, I told Dell I'd take him for a hack around the show grounds, but Dell said not to bother. I did it anyway. He...fell just as we passed the stabling entrance. Last thing I remember is hearing his breathing go ragged and then...nothing. I woke up in the hospital and he'd been dead for hours."

"I'm so sorry."

"Don't be. I'm over it."

Holly arches one brow, but wisely says nothing. I'm glad for both of us. I don't trust myself right now. The coffee machine beeps and I take a minute to fix myself a cup, pretending like I'm concentrating on the coffee so I don't have to face her. "All I know," I say, dumping a metric ton of sugar into my mug, "is Parish was seen leaving Arch's stall an *hour* before I arrived to take him back out. People noticed because the horse was thrashing, making a huge racket, as Parish came out. He shouldn't have been in there, and no one will give me a real answer about why he was."

A pause. "Checking Arch's water buckets?" she suggests. "Maybe he was out of hay?"

"They were fine." I stir with a shaky hand, slopping coffee onto the countertop. "I did them myself, and furthermore, we have our own people who do that. Charlie was on top of things."

"Well, Parish works for Dell. Maybe he was asked to check on him."

"Why? Why after two years of using Twelve Oaks' staff would Dell send him in?"

I sound like a paranoid lunatic, and I turn back to Holly fully expecting her to be wide-eyed with disbelief, but she isn't. She's sitting very still and watching me closely, something calculating in her expression.

"You said you didn't get a real answer?" She leans forward a bit. "What *did* they tell you?"

"One person said Parish was there for another one of Dell's horses, but he didn't have any at the competition. Parish said he heard Arch thrashing and came running. He said a bee or something must've stung him."

"Did you find any marks?"

"Absolutely not."

"Maybe he hung up a leg? Got cast?"

I consider her again. They're not bad suggestions. Sometimes horses lie down too close to their stall walls and get wedged, or they catch a leg on something and get stuck. Holly's trying to think through all the possibilities. Months ago, I did the same.

"Maybe," I say at last. "Or maybe he was thrashing because he'd been injected with something." It's the first time I've been able to say it out loud since I first argued with Adele about it almost a year ago. I half expect for Holly to react the same way with the same excuses: "Dell would never order his staff to do such a thing!" "Nothing was found in the necropsy!" "Surely not!"

After all, Dell's a millionaire land developer. He's a fixture in the equestrian community. He sits on a bunch of boards and contributes to various charities, but there are rumors too—rumors about grooms not getting paid and feed store checks bouncing and how he's known to take a swing at his wife.

If you don't respect women enough not to hit them, how would you feel about an animal that you legally own? If I had to guess, Arch was one step up from a tennis racket.

So, yeah, I expect Holly to bring up all sorts of excuses for Dell because even though she doesn't ride, she's in the industry. She knows all the same people I do.

But once again she surprises me because she doesn't get swayed by the emotion of the situation, she gets quiet. Her mouth turns down in determination. "Why would you think Arch got injected?"

"Because he was such a pain in the ass about needles. Everyone knew it. He practically needed a sedative before his annual shots and forget pulling blood without a fight. If Parish injected him, Arch would've pitched a fit."

"Like the one that was overheard?"

"Exactly."

She goes quiet again, plucking at her shirt's hem and staring out the window. "That's a pretty big leap, but when you consider what happened an hour later..." She trails off, swallowing.

"They did something. I know it. I can't prove it yet, but I know they did."

"Or, it was a horrible coincidence. Parish works for Arch's owner and he happened to be walking by when Arch needed something." She recites the words like she's memorized them, which she probably has. I'm sure Adele told her everything—or at least the commonly known version of the story.

"And," she adds, "Arch could've flipped out because he was stung by a bee, or he startled himself, or a million other reasons horses spook and *that's* the reason Dell went in to check him. It doesn't mean he was injected with something."

"It doesn't mean he wasn't either."

"Jeez, are you for real?" She blows wisps of blond hair out of her eyes and glares at me. "Please think about this, Beau. You're making unsubstantiated accusations and it isn't just Dell Landers's reputation you're playing with. It's Mrs. Mar's too."

"I know."

"You 'know?'" Her blue eyes open wide and mouth hangs open. "She's been your sponsor for almost twenty years! You are who you are *because* of her!"

"Yeah." I nod, the heaviness of it all getting to me again. I don't want to drag Adele into this. I know without a shadow of a doubt she had nothing to do with this, but if the truth comes out, she'll get tarnished just the same. The smart thing would be to move past Arch and I can't. I lost my career—my *life*—and Landers and Parish tortured a defenseless animal. "I know how much I owe her. She's given me everything, but it would be wrong to let this go. I mean, surely you get that, right?"

Holly hesitates, something zinging through her eyes, and it stops me dead. She does get it. She doesn't want to, but she does.

She leans back against the countertop, studying me. "Since when are you interested in integrity?" she asks at last. The dig's half-hearted though and we end up staring at each other, saying nothing.

Then again, her eyes keep dipping to my mouth and my dick keeps noticing and this might be a good time for some angry kissing, but I can't bring myself to do it. There's something...different simmering between us. She's different. Or maybe I am.

I clear my throat, forcing myself to look away. "Help me find out the truth, and I'll make sure you get that bonus."

A pause. "How would I help you?"

"I found another witness and I need to talk to her—we need to talk to her."

"Why both of us? Worried your charm will fail you?"

"Cute, and *no*, I'm not." I lean my good hip against the counter edge and cross both arms. "I *am* worried she won't talk to me at all because my temper got the better of me, and everyone knows where I stand. She likes her job. She isn't going to want to get involve in what everyone else considers drama."

"Who is it?"

"Kat Bowman. She's a groom for the Fisher family. You know her?"

Holly shakes her head.

"I think if we catch up with her together, she might be more in-clined to talk. You're approachable when you're not pissed off. People like you."

For a moment, Holly says nothing, but I can tell she's thinking a *lot*. I push away from the counter and her hand finds my elbow again. She tugs me back around. We're in each other's space again, and everything inside me tightens. I want her again.

You want her still, I think.

"Are you serious?" she asks finally. "If I do this, you'll be good?"

I smirk, taking enormous satisfaction when the accidental innuen-do hits her. Holly's whole face goes bright pink.

"Honey," I whisper, leaning in. "I'll be *very* good."

CHAPTER 14 | Holly

Ten hours later, I park the Bronco in the closest spot I can find and peer through my windshield at the darkened buildings ahead of us. The Hole In The Wall is tucked downstairs from a swanky southern restaurant. Dimly lit with a narrow staircase leading down to the door, you'd miss it if you didn't know it was there. According to Kat's Facebook page, she's here almost every Saturday night.

"I can't believe I stalked this poor girl," I mutter.

"We didn't stalk her." Beau slides gingerly out of the Bronco, wincing a little when his feet hit the ground. "It was on her Facebook page. Anyone could see it. Our arrival can be a life lesson about the importance of privacy settings."

I stare at him, and for the billionth time that day, I think about how I should call Ellie so she can talk some sense into me. I have actually teamed up with Beau Kent to score a financial bonus. I'm either delusional or really desperate.

Or both.

"You know what?" I ask at last. "Just don't say anything. Let me do the talking."

He shrugs, and I can't tell if that's an agreement or a "Maybe."

More likely, it's 'I'm Beau Kent! I do what I want! I think, gritting my teeth and hopping out of my car.

Inside, the bar's just as dimly lit as the street. High top tables are scattered around the main floor, a huge oak bar lines one entire wall, and the walls...well, the walls are covered with taxidermied animals—raccoons, deer, squirrels—and all the animals are dressed in costume.

"Now that's just fucked up," Beau announces, peering close at a snarling warthog in a top hat. "I can't tell if he's grinning or if he's going to eat my face."

Honestly, I can't tell either, and in another lifetime, I might've giggled, but I refuse to encourage Beau any more than I already have by showing up to this monumentally bad idea.

If you do this, he said he'll behave, I remind myself and scan the crowd, eventually spotting a slender redhead at one of the high tables. It's definitely Kat. I recognize her from her Facebook pictures. She's scrolling through her phone and sipping a beer, probably waiting on someone.

I nudge Beau and he reluctantly pulls himself away from the warthog. "Over there," I say, already moving toward Kat. He follows me, and as we thread our way through the crowd, his fingertips brush my spine.

I shiver. "Kat?" I ask, giving her a huge smile as we come closer.

She looks up, brows drawn together. "Yes?"

"I'm Holly Benson. This is Beau Kent."

Recognition makes her expression shutter. Kat slides her phone into her purse, and pulls her purse to her chest. "Nice to meet you," she mumbles.

Not good. I pull my smile wider. "I had a couple questions I was hoping you could help me with."

"I already talked to Charlie. I told him everything I saw. I don't—"

"I promise it won't take long," I say. Her eyes are still fixed on the door and I step a little closer. "And I promise no one will know you talked to us."

Slowly, Kat turns back to me. She can't be more than twenty, twenty-one. Hours in the sun have given her freckles and pinkened cheeks, and even though she's wearing a fancy strapless dress and heels, her auburn hair is scraped into a plain, high ponytail—probably the same one she wears to the barn every day.

"Please?" I add.

Finally, she nods. "Okay."

Relief makes me sag. "Awesome. Thank you." I hop up onto the closest stool and Beau takes the one next to me. "I heard you work for the Fisher family."

She nods again.

"And their horses were stabled down the row from the Twelve Oaks horses at the Fall Invitational?"

"Yeah, we were there for the whole week. Their daughter has two ponies she competes and Mrs. Fisher rides in the amateur jumper division."

"That must keep you really busy."

"No joke." Kat puts her bag on the table and holds up one hand to catch the waitress's attention. This is great. If she's planning on settling in, she must be ready to share. "It's not too bad. I mean, two horses and two ponies, but I could've used some help—especially because it was championship's that weekend."

"Evening!" the waitress says when she joins us. She's a small boned thing with sculptural tattoos looping out from under her shirt collar. "What're y'all having?"

Kat and I order beer, but Beau gets a bottled water. Surprise trickles through me. I've never seen him voluntarily turn down an opportunity to drink. Our eyes meet and he lifts one shoulder in a half-hearted shrug.

After the waitress leaves, I shift around in my seat to face Kat again. "With that many horses, you must've been around a lot. See anything unusual going on down by the Twelve Oaks horses?"

She frowns. "It didn't seem unusual at the time, but when I thought back on it...yeah, I saw Parish coming out of Arch's stall. I looked up because I heard all the commotion. It sounded like the stall was being kicked down."

I pause, thinking this over. "So he wasn't coming *in*? I'd heard he was running in to help, not leaving once Arch started thrashing."

"Not from what I saw. He stood outside the stall door, watching, and then he noticed me, and went back in. *That's* when I heard him start yelling about needing a hand."

Our waitress reappears and passes out our drinks, taking away Kat's empty bottle and promising to check on us later. Kat takes a long swallow of her beer before saying, "After he started yelling, a couple other grooms ran over. I didn't think anything more of it until..."

She shakes her head, wincing.

"Until Arch died," I finish.

Now Kat and Beau both wince, and we all fall silent. Up on the low slung stage, the house band begins tuning up. It won't be long before music renders conversations impossible, but I can't think of anything else to ask. This is awful enough.

"Have you heard anything about Dell's staff getting paid late?" Beau sounds utterly casual, but the line of his shoulders is tight. "Like after Arch died?"

Kat frowns. "I mean, rumors, yeah. One of my friends was hired to take care of his horses at another show and he *never* paid her. She mentioned it to the show's farrier, and *he* said he hadn't been paid either. Money problems. My friend was really upset, but who's she going to complain to, you know? It's not like they had a contract."

Beau and I nod. Unfortunately, verbal agreements are pretty much standard in the horse industry. If people want to take advantage, it's easy to do. But, of course, that wasn't really why Beau asked about Dell's payment history. His eyes meet mine and I know what he's thinking: more circumstantial evidence proving Dell needed cash, and killing Arch was the fastest way to get it.

"I'm sorry that happened to her," Beau says, tapping his fingers against the stained tabletop. "Can you remember anything else you've heard? Anything else you might have seen?"

"No." Kat turns her beer bottle around and around. "And I couldn't have done anything anyway. I mean, what would I have said?" The defensive note in her voice skews the question even higher, and I start to tell her of course, she couldn't have done anything, but Kat's attention is pinned to Beau. It makes my heart hurt for her. People like him are industry gods. I can't imagine how she must feel admitting to him she saw something, but didn't know what that something was until it was too late.

"It isn't your fault," Beau tells her. "Believe me, no one blames you."

Something—hope, worry, or maybe gratitude—zips through Kat's eyes.

"And I appreciate your honesty," he continues. "I promise your name won't come up again. Technically, what you saw doesn't prove anything, but when I add that to what I already know..." Beau pauses, swallowing. The muscles in his jaw tick twice and his fingers clench around his unopened bottle of water. "You've helped me know I'm on the right path," he says finally. "I won't forget that. If you ever need anything, let me know, okay? The Fishers' aren't the only family in need of excellent grooms. If you ever decide to leave, call me. I'll reach out to some of my friends."

Kat's eyes widen as he passes her a business card. I watch them, feeling slightly out of my body. Since when does Beau carry business cards?

And since when is he this considerate? I have a hard time reconciling the understanding, but scruffy-looking guy in front of me with the drunken and scruffy-looking guy I usually have to wrangle.

Kat tucks Beau's business card in her wallet. "I will," she says. "And Mr. Kent?"

"Call me Beau."

Even in the shadowy light, I can tell Kat flushes all kinds of red. "Beau, I'm really sorry about your loss. If this is true, it's beyond horrible. Please be careful."

CHAPTER 15 | Holly

Outside the Hole in the Wall, evening chill is setting in. Beau and I keep our heads down as we head for my car, trying to stay inconspicuous, but I don't think it really matters. Everyone else is eagerly hurrying inside, ready to get their evening started. They're not carrying around this awful weight.

I sneak a glance at Beau. His jaw is still set and there's dangerous determination in his eyes. Honestly, I've seen the look before. Ellie gets it too—Parker and I called it her Take No Prisoners expression. Top athletes are just wired differently than the rest of us. They have more grit, more determination.

But I never considered how scary it would be when that determination became focused on something else. Taking Dell Landers and Parish down is Beau's whole world now. There's no room for anything else.

I unlock the Bronco and we both get in, sitting in silence for a moment. "Okay." I take a deep breath of cool fall air, hoping it will clear my head. It doesn't. I feel...slimy. "So the timeline would fit with your theory. Arch was fine until Parish went into his stall. He started thrashing—presumably because Parish injected him with something—and Parish stepped outside to keep from being stomped."

Beau nods, both hands flexing against his knees. "But then he noticed Kat watching him and had to go back in and pretend to be worried. He calls for help and tells everyone he went in only because Arch *was* thrashing."

We both pause, considering it. As much as I hate to admit Beau's right, the timeline works, but unless he can prove something's funny with the horse's bloodwork, it's still just conjecture.

I crank the Bronco. It rumbles to life as an uneasy thought hits me. "You think Dell or Parish are worried about Kat?"

"Doubtful." Beau clenches and unclenches his hands, staring out at the darkened street around us. "If she did accuse him of something—and really what could she?—he could always deny it. She has the same problem I have: lots of circumstantial evidence. No smoking gun."

I pop the stick in reverse, and we wheel out of the parking space and turn for home. I drum my fingers on the steering wheel. "I don't get it. I mean, if you're going to do a secret injection, why do it in the middle of the day? The risk of witnesses is pretty high."

Beau shrugs, but his hands clench again. And hold. "If you're experienced, injections are quick. Plus, if they want to make it look like the death was related to his performance earlier in the day, time was of the essence. They couldn't wait around."

That's true. Just because *I* couldn't pull it off doesn't mean Parish couldn't.

"We should celebrate," Beau says, turning to me.

I eye him. "Why?"

"I'm going to win." He settles back into my seat with a smug smile, manspreading his knees apart as, presumably, he anticipates revenge on Dell Landers and Parish.

One of those spreading knees brushes my knuckles as I grip the gearshift.

Move your hand, I tell myself. But my hand doesn't move, and neither does Beau's knee, and I know this doesn't even qualify as *remotely* near first base, but my stomach still heats.

He's not even trying to get me all bothered, I realize, and then shiver because what would I do if he *did* try?

Dissolve into a whimpering puddle seems like a distinct possibility.

Beau stretches both arms above his head, his hand coming down on my seat...and then sliding to my shoulder. I white-knuckle the steering wheel as the backs of his fingers graze up my neck and along my jaw.

"Did you lose something?" I ask, silently congratulating myself that my voice doesn't waver.

Which is some kind of miracle because he's trailing stars across my skin.

Beau touches me like I'm breakable—no, like I'm perfect. It makes me shiver.

"Celebrate with me," he murmurs, fingertips tracing my ear.

I nearly run off the damn road. *Get it together*, I think as he gently massages my earlobe. The streetlight changes to red and I stop behind a low-rider sports car. *Are you really this desperate? Ask him if all his dates are this pathetic. Ask him if he thinks that's sexy.*

It doesn't matter if he thinks it's sexy. Clearly, my body thinks it's plenty sexy because delicious chills pass over me in waves. I flex my hands against the steering wheel. "What do you have in mind?"

"Mmmm."

Beau's groan makes me go wet in a rush. I snatch a glance at him, and his thumb finds my lower lip. He grins.

And nudges his thumb into the seam of my lips.

My nipples tighten. My stomach tightens. He's daring me.

Don't back down now, I think and suck his thumb into my mouth. He makes a strangled noise. I suck it deeper, staring him down as I circle my tongue around his thumb.

Then I pop it out and smile like *I'm* winning.

Because I am. I'm in control. I could make him *beg*.

Except when I look back at Beau, I realize what I'm playing with. His eyes have darkened, and his attention is fully mine. This isn't just a man who's used to winning. This is a man who's used to getting everything he wants.

And right now, he wants me.

CHAPTER 16 | Beau

It's taking everything in me not to reach across the Bronco, and kiss her. The only thing holding me back? She drives like a bat out of hell and even though the SUV rolls around like a freaking tank, I'm pretty sure we'd die if we crashed.

I might die if I *don't* kiss her though.

Then Holly sneaks a glance at me, smirks, and it shouldn't be remotely possible, but I go even harder.

I shift in my seat, trying to ease the pressure. This is what happens when you spend entirely too much time fantasizing about your assistant/keeper/pain in your ass, the slightest look turns you into a hormonal fourteen-year-old.

"Is that how you usually celebrate?" she asks me, eyes on the road ahead of us.

"Not precisely." Holly hits a pothole at 50 mph and we bounce hard as she rights the Bronco. "But I'm sure you can imagine the rest."

Her hands flex against the steering wheel again and I grin. I might be sitting here with blue balls, but Holly's not unaffected.

She makes the last turn for Twelve Oaks and I crack my window, hoping some cold air across my face will clear my head. It does, but of course, now all I can think about is Arch and Dell and Parish. I'm sorry Kat was put in that position, that she'll have to carry this horrible moment with her for the rest of her life.

There. That's the downer I needed. Holly and I drive on in silence, eventually reaching Twelve Oaks' moonlight drenched driveway. We speed between black-painted fencing, all the paddocks empty of horses until morning.

One more turn, and my place comes into view. Holly parks next to my farm truck and turns to me, leaning across the space between our seats until I can barely keep from dipping my eyes toward her cleavage. It should be sexy as hell, but there's an intensity to her expression that stops me dead. It's like she's reading everything I've ever thought, examining every memory.

"You were kind tonight," she whispers. "I can't figure it out."

I arch one brow. "Figure what out?"

"Are you an arrogant ass who can be kind when he needs to be? Or are you *actually* kind and only an arrogant ass when you need to be? Who's the real Beau Kent?"

Something very close to alarm ripples through me. I tilt my head toward her. "Want to find out?"

"Yes," she breathes.

And kisses me.

I'm stunned. Her mouth is perfect, fitting against mine so sweetly I'm almost lost—and then her tongue touches my lower lip and I'm back, sliding my hands into her hair, tilting my mouth against hers.

Holly's fingers knot in my T-shirt. She drags me closer, and I take her mouth harder. She makes a tiny mewling sound of pleasure, arching her back so her breasts press against my chest. My dick nearly punches through my zipper. Christ. She is the hottest thing I have ever known.

I grab her waist, hauling her across the console to straddle me and almost yelping with excitement when she grinds right *on* me. She slides over me once, twice, again. My tongue is in her mouth. Her fingers are in my hair. She cranks back my head to look at me, and my hands go to her ass, squeezing.

She grinds down harder and I groan. "Again," I whisper.

Holly lifts and lowers herself, eyes hooded and pinned to me. She's watching her effects, watching my reaction. Fine.

Because I'm watching hers. Holly rides me exactly how she needs to. Lift, down. Lift, down. She sweeps her hips against me, and we both shudder. She needs it hard and fast.

So I slow her down. I catch her face between my hands and kiss her lightly, teasingly. Her mouth opens, begging for more and I deny her, sucking her lower lip, tracing the edge with my tongue. I kiss my way up her jawline to her ear and as I whisper, "You drive me mad," my hand finds her breast. I thumb her tightened nipple and she rewards me with another frantic grind.

She's sensitive. So fucking sensitive. My dick throbs. "Imagine how good it will feel when I put them in my mouth, sweetheart," I whisper, feeling her shiver. "Should I play with one like this"—I tweak her nipple between my fingers—"while I suck the other?"

Holly moans, rubbing herself against me, head lolling so her hair falls around us. She loves my dirty talk. I need to remember that.

The thought excites me even more. I would love the opportunity to tell her exactly what I'm about to enjoy.

Or am already enjoying.

My brain flashes to kissing up her silky thighs and parting her legs so I can tongue her, keeping her on edge for as long as I can. My dick throbs. We need to go inside. Now.

My hand gropes for the door handle, and after freaking forever, I find it. The door swings open and cold air rushes in. Holly shrinks back, blinking. She's panting hard and looks disoriented as hell.

Gotta admit, I like the look. A lot.

My hands return to her ass and squeeze. Curves and heat and *curves*. She's fucking perfect. "God, I want you. Inside. *Now*."

A tiny smile. She shakes her head, and my stomach plummets.

"C'mon, indulge." There might be begging inching into my tone. Might be.

Fine. There's begging.

"Everyone indulges you. That's your problem," she whispers, and then slips off me and disappears into the dark. I sit there with a hard on *again*, feeling like a dipshit *again*, and listen to her boots crunch across the gravel drive.

Even so, I'm grinning. I really like our games.

CHAPTER 17 | Holly

Just go ahead and indulge, I think, splashing cold water from the bathroom sink onto my face. Sadly, it does jack all to cool me down. *Why not indulge? It isn't like you haven't been thinking about it.*

Way *more than you should.*

I frown at my damp reflection. Coming in from the Bronco, I'd gone straight to the bathroom, planning the coldest shower I could get. Only it ended up backfiring because I got a *really* good look at myself in the mirror—tangled hair, faintly swollen lips, starry eyes. There wasn't a cold enough shower in the world that would fix this. I want him.

"Ugh," I mutter, resisting the urge to bang my head against the wall. What *is* it about this guy? Why do I keep...lingering?

I grab a fluffy towel from the shelf, and dry my face. I should feel better, but my libido is still out of control. My nipples are too sensitive, rubbing against the thin fabric of my top.

"Should I play with one like this, while I suck the other?" he'd asked.

Honestly? I'd nearly combusted on the spot. Hell *yes*, he should play with me.

But then he'd opened that door, and cold—literally—reality came rushing in and my brain asked me what the hell I was doing.

I hang up the towel and study my reflection again. Washed face or not, I still look like I've been making out. There's the starry, wide eyes, the tousled hair...the grin trying to spread across my face.

Just jump him, I tell myself. Sex is just sex. That's not to mean I hop in bed with anyone I meet, but I've been able to have a couple partners where we both knew it was just for fun. Work made it difficult to have real relationships, but that didn't mean my need for orgasms lessened.

And, hell, sometimes I just needed to touch someone.

And—and I'm trying to justify this to myself and I shouldn't have to. Like I said, sex is just sex, and sex with Beau Kent would be great sex, but also just sex. No strings attached.

So why am I balking at what could possibly be the greatest orgasm of my life?

Because I want more. I want the real thing. It's a little voice inside my head, but it rings true. I want more, but I also know I can't have it. I take care of my mom. I work for Mrs. Mar and I'm working on my fashion line dream. I take care of everyone else—there's nothing left for "real," definitely nothing left for "more."

No matter how much I might want it.

I grip the sink edge and lean closer to my reflection in the mirror. Maybe I need to settle for good enough.

There's a champagne pop from outside the bathroom, and I pause. Beau wasn't kidding when he said he wanted to celebrate, and after the week I've had?

"Getting buzzed and laid sound perfect," I mutter, shoving away from the sink and opening the bathroom door. Beau's in the kitchen, bottle in one hand. He looks up and there must be something in my expression because he pauses.

Swallows.

He wants you, I think and the reminder is so powerful I go wet again. "Pour me a glass?" I ask, stripping my jacket and tossing it on the floor.

A smile tugs the corner of Beau's mouth. "Come and get it."

I walk toward him like my panties aren't damp and my nipples aren't already hard. I don't stop until we're toe to toe, until we're almost touching. I can smell the champagne on his breath, but I can also smell *him*: a mix of mint and soap.

"I've reconsidered your offer." I meant for it to sound light and flirty, but it comes out half desperate and Beau hears it.

"My offer?" He slides his hand into my hair and grips, making my nipples tighten even more. He irritates me to no end, but I love how he touches me. He pulls me forward and I let him. Our lips brush. "Oh, you mean the one where I touch and suck you until you scream?"

It sends shivers down my spine.

"That's what I thought," Beau murmurs, massively smug. His tongue teases my bottom lip, begging for me to open for him, and it sends my already spinning brain into over drive.

It's just for fun, I remind myself. *In the morning, you can play it off like it wasn't good enough to mention.*

Or like it doesn't matter.

Yeah, I think, relaxing into him. *That's the one.*

So I let myself indulge.

I loop my arms around his neck, earning a surprised growl from Beau. My mouth opens and his tongue teases mine. His other hand cups my cheek, thumb skimming over my skin.

I close my eyes. How long has it been since I relaxed like this? Since I *indulged* like this? I press into him and he rewards me with a deeper kiss.

He feels amazing, I think. His body is so hard against mine, all wiry muscle and heat and I need it *closer*.

I yank his worn T-shirt up, half-expecting it to rip in my hands it's so thin. By some miracle, it doesn't, and I'm treated to the sight of Beau's bare chest. It makes my mouth go dry.

Broad shoulders, muscled chest narrowing down into abs I want to trace with my tongue, he's perfect.

And he grins like he knows it.

"Fair's fair," he murmurs, fingers already finding the buttons on the back of my dress. In seconds, the lace puddles around my boots. Not that I notice. I can't take my eyes off him. The smooth skin, the tight muscles, the tattoos.

So it is *true*, I think, fingers tracing the small roman numerals that start just below his collarbone. *All these wins.*

They reach all the way to his hip bone.

Then Beau lifts me, wrapping my legs around his waist, and carries me to the couch. He tosses me down and grins, grabbing my boots and tugging them off. "Let's do this right," he says.

I laugh. It's probably nerves because I can't help it, and when I open my eyes again, his gaze isn't on my face. It's sliding over and over my body.

"I've wanted this," he breathes.

In spite of my confusion, heat pools in my stomach—and spreads lower. The leather couch cushions suddenly feel hot against my bare back as Beau bends over me. His knees spread my legs apart. His hands pull down my bra, baring me.

"Mmm," he murmurs as I arch into his chest. The quickest flick of his fingers and my bra pops open. He tosses it away, everything in me clenching. He traces the hem of my panties over and over until I squirm. "You're even more perfect than I thought you would be."

He's thought about what I look like naked? For all of two seconds, I'm appalled and then I remind myself: this is Beau. He's probably imagined everyone naked.

But there's something about the way he turns the words that makes it sound almost...reverent. I push against his teasing fingertip, unable to look away from him.

Beau's eyes lift, meeting mine. "Mmm." His smile lights me like a fuse. "You like watching, sweetheart?"

Before I can answer, he slips his finger beneath the lace, going straight for my clit. I jerk.

"Even better," he whispers, easing closer. That inked collar bone brushes my mouth and I have to resist the urge to kiss every single one of his wins. "Should I make you come hard and fast?"

Yes. My legs fall even further open. Yesyesyesyes!

A low, dark chuckle. His touch lightens. "Or should I make you wait for it?"

I shake my head. "No," I manage, pushing against the cushions to lift myself higher, *firmer* against him. "Please don't."

"Christ, I could get used to you saying 'please.'" Beau replaces his finger with his thumb. He rubs my clit in soft circles, driving me higher, faster. I'm panting. "In fact..." He rubs my clit once—firmly—and my hips buck. "Say it again."

"Please." The word escapes before I even realize it's gone.

Another firm rub. It streaks lightning across my skin and my head falls back.

"Now see, darlin'." Beau's Southern drawl deepens and I get wetter. "Isn't this better than when you're snapping at me?"

"I only—" another rub that makes my toes curl "—snap at you when you're being an ass!"

"Ah ah." He begins those maddening circles again. "That was a tactical mistake. Never insult the man who wants to make you come."

I glare at him and he laughs. The asshole *laughs*. "You—" I start to rear up and his thumb taps me, sparking a wave of pleasure.

"You want to leave now?" he asks, blowing cool breath across me. "We're just starting."

I twist, desperate for a firmer touch. It doesn't matter though. Any way I move, he keeps it light, teasing. "I thought you said you wanted to make me come."

There's an embarrassing whine to my voice now and he leans down, sucking one nipple into his mouth and tugging until I gasp.

"I *am* going to make you come. I just haven't decided how yet."

Like it's his freaking decision, I think, gritting my teeth so I don't moan as he begins to play with me again. I dig my heels into the cushions, lifting my hips, and he backs off, chuckling.

"I bet you can't," I moan. I can't help it.

"Can't what?"

There's a tightness in his voice now and I turn my face into the couch cushions so he can't see my smile. Beau might be breaking me into pieces, but I'm not so far gone I don't remember who he is: a walking, talking ego. "Maybe you can't make me come."

Another light touch that makes me want to crawl the walls. "That so?" he asks.

"Might be."

"Good thing we have all night."

All night? My eyes fly open, meeting his. Beau's doing that annoying, smug smirk thing he does when he's winning.

I glance down, slightly horrified to see how I'm riding his hand and arching under his gaze. Beau gives me a languid smile. His whole body's relaxed, his movements somehow lazy and precise.

He could *do this all night*, I realize, shivering.

It makes him grin. "Still think I can't make you come?"

CHAPTER 18 | Holly

Still think I can't make you come? The words ripple through me, and I pull up my chin. "Nope."

"Good." Beau's smile never wavers. His body doesn't move.

But his fingers do.

He pinches my clit between his thumb and forefinger, and I come in an instant rush. My head flies back and my hips push into his hand. Another pinch, another wave, and dimly I hear Beau say my name. Say it again.

"Look at me," he says.

Still panting, I do.

He grins. "Still think I can't make you come?"

I open my mouth to answer, but he drops to the floor by the couch, lowering his head and holding my gaze as he slowly licks my already throbbing clit. I gasp and try to wiggle away, but his hands slap down on my thighs. His fingers dig in. He holds me to him.

"No!" I writhe, unable to escape. "It's too soon! I'm too sens—"

He licks me again, a firm stroke that softens over my still throbbing clit. He circles me, holding me effortlessly as I thrash. *I can't*, I think. *I can't.*

But my body disagrees, already he's making me grow wet again, needy again. His tongue slides into me and I'm suddenly desperate to fuck his face. Then he withdraws, sucking my clit before I can complain. He pushes me over again, licking me until my screams go hoarse, until he's pulled everything from me and I'm boneless. His hands hold me up.

"Now who's playing with who?" he whispers, nipping the inside of my thigh.

My cheeks go hot as chills climb all over my skin. Fine. Whatever. So he knew I was manipulating him. Who cares? I don't. I just came three times.

I summon a shaky smile, fully ready to tell him so when Beau sits up. His shoulders tighten, tattoos standing out dark against his skin, as his hands go to his jeans' top button. He undoes it and my legs open.

He smiles. "Wider."

Trembling, I obey. It makes his eyes go bright. Taking his time, he unbuttons his jeans, working them down over his hips and I have to stuff down a gasp. No boxers. No briefs. Just *him*.

He's bigger than I expected, and I should probably be nervous—it's been months and *months* since I've had sex—but just looking at him makes me want more.

"Lift your knees for me."

I do. It slides me a little further down the cushions and he hisses something under his breath as I open even wider. His hand grips his shaft, stroking it once. Twice. I whimper.

"Now put your arms over your head," he orders, voice gone rough.

I lift my arms, shaky hands grabbing the armrest behind me. He makes a low sound deep in his chest.

"I could look at you like this all damn day."

I blink, coming back to myself and realizing how bare I am, how exposed. He has me naked, spread, *needing* him. "Beau—"

His eyes flick to my face, holding my gaze as he slides on a condom. "Holly," he murmurs and lowers himself on top of me, his length hard and hot against the inside of my thigh, his weight delicious. "The things I want to do to you," he whispers, sounding utterly in awe.

It makes me whimper. I reach for him and he grabs my wrists.

"Ah ah," he says, moving my arms above my head and holding them in place. "This is about you."

What? I squirm and his grip tightens. "It's *been* about me," I whisper, suddenly shy. My face feels about a thousand different shades of red, but I don't think he even notices.

Beau repositions, taking both my wrists in one hand while the other skims down to my ass. In one firm movement, he lifts me, his shaft pressing my entrance. I gasp. He grins. "Tell me again how I can't make you come," he says.

And he enters me with a hard thrust.

Now we both gasp. He's stretching me to the point of over-fullness, and like he senses it, he gentles his strokes. One. Hold. Two. Hold. Three—my hips follow, and he lets out a hiss. "*There*," he mutters, finding a brisker, harder rhythm that makes me moan. "There you are."

I arch, my already aching nipples brushing his chest. His fingers dig *hard* into my ass, each fingertip blazing against my skin. Friction. Heat. My head rolls back as my body gives into his. In this position, I can't fight the pleasure. I can't get in my head. My whole world is suddenly made up of Beau: his grip, his thrusts, his hardness.

I'm rushing toward another release and suddenly he slows, dipping his head to kiss me like we have the rest of our lives to tease.

"Tell me," he whispers against the corner of my mouth, his drawl gone honey warm. It makes me want to moan. "Tell me how I can't make you come."

"No." I love denying him. I love the punishment I get. He gives me two short, hard thrusts and I'm moaning again.

"Tell me," he says, and I shake my head, sinking my teeth into the dip between his neck and shoulder. He rewards me with another rock of his hips, his fingers twisting my sensitive nipple. Pleasure washes through me, building and building and—he slows his rhythm.

I glare up at him, and Beau kisses me hard, finally breaking away to say, "Won't admit when you're beat?"

The slow, full thrusts turn into slow, half-thrusts as his hand leaves my ass and returns to my clit. One touch lights me up. One more stroke, and I go wet in a rush. I jerk against him, a heartbeat away from release and we both know it.

"Would it be so awful to just admit you like how I ride you?" he continues, both hands going to my hips now, shifting our position so he can take me deeper.

Oh my God, I want him to take me deeper.

He rolls his hips and my hands fly to his. I grip, scrabble, pull. Nothing. He gives me another half thrust and makes a *tsking* noise. "Incapable of taking direction and incapable of admitting when wrong. I'm going to enjoy writing up your yearly review." Then he leans close, loosening one hand from my hip so he can hold my chin. I freeze, staring up into his eyes as he gives me a long, lazy thrust. "I really enjoy making you eat your words."

A deliberate thrust.

I cry out.

He strokes me again. I lift my hips and he curses, bucking against me as I tighten my legs around him. I take him deep and watch his eyes roll back. I know the feeling. I'm coming again. It washes over me in an unending wave as he pulls me against him, and I urge him on. I dig my heels into him, arch my breasts into him. I watch as he buckles against me.

"Can't stop myself! Can't—" His head flings back as he comes, pumping me hard as my pussy grips him harder. "Holly. Holly. *Holly!*"

He holds me against him as he comes down, giving me shallow strokes that make me shiver.

"And I can make you come too," I whisper.

His eyes pop open, and we stare at each other, panting. There's a calculating look in Beau's eyes—one that makes me shy all over again—and I *know* if I look away now, he'll have me.

He already has you, I realize, cold coiling in my gut. Because all of this? I want to do it again.

And again.

A quirk of a smile. "You're not what I thought."

I frown. *Neither are you,* I think. Not that I'm going to tell him. I arch one brow in (what I hope) is a mysterious fashion and roll out from under him. I pop my feet and force my shaky legs to straight.

Beau slaps my bare ass and I gasp, the burn lingering. I narrow my eyes at him, but he's flopped back onto the couch, treating me to another long look at his perfect chest. "Trying to control the situation—now *that* I should've expected that from you. Next time, I'll take you from behind. We'll see how well you can control things when you're bent over the bed."

Next time. I swallow and he grins. "Not sure what to do about that, darlin'?"

The southern accent isn't as thick. He's coming back to himself, getting cockier by the second. I consider him for a beat and then take my time with a luxurious stretch, arms over my head, back arched. Beau swears under his breath, hands clenching as he stares at me.

Now *I'm* grinning. "Oh," I say. "I'm pretty sure I know *exactly* what do to about that, 'darlin'."

And while he glares at me, I hop up and sashay toward the bathroom, shutting the door before he can see I'm still grinning.

CHAPTER 19 | Beau

I wasn't shocked that sex with Holly was even better than I expected. I was, however, shocked to find myself passing out at eleven and waking up at six.

Almost like I used to.

I guess 'passing out' is a bit of an exaggeration—I hadn't even touched the champagne last night. Perfectly good waste of an *extremely* good bottle too—but I was so tired I just crashed.

Last thing I remember was kind of sort of hoping Holly would wander in to sleep with me after she showered, but she didn't. The light under her door went dark and I was vaguely amused to realize she'd used me to relax.

All the more reason to annoy her, I think the next morning as I pour myself coffee. *Then she'll need more relaxation and we can go again.*

The idea makes my dick hard enough to hurt. I cram a plastic top onto my coffee mug and head for my truck. Holly's...not at all what I thought and I don't quite know what to do about that.

Outside, the farm is dark and shadowy with the faintest edge of gray in the distance. Of course, the barn itself is lit up and busy. Horses are being fed. Stalls are being mucked. A couple people slide glances in my direction, but no one says much past the usual good mornings as I walk up the aisle and into the tack room. I could almost pretend I do this every day.

Inside the tack room, the desk light is on, and Maisy's sitting in front of the computer, muttering at it.

"Everything, okay?" I ask.

Maisy blinks at me, eyes huge as saucers. I can't decide if that's just the way she rolls, or if I made that bad of an impression on her. Probably a little of both.

"I was—I was trying to check our SmartPak order, but the Internet is down."

"Probably need to reset the router."

More blinking. She's either terrified of me or has no idea what I'm talking about.

"I'll take a look," I say, carefully lowering myself to the floor and sliding under the desk. For whatever reason, we installed our router in the most inconvenient spot possible and it takes me a minute of stretching behind the desk before I can turn it on and off. "Try that," I say, lying on my back and staring at the desk's underside.

Maisy clicks the mouse back and forth as the tack room door opens and shuts. High heels click across the old heart pine floors, and I know without even looking, Adele is here.

She toes my foot. "You're up early."

"Yeah."

"Do you have a moment to talk?"

I slide out from under the desk as Maisy hops to her feet. "I'll just..." She flees without finishing, shutting the door behind her without a backward glance.

"Is she always so nervous?" Adele asks.

"As far as I can tell." Trying to look casual, I lean one hand on the desk chair as I stand, careful not to wince when my hip twinges. "What did you want to talk about?"

She takes a moment to adjust her watch band, and I'm not sure if she's stalling or if she's just touching up her outfit. It's not even seven AM and Adele is the picture of elegance in high heels, sleek dress pants, and a white collared shirt. It's like her super power to look polished. Personally, I've never cared enough about that stuff—except for my horses. When it comes to them, I want everything perfect. Or I did.

Adele takes a deep breath and looks up at me. In the shadowy light, she looks older than she usually does, way more tired. "I want you to tell me what you've found out about Dell, or what you suspect. If there's truly more to this, tell me."

I pause. What I know is still pretty circumstantial: Kat saw Parish coming out and going into Arch's stall at very different times than what Parish said. If I tell Adele, she'll only come up with a million reasons why it could mean anything other than what I'm *sure* it is.

Then again, she's also Adele, and she's the closest thing I have to family. We've worked together for years and she's an amazing person.

Which is probably why she can't see the bad in other people.

I sigh. *What the hell?* I figure. "I have a witness who saw Parish come out of Arch's stall while he was thrashing. Parish only went back in because he knew he'd been spotted."

"Who's your witness?"

"Can't say. She wants to stay out of this."

Adele stiffens. "Cowardly."

"*Smart.* She knows how much trouble this could buy her."

"I would say so. Eyewitnesses are wrong all the time, Beau. She could be misremembering."

"Sure." I nod. *Not bloody likely,* I think, *but sure.* "But when you put her story next to confirmed rumors Dell wasn't paying his people, it starts to look...really suspicious."

Adele's dark brown eyes are huge. She swallows and her hand drifts to the pearls at her throat. "What do you mean 'confirmed?' He said that's a rumor, that everything's fine."

"I asked around. It's definitely true." My back is starting to ache and I lean against the desk for support. "He's broke—or he *was* broke. Arch's insurance policy helped with that."

Adele pales. "That's not enough proof, and you know it. I've known Dell all my life. He's never..." she trails off.

This is pointless, I think. *It always comes back to Dell being a family friend.* I shake my head and start to push past her.

Adele catches me, holding onto my elbow with an iron grip. "I do *business* with the man. I know him."

"Are you sure?" I pause, knowing what I need to say and hating that I have to say it. "Adele, when this comes out, it's going to be bad. You need to be prepared."

Her hand drops. She stares at me like I'm a stranger.

"Just let it go. You're not going to believe anything I say—"

"I've known you for almost as long as I've known Dell, and I don't believe a word he's saying about you either."

Silence stretches between us, barn sounds filtering in. One of the horses neighs, and jazz music—Adele swears it's Ace's favorite—drifts by in disjointed snatches. It's so familiar I don't even need the full tune: Strange Fruit by Billie Holiday. She's been playing it for Ace for ten years now. The way the morning light slants across us, the smell of Adele's Chanel perfume, it's *all* so familiar.

I damn sure don't know who I am without riding, but I might not know who I am without Adele too. She's family.

The realization makes me think I might be sick. First, Dell took Arch. Now he's going to take the only family I have. If Adele sides with him, there won't be anything left between us.

"He's never given you any indication ever that he's capable of something like this?" I ask at last.

Adele's lips clamp together. "People can do terrible things—especially for money." She hesitates, something nameless playing behind her eyes. "If this is true, it's animal cruelty and insurance fraud."

"Yes."

Her eyes swing to mine. "And it's *horrible*. It's not anything I want to be associated with, anything I would *ever* condone."

"Then don't. Help me find the truth."

"What if you can't prove it? What if he…gets away with it?"

I give her the smile I used to use on reporters, the confident one, the one that says 'I can't lose' because I didn't usually. "He won't," I say.

Because one way or another, Dell Landers and Parish will pay for this. I'm going to make sure of it. There's more than one way of taking people down, and I don't need a court decision to do it.

CHAPTER 20 | Holly

I wake up after seven and it looks like Beau's long gone. The coffee machine's cold and the truck's already parked up by the stables. If I look through the living room's picture window, I can easily spot it.

Not that I was looking necessarily.

I'm fiddling with the coffee machine when I hear someone drive up and park outside the cottage. Briefly, I think Beau might've returned, but then I hear heavy boots galloping up the steps and grin. Ellie. Has to be.

"Hello?" she shouts. "Anybody home?"

"Hey!" I stick my head around the corner and wave. "C'mon in. You want any coffee?"

"Nah." Ellie eases through the door, looking from side to side. She's dressed for the day in fawn-colored breeches and a gorgeous pair of cognac riding boots. Her huge purse hangs off one shoulder. "I just wanted to see how life was going at Camp Cargo Shorts."

"Shockingly clean."

"You sure? Like checked-it-with-a-black-light sure?"

I laugh. "No. I probably should've, but he hasn't had a girl over since I moved in."

She arches a brow in amazement, and wanders into the living room, gaze wandering from the tasteful beige rug to the tasteful beige walls to the equally tasteful leather couch. In the morning light, it looks like any other leather Chesterfield, but now every time I look at it, I think about what Beau and I did on it and my face goes red.

Normally, three orgasms is plenty to hold me, but clearly my body disagrees because in addition to flaming cheeks, my nipples are now aching. I almost wish Beau had been returning.

Ellie drops onto the couch and opens her purse. "I saw Beau at the barn so I figured we were safe to talk because..." She takes a huge breath before grinning. "I have pictures!"

I gasp. 'Pictures' can only mean wedding pictures! Ellie's beautiful sister, Wren, was married two months ago in a whirlwind wedding. I helped with the dress, decorations, and drinking as much champagne as possible. It was a killer night. We had so much fun.

"What's your Wifi password?" Ellie asks, flipping open her laptop. "Everything is still on the photographer's website, but Wren gave me the log-in."

Minutes later, we're watching Wren and her husband, Tate, smile up at us from the screen. I put my coffee cup down and lean closer, trying to see the dress's pleating. I so nailed that alteration. I *told* that seamstress she was doing it wrong. "She looks amazing."

"She looks amazing thanks to you—and stop obsessing over the dress. I can tell you're checking your work."

I shrug, and for a moment, we sit in silence and flip through picture after picture of an incredibly radiant Wren. It's only been two months, but it seems like a lifetime ago.

"I wish Parker had come to the wedding," Ellie says absently, fingers trailing over a shot of the camellia centerpieces. "She said Matthew wasn't feeling well, but he *always* seems to be sick whenever she's supposed to visit, and we pretty much never talk anymore."

I nod. I've noticed the same thing. Parks married Matthew right out of high school. He'd inherited some remodeling firm over in Seattle so they packed up and moved so he could learn the family business. At first, we made the separation work, but little by little, Parker's been vanishing from our lives. Something else I need to fix because I don't want to lose her.

I lean my cheek against Ellie's shoulder. "How's Wren enjoying New York?"

Ellie frowns. "Loves it, and I love that she loves it, but, you know..."

I sling my arm around her shoulders. Losing Wren was really hard on her. After their parents died in a car accident, Ellie and Wren were pretty much all each other had. Then Wren fell for Tate and Ellie kind of sort of lost her mind for a bit, but it all worked out—especially for Ellie because now she has Caleb.

"Hello? Earth to Holly." Ellie waves her hand in front of my face. "What's up? I thought you'd be more excited about this."

I shake my head. "Sorry. I have a lot going on."

"Yeah, I bet. I have to speak at a course designer seminar this week. Want to come? We could tranq Beau, leave him locked in your closet, and get you away for a bit?"

I grin. "Tempting as that is, I better not." I take a deep, deep breath before saying, "Beau thinks Arch was killed for the insurance money, and I think he might be right."

Ellie sits up straight, staring at me like I've just spoken in tongues. "Are you serious? How—" She shakes her head as if trying to clear it. "I mean, what proof does he have?"

"So far, just witnesses who saw some suspicious behavior."

"Like what?"

I recount everything Beau and I know now so far and Ellie listens without interrupting me even once. At the end, she sits quietly, looking at her folded hands and then says, "This is horrible. If it's true, Dell is a vile human being. It's one thing to put down a horse because it's sick or dying, but to kill it for insurance? He could've sold him."

"Yeah, but he wouldn't have made as much money. Remember Arch had a refusal in his last competition. Beau was sure he just needed time off, but Dell thought Arch was breaking down."

Ellie nods. "That was before I came to Twelve Oaks, but I heard about it. Either way, Beau walked into that competition with a horse worth over a million and walked out with one worth far less."

It's one of the horrible truths of show horses. They're only as good as their competition records. Winning prestigious classes can triple your horse's value, but it's a precarious thing because losing prestigious classes takes prices the other direction. Fast.

In Arch's case, he went in being a recent gold medalist and he came out looking like something was wrong with him. It probably lowered his worth by several hundred thousand and for an owner who was counting on the sale to make ends meet, it would have been a devastating blow.

Looking at Ellie, I can tell she's thinking the same thing. "If Dell really needed the cash..." she trails off, looking ill.

"He still could've sold him. He could've done the honorable thing—the right thing—and made up the difference."

She nods, tears making her eyes shine. Ellie's a true horsewoman. She loves her horses, so much so that it really bothers her to sell them on, but she's always understood the reality. After all, this is the way she makes her living.

"What's Beau going to do about it?"

"Get to the bottom of it. I have to admit I'm...impressed. You're the only pro rider I've ever been able to stand. The rest of them used their horses like tennis rackets. Honestly? I expected Beau to be the same. I mean, he's had how many horses so far? Forty? Fifty?"

Ellie thinks for a moment. "Way more than that. It's the nature of the game. Horses work out or don't work out. Mrs. Mar has always had an impeccable reputation for taking care of them though. She doesn't sell on to just anyone."

"Which is why this will look even worse if it goes public."

"He really isn't going to give it up?"

I shake my head. Beau Kent is a lot of things, but I'm beginning to realize he has more integrity than I would ever have given him credit for. "I don't think he's wired to give up on anything."

Ellie blinks. "You *like* him!"

"He has his moments."

She continues to study me and heat begins to creep up my neck and across my cheeks. Ellie's eyes widen. "Oh my God, you *really* like him!"

The world's stupidest giggle escapes me and Ellie shrieks. "You're *sleeping* with him! I can't believe you didn't tell me!"

I cringe, still shaking with laughter. "It was…" I have no idea what it was. A bad idea? Cheaper than a massage and three times as relaxing? A lapse in judgment? Well, I can't really say it was a lapse since I fully intend to do it again.

"Yeah." I sigh, rubbing my face with both hands. "I'm sleeping with him. He's gorgeous and it was *good*. Oh my God, it was good."

I drop my hands, realizing what I just said. Out. Loud. Ellie and I stare at each other. She grins. "So what's the problem?"

"Who said there was a problem?"

She raises both brows, waiting.

I sigh heavily. "He's *Beau*. He's a manwhore. The only real feelings he gets are in his pants."

"But?"

I scowl. Ellie reads me too well. "But, sometimes there's more to him. Lots more. Like with Arch. He knows pursuing this could tank him, but he's doing it anyway because it's the right thing to do, the honest thing to do. I really like that about him."

"I like that too." Ellie slides lower. "But I'm scared the bad stuff will outweigh the good. I don't want him to hurt you."

I smile. "He can't. I won't let him. This doesn't mean anything. It's just for fun," I add and I sound *great*, like it's the most natural thing in the world.

And it is, but Ellie doesn't look like she believes me.

CHAPTER 21 | Beau

Adele and I make small talk until she has to leave for an appointment. I wouldn't say we're good, but we're...better. We walk out to her car together, and as she drives away, she studies me through the window, lifting one hand in a wave. I wave back like everything's fine and I'm not seething.

Parish and Dell Landers are going down. I'm going to make sure of it.

And realizing that? Committing to it? Suddenly the seething stands down. I feel more centered, more like myself.

Not sure what that says about me honestly. This is revenge. That's what I'm talking about, isn't it?

Pretty much, I think, turning for my truck. Ellie will be here any minute now to start the day and I don't want to be here. I can't watch her ride, not while I'm still sidelined. I ease into the truck and pop it in reverse, maneuvering out of the parking spot and onto the farm road.

So what's my next step? I need proof, which at this point would mean bloodwork. I need to show something was in Arch's system, but I know the vet that did the necropsy after he died. Nothing was found.

Or so I was told. I roll down my window a little bit, letting cold rush across my face. I've known Dr. Jenners for years, but I don't know if our relationship would extend to asking awkward questions about one of her patients.

Ahead of me, Adele turns onto the main highway and I keep circling around, taking the long loop down toward my place. As I round the bend, Ellie flies by in her car. She waves, laughing.

The hell? I wonder, scowling at her. She doesn't slow down and I swing into my driveway. Holly's standing on the front porch, coffee mug in hand. She looks amazing in skinny jeans and a slouchy gray cardigan. It spills off one shoulder, revealing the lacy camisole under-neath. Whatever satisfaction I got last night evaporates on the spot. I need her again. Immediately.

Then I remember Ellie coming from this direction and my dick stands down. They must've been catching up. The idea makes the hair on the back of my neck prickle.

"Did I miss the pillow fight?" I ask, sliding out of the truck.

Holly lifts one brow. "Har har. You're up early."

I shrug. Looking at her now...I suddenly don't know what to say and I don't know what that means. Actually, I do. I like her. More than I should. It's irritating.

"Coffee?" Holly asks.

"God, yes." I follow her into the house and get hit with the smell of something delicious cooking. I take a deep breath. Eggs and cheese? Gotta be.

I'm right too. Holly's put together some sort of casserole. Plus bis-cuits. Plus fruit salad. She pulls a plate out of the cabinet and forks a huge wedge of casserole onto it, dumps a bunch of fruit next to the casserole, and passes it to me.

I hesitate. I'm really not used to people being this nice.

Actually, that's not true. I'm not used to Holly being this nice. Usu-ally, we annoy each other. Is this because of last night?

"What's this about?" I ask.

Another brow arch. "Some of us like to consume things other than alcohol and cereal."

I frown. *Okay, I deserved that*, I think. The barb should put us back on our usual footing, but I can't seem to find it. Looking at her, I feel unraveled.

Clearly, I'm the only one though because Holly's wandering around the kitchen like this is no big thing.

Which leaves me wondering *why* it feels like such a big thing to me.

I sit down at the kitchen table and scowl at her. I'm not used to being the one who doesn't know what to say, or what to do, or why my lungs feel two sizes too small.

Oh, for God's sake, Kent, I tell myself. *If she can play it cool, so can you.*

"So what's the deal?" I ask in between bites of breakfast casserole. It's amazing and somehow that makes me even more irritated. "Why are you really doing this for Adele?"

"Feeding you, or making sure you behave?"

"Why do you need the money so bad?" I look her up and down and regret it. She looks so...touchable. I want to rub my hands all over her cardigan and then pull it off. "You want a dress shop?"

Holly takes a deep breath through her nose and pushes it back out her mouth before saying: "It's more than a *shop*. It's a *line*. My line. I want to design clothes."

"Oh." I pause, thinking it over. I almost can't because I've taken another bite of breakfast casserole and my eyes nearly roll back into my head it's so good. "I can't even draw stick figures."

A tiny unwilling smile. I wouldn't exactly say it's a win, but I'll take it.

"And that's what you're going to use the bonus for?" I ask.

She nods.

"How will that work out with your mom?"

Her shoulders tighten. "How do you know about my mom?"

"Ellie's mentioned her before. Said something about you're taking care of her. Is that why you came home?"

"Not really. The design firm I worked for went under and I needed a place to crash. Then she got sick and I helped out."

"Oh." I think this over. "So will she come with you back to New York or what?"

"I don't know. I haven't figure that part out. The thing is—" Holly stops abruptly, like she suddenly realized she was sharing something she shouldn't. If I wasn't already intrigued, I really am now.

"What's the thing?" I ask, turning so I can face her.

There's a war of emotions going on in her expression right now and I wait it out. Eventually, something wins. It makes her mouth stamp into a firm line.

"The thing is," she says slowly, refilling her coffee cup and then carrying it to the table. She sits down next to me. "I love New York, but I love being here too. I feel really...torn."

"Oh," I say again. Somehow none of this is what I expected. "What kind of stuff do you want to design?"

Holly straightens in her chair, casting me an unreadable look before saying, "No one ever asks me that."

"Well, I *am* extraordinary."

"Not the word I generally use to describe you."

"Amazing?"

"No."

"Breathtaking?"

"Also no."

I sit back. "You should expand your vocabulary then." I smile so she knows I'm kidding, and after a beat, she smiles back. "I'll get you flashcards," I tell her. "So tell me: what do you want to design?"

"Everything." She takes a shaky breath, and I realize she's forcing herself to be brave. She thinks I'm going to give her a hard time.

Is that what she thinks of me? I wonder, horrified, and then realize of course it is. It's not like I've been easy to be around.

"I'm really obsessed with vintage styling and I'd like to bring that to a ready to wear dress line, but I want the designs to fit the everyday woman, not just someone shaped like a model."

"Something for the rest of us."

"That's almost hilarious coming from someone like you."

"What?"

Holly wave one hand in dismissal, eyes wandering to the windows and the horses beyond. "You're so rare. You're like a model. You're the one percent of the one percent. You're...not like the rest of us."

"I still don't understand."

She gives me a wry smile. "How many people in the world can do what you do?"

Oh. I get it now, and the recognition must show on my face because her wry smile turns into a grin.

"Models are the same way," she continues. "It's a combination of all sorts of things that makes a great model. Great riders are the same way. Most of us can diet or practice until the cows come home, but it doesn't mean we'll ever be as good as the people born with that innate *something* that makes them so special."

I pause, feeling like she's just pulled back a layer of me. I know what she's talking about, but I rarely acknowledge it. Then again, if she can be brave and honest so can I.

"Yeah," I say at last, pushing a red grape around with my fork. "I know what you mean. I don't get why some people—most people—can't ride like I do."

Or did, I think, and for a second I can't breathe. I shake myself. "For me, it's like breathing. It hasn't always been easy, but it's always been attainable. I know that's not true for everyone."

She shrugs, and I feel like I could leave it there, but for some reason I can't and say, "I've never understood why professionals look down on the people who can't ride as well as they do. I mean from a financial sense, it's incredibly short sighted: there will always be more of them than us and they want to ride with us. They want to pay us to teach them what comes so easily to us. So they'll never ride as well? Who cares? Doesn't mean they don't deserve nice horses and compassionate trainers."

I concentrate on the fruit salad, waiting for Holly to respond, and when she doesn't, I dare a glance at her. She's staring at me like I have two heads. "Holy shit," she says at last. "I think we agree on business models *and* ethics."

I pause, knowing I should come up with some sort of smartass reply and not really having one. The idea we agree on something isn't a big deal. It's the idea that we agree on something I hold as close to me as this...bothers me.

I deliberately look Holly over, trying to annoy her and only noticing how the sunlight turns her blond hair almost white and how perfect her breasts are in that lacy top. My dick goes insta-hard. Christ, the woman is always so sexy.

"That's definitely a first for us," I tell her, shifting so my blue balls have a chance of not crippling me. "I have some lingerie ideas if you're looking for a way to reward me."

"And then you ruin it. Typical." But there's no animosity behind the words. Holly's looking me over now and I'm not sure what to do. I give her the lazy, satisfied grin that should make her roll her eyes, but it doesn't.

"You do that every time, don't you?" she asks suddenly.

My stomach curdles. "What are you talking about?"

"When you finally say something real, you follow it up with something obnoxious to cover it up."

"No."

"Yes." Holly's nodding to herself now like I'm some problem she's just unraveled. She takes a sip of coffee and grins. "I see through you, Kent."

I scowl. "No, you don't."

Except every time she looks at me, I feel like she does.

CHAPTER 22 | Holly

I can't believe I actually said that, but I did and it's out there and I fully expect Beau to swish off in a huff, but he doesn't. He shovels another two helpings of breakfast casserole onto his plate, and then reaches for the fruit.

"Is that another dare?" he asks, grinning. "Like when you said I couldn't make you come?"

My face goes hot, and it's totally and *completely* irrational, but I can suddenly feel his hands on me. The promise in his eyes makes me want to strip right here and jump him.

"You tell me," I finally manage and Beau laughs. I don't blame him. It's not my best snappy retort. He makes my brain go fuzzy. Inside my sweater pocket, my cell vibrates. I check the screen. Home number.

"Gotta take this," I say, standing up and turning away. My spine heats like he's watching me. Even stepping outside onto the front porch does nothing to cool me off. "Hello?"

"Holly."

"Hey, Dane. How goes it?"

"It goes." He sounds pissy and I swallow, sitting down on the top step.

"Are you okay?"

"No, it's a little hard to get a merger finished from here." His voice is tight and I flinch. "I need you to talk to Mom. She wants me to take her to the grocery store. She has some party coming up."

Oh boy, I think. There's no way she told him what kind of party she's having, and I decide not to enlighten him. Some details are best left out. "Why don't you want to take her to the store?"

"She's in a mini-skirt, Holls. A *mini*-skirt. It's probably one of yours."

I laugh. I can't help it. "Actually, I'll be it isn't. She thinks mine are too long. She's your mother, Dane. Let her wear what she wants."

"Hold on."

There's a thump on the other end and I hear someone breathing. Holding the phone a little closer, I ask, "Mom?"

"Holls?" Her voice is a little wavery and thin today. "How are you, honey? How's work?"

I smile. Might be wavery and thin, but if she's wearing mini-skirts and going to the store, she's doing great. The realization makes my heart soar. "Beau's..."

Even sexier than before.

And not what I thought.

It's the last realization that makes me really pause.

"I'm managing," I say at last, stretching my legs out until my feet almost reach the bottom step. "It's a day by thing."

"I'll bet. What have I always told you, girl? If it has tires or testicles—"

"It will cause you problems," I finish, grinning.

"Your brother's in a mood. It's getting quite wearing."

"I'll be home soon. Only another week."

"Just in time for Wendy Holviak's movie night. Her grandson came home from college and taught her to make hunch punch. We're going to drink and watch Magic Mike again. You and Ellie should come."

We lose the next twenty minutes in funny, little asides. Our conversation spinning back and forth and away on tangents. It's probably maddening for anyone to listen to, but I love it. She's my mom and my friend and I'm so lucky to have her. I think it was the round of flu that really brought the whole thing home: she won't be here forever. I want to stay close, but I also want New York.

You need something for yourself, a little voice that sounds remarkably like Scott whispers.

And now I feel conflicted and guilty and unsure all over again.

"Oh, dear," Mom says, blowing out a sigh. "Your brother's fussing. We're being too loud. Can we talk later?"

"'Course. Love you."

"Love you too." After she hangs up, I take a couple minutes to sit on the step and breathe. I need to figure out what I'm going to do, who I'm going to be—and soon too. I push to my feet and let myself back inside.

Shockingly, Beau is at the sink, doing the dishes. His hair stands up in the back like someone dragged him through a bush backward, but he's considerate enough to clean.

I don't get you, I think.

"She okay?" Beau doesn't look my way and I'm glad. He's caught me off-guard. Why would he ask?

Why would he *care?*

"Yeah," I finally manage, tugging my cardigan tight around me. "She's great. My brother's annoying her, but that's normal for us."

We look at each other. I'm not sure what Beau's seeing and I'm not sure I want to know. He blinks first, swiping his truck keys from the table. "I'm glad. C'mon. We have places to go."

"Like where?"

"Dr. Jenners," he says and stalks off, leaving me to follow along behind like a good little assistant, and I take a minute to fantasize about kicking him.

But where? I wonder, eyes running down his lean back to his perfect ass. Even in ratty cargo shorts, Beau looks damn near perfect.

"Want me to drive?" I ask suddenly not sure if I want to kick him in the ass or grab his ass.

"God, no. I want to make it there alive."

Definitely kick him in the ass. Beau holds open the door for me, and as I pass, I ask, "Why Dr. Jenners?"

"We need proof." His tone—dark and tight—gives me chills. "And she's my last shot."

***

Dr. Elizabeth Jenners is one of the top equine vets in the southeast. Her practice includes hundreds of clients and her office location probably take up three or four acres between the cutting edge barn and the paddocks for sick or lame horses.

As we drive in, three truck and trailer rigs are already parked and empty, their high-priced performance horses inside being evaluated. Beau parks us next to the office's entrance, and as we go inside, smiles his "Aw, shucks, it was only *two* gold medals" at the middle-aged woman who gawks at us.

Inside, the lobby is crowded with riders, owners, and several barky, little dogs. Beau goes to the receptionist's counter and I grab the closest seat, noticing again, that he isn't moving right. He's not limping like he did the night of the party, but he isn't moving smoothly either.

It's troubling—ironic too, because as naked as we got last night, we still don't really know each other. He's hiding something.

After a few minutes of whispering with the guy behind the desk, Beau returns to me. "We go next."

"Wait." I sit up, suddenly realizing he didn't have an appointment. "They're just going to see you right away because you're...you?"

"Great, isn't it?" His grin is thousand watts, but there's something flat behind his eyes, like I'm getting a glimpse of another Beau Kent, a ruined one I never would've guessed existed.

"What—"

"Beau?"

We turn. Dr. Jenners is standing at the lobby door and her smile is solely for Beau. Cold trickles down my spine. He didn't get in because he's Beau Kent—well, I'm sure it helped—he got in because they've slept together.

Or she wants to sleep with him.

And he's using it.

"Let's talk back here," she says, motioning for us to follow her. Beau nudges me ahead of him and we walk into the back. I've only seen Dr. Jenners a few times at our farm, but even at her office, she looks the same: barn clothes, smooth, brown ponytail, and cup of coffee in one hand. It's not hard to see why Beau would be into her. She has a great smile, and is supposed to be some sort of veterinary genius.

"Thanks for seeing us," Beau says to her.

"Of course. Let's talk in my office." Dr. Jenners points to a door down the hallway on our right and leads us into a sunny office, its walls lined with filing cabinets and vintage foxhunting pictures. The desk is messy and she has to push papers aside before finding a spot to sit. "What did you need to see me about?" she asks Beau.

I curl into an armchair and study them. Her tone is light, her smile is still huge, and even though Beau's shoulders are tight and coiled, his own smile is pure promise.

"I had a few questions about Arch," he says. "I know you're too smart for my bullshit so I'll just get straight to the point: what can you tell me about the necropsy?"

It sucks all the air from the room, and for a second, I think—flirty Beau or not—Jenners is going to throw us out. Her expression hardens, but when she sighs, I realize it isn't hardness so much as exhaustion. Briefly, she looks utterly beaten down.

"It was normal," she says finally, rubbing both hands over her face. "Everything seemed normal."

"That can't be right."

"I agree."

Beau sucks in a breath like he's about to argue and stops. "You agree? Good. That's...good."

He glances at me and I don't know what to say. I'm not seeing the cocky Beau from seconds before who was flattering his way into information. I'm seeing the raw Beau from *days* before, when I said I believed he had a point. I'm not sure which to believe.

"So what didn't look right?" Beau asks her.

"All of it? None of it?" She frowns and looks away. "I'd been seeing Arch since Adele and Dell purchased him. He was healthy as could be at our last insurance assessment. Between his exemplary performance seemingly excellent health, I had no problem signing off on the insurance bump. I think it took him from eight hundred to one point five."

Beau tenses. "When was that?"

"Three weeks before he died."

"Are you fucking *kidding* me? Little suspicious, don't you think?"

"Yeah, but what can I *prove?*" Jenners's voice skids up and her eyes turn haunted. "As far as the necropsy went, everything looked fine."

Beau cocks his head. "That has to be impossible. There has to be something."

"But there isn't." Jenners pauses. "If this is true, they thought of everything, Beau. You're not going to pin this on Dell Landers—or Parish."

He goes quiet, and she gives us a bitter, brittle smile. "What? You think I didn't know that's what you came here about? That's why we're back here instead of talking out there. Yes, it seemed suspicious to me too, but Beau? I can't prove it and I'll be damned if I put my practice and all my employees' jobs at stake with conjecture."

I wilt. I can't help it. I understand her predicament, but it's so damn disheartening. I take a shaky breath. "What about the blood-work? That's a normal part of a necropsy, right?"

Dr. Jenners tugs one hand through her ponytail, and loosened strands fall around her face. "In this case, yes, absolutely. I sent several vials off for testing."

"*And?*" Beau demands.

"It came back clean."

He makes a half-strangled noise, but before Dr. Jenners can say anything more there's a knock at the office door. A young woman sticks her head inside. "Dr. Jenners? You're needed in the paddock. We're ready to start radiographs."

"Thank you, Hannah." Jenners gives her a small wave. "I'll be there shortly."

"Great."

The vet waits until the door shuts before turning back to Beau. "Yes, it came back clean."

"Except for the D-M-S-O," Beau says. He sounds like he's reminding Jenners and she pauses, her eyes boring into him.

"What do you mean?" I ask.

"There should've been D-M-S-O in Arch's system," Beau explains. "In controlled amounts, it's a legal anti-inflammatory. In large amounts, it's illegal in international competitions. We use it, but we're always very careful to stay well under the limits. It still would've tested though."

Jenners's jaw flexes twice before she says, "Mr. Landers said you were no longer using any type of anti-inflammatories on him. He said the bloodwork was clean because the horse was clean."

Beau studies his shoes for a beat, and then one more. "Someone at the lab must have tampered with the bloodwork."

"That would be my guess as well," Dr. Jenners says slowly. "I'll bet it was swapped for another horse's, but you'd have to prove it. Right now, this is your word against his." She slides off the desk, her boots thumping against the tile floor. "I wish I could be more help. He was an amazing horse."

"Yeah." Beau's gaze skitters around and around the room, landing on nothing. "And look what we let happen to him."

CHAPTER 23 | Beau

Swapped. It's like someone's kicked all the air out of me. I bang out of Jenners's office and I don't care who sees me. Holly walks behind me, saying nothing, but I can feel her watching me, *thinking*.

Thinking what though? It shouldn't worry me, but it does.

Outside the vet office, the noonday sun's over bright, pooling shadows under everything. I fish sunglasses out of my shorts' pocket and cram them on. Fucking *swapped*.

It's times like these I need a drink. Or several. I lean one shoulder against the truck's passenger door and try to force my jaw to unlock. It doesn't work. My brain can't stop replaying my conversation with Dr. Jenners: how she'd tried not to cringe when she told me about the necropsy, how Holly had stayed so quiet, and then she'd spoken up, her voice so clear and strong when everything inside me was shattering.

Shit. "I didn't even introduce you," I say.

"What?"

"I didn't introduce you to Dr. Jenners. Sorry. It was rude. I get...tunnel vision."

A pause, and then she gives me a half-assed laugh. "Don't be sorry. It was a good reminder for me."

"Reminder of what?"

"Of what this is: a fling." I snatch a glance at her, but Holly's not looking at me. She's studying the rigs still parked in the lot. "Swapping bloodwork. How could someone pull that off?"

"I don't know, but we're talking more than a million in payout. Plenty of money to grease the wheels."

More conjecture, yeah, but it makes sense. *So* much money was at stake—plus Dell's reputation as a supposedly successful businessman. He knew it wouldn't be long before people started talking openly about not being paid. He had to move fast. Killing Arch and cleaning up the necropsy results were the only two things that stood in his way.

Holly joins me at the truck, resting one arm on the side view mirror. She doesn't say anything else and I can't bring myself to keep going. I keep noticing her breathing—measured and deep. It starts to slow mine.

"We'll never find out who swapped the bloodwork for them," she says after a moment.

"No." Depending on the lab, there could be anywhere from a dozen to a hundred technicians on site. I wouldn't even know where to begin—and who would be motivated enough to tell the truth? No one, that's who.

"That means it's over." Holly's dropped her voice to a whisper. It's so soft I almost think the words aren't meant for me.

I straighten and pain rides up my spine. "No, it just means I have to find another way to hurt them."

She turns to me, moving so slowly it's like she's underwater. "What are you talking about?"

"They're not going to get away with this, Holls. I'm not going to let them. They killed a defenseless animal and took my *life*." I didn't mean to say that. It slips out before I realize it's going and Holly pales.

"Beau, you can take your life back any time you want."

It's meant as a statement, but we can both hear the question hanging between us. You can take your life back any time you want, *right?*

She wants the truth and I can't bring myself to say it. I lean against the truck, watching two women—probably a mom and daughter—lead their horse out of one of the paddocks and toward the rigs. They're ready to load up and go home.

Holly steps in front of me, expression deadly focused. "So you're going to do *what?*"

"Frame them. You heard Dell at the party: he's going to buy another horse. I'll make it look like he was going to kill that one too."

She gapes at me. "That's not...you're not...that's *revenge*."

"I prefer the term: returning the favor with interest."

"I prefer the term: possible felony. You're a lot of things, Beau Kent, but I never would've guessed you'd stoop so low."

I blink. The observation actually...hurts. "What's that supposed to mean?"

For several seconds, we stare at each other. Holly looks even more golden than usual in the overhead sunlight. Her blond hair is coming loose from its braid, tendrils brushing her cheekbones. She dashes them away with one hand. "Nothing," she says at last. "I guess I just thought you were different."

I laugh. I can't help it, but it still sounds mirthless and half choked. "Are you trying to say you thought I was honest? I *am* honest. I know what they did and I want them to pay for it. How I'm going about it is...creative. But it's not dishonest."

Holly's mouth flattens. She disagrees and I don't care. Satisfaction, hard and round, is rolling through me. Landers and Parish think they're untouchable. They think they've covered all their bases.

Payback's a bitch, suckers, I think, grinning.

"And how are you going to do it?" Holly asks.

"I haven't figured that part out." The honesty surprises both of us. I open the truck's passenger door. "After you," I say, and after a beat of hesitation, she brushes past me to climb in. That soft floral perfume hits me, and before I even realize I'm doing it, my hand reaches for her. I run my knuckles down the back of her bare neck and she shivers.

I love that. She's so responsive. She looks up at me from under a curl of hair and it's like a gut punch.

"Want to celebrate again?" I whisper, feeling a little like I'm losing because I'm bringing up last night first, but I want her. She makes my bones hum.

"Celebrate the decision to frame two men for a crime they didn't commit? No thanks." She starts to shut the door in my face and I catch it. I lean into her—a mistake because now I want to kiss her and argue with her.

"You and I both know what they did," I say carefully.

She nods.

"And you and I both know they're capable of doing it again."

Another nod. She's agreeing with me, and it just pisses me off. I still want to kiss her, and now I want to shake her.

"Then what's the problem?" I grate.

Behind me, the clinic's door opens and someone laughs. Holly's eyes flick from mine, watching whoever's behind me. "Let's go," she says softly. "Please?"

It's the 'please' that wrenches apart my gravity. Or maybe it's her expression. There's something almost tender in the way Holly looks at me. Almost broken.

I see through you, Beau Kent, she'd said. Chills wash over me. I slam the door and stalk around the truck. We pull out of the parking lot, heading back for Twelve Oaks, and Holly curls her legs under her.

"What do you friends think of all this?" she asks.

I glance at her, replaying the question, but I can't see the angle. "Huh?"

Her gaze slides to mine. "You do have friends...right?"

"Um, have you ever seen me leave a party alone?" I'm being an ass and she ignores me.

"I don't mean hook ups," she says. "I mean friends. Friends you could talk to about Archc, about what you want to do."

"I don't need them. I'm not lonely."

The corner of her mouth quirks up and she waits, studying me. I give her a lazy grin. *Stare me down all you like, darlin'*, I think. *It doesn't change anything.*

"I think you *are*," she announces, "and I think you've been lonely for so long you don't even know what lonely looks like anymore."

"I think you're full of shit." There's more force behind the words than either of us expected. Holly blinks in surprise and then leans across the truck's console, refusing to back off.

"Oh yeah?" she asks. "When's the last time you hung out with people who like you just because you're you—" I open my mouth to argue and she holds up a finger to shush me "—not because you're Beau Kent, *Olympian?*"

"I do dinner with Adele sometimes."

"Someone who benefits from your riding."

"I go on a lot of dates."

Amusement makes her eyes light up. "We need to work on your definition of date, but I'm listening, do go on. Tell me how you're well rounded and not lonely and haven't completely isolated yourself from anyone who could help you."

I open my mouth, and then close it. I can't. She's right. I don't have friends. I have work, and for three whole heartbeats, we're silent. I'm gripping the steering wheel so hard my hands are screaming, but it's like it's happening to someone else.

"It's not surprising with the kind of hours you do," Holly adds softly. "Ellie's the same way—but still it's something to consider. There's more to life than...this."

Blood thumps in my ears. "I love *this*. I've devoted my whole life to it. If I don't have riding, I don't have..."

Anything. I don't say the word, but Holly seems to hear it anyway. Her whole body softens. "There's more to you than riding," she whispers.

There's pity in her eyes and it spikes my anger higher. I don't want pity. I don't want people to feel sorry for me. I want my old life back, and I want Landers and Parish to pay.

CHAPTER 24 | Holly

Back at Twelve Oaks, it's another gorgeous Fall day: cool and dry, with impossibly clear blue skies. Though the board meeting will be held in Atlanta, Mrs. Mar always hosts a party at her home afterward. It'll be filled with the usual suspects—riders, owners, trainers, and friends—but also reporters. If all goes well, the charity program funding will be approved and she can announce her plans and I can collect my bonus and be done.

I climb out of Beau's truck and turn my face into the sunlight, closing my eyes and enjoying the pale pink behind my lids. It takes me only a few seconds, but when I open my eyes again, I catch Beau staring. His expression is hungry and it makes my joints go heavy, hot.

He isn't what you need.

But he is *what I want.* Being with him can be infuriating, but sleeping with him? It blocks everything else out. It's like he makes space inside me for me.

I sigh, trailing up the porch steps and into the cottage. It's probably just my libido talking. Everything about Beau Kent is beautiful and *broken.* This quest for justice he's on? It's self-destructive as hell.

Doesn't mean you can't enjoy him, I think. *I mean you're stuck here for another week, right?*

I frown. My libido has a point. Maybe more than a point.

It makes you a groupie, I remind my libido. Or does it? Because I know what Beau is and I know what I want from him: a hit of feel good endorphins. I might want more from relationships in the future, but right now all I need is distraction, and the guy is practically electric.

Every time we touch...I feel like he's conducting lightning across my skin. The memory of it turns my mouth dry, and I try to swallow.

122

Inside, Beau stalks to the kitchen and then loops through the living room and paces back into the kitchen again. *Shit*, I think, studying his mutinous expression. I'm not the only one who needs a distraction.

Rage simmers beneath Beau's surface. He's thinking about another angle to nail Parish and Landers, but that will only lead him to thinking about revenge again. Honestly? It's terrifying.

Part of me knows I need to go straight to Mrs. Mar, but another part of me wants to hold back. He doesn't have a plan. Maybe he's blowing off steam?

Or maybe it's because you agree with him? I wonder. Landers and Parish are horrible, horrible people. Maybe it would be better if Beau brought them to justice.

Except, of course, it isn't real justice. It's revenge.

Even *if* he gets away with it—Mr. Landers and Parish get framed and no one connects it to Beau—his soul won't survive. He won't come back from this. He'll never heal.

And you're worried about that...why exactly? I wonder.

Because I like him. The thought should hit me like a thunderbolt, but it doesn't. It's quiet. It's calm. It's so right and so true it feels like it's been waiting for me to notice. I like Beau—and right now, I'm scared for him.

I sink onto the couch's armrest, legs gone suddenly shaky. "Beau?"

His stride hitches, but he doesn't look at me. "Yeah?"

"Promise me you won't do anything stupid."

He doesn't respond. The pacing resumes—quick, jerky strides that make him wince.

"There has to be another way," I continue as he brushes past.

"Don't worry, sweetheart. I'll wait until after the board meeting."

I gape. "Don't 'sweetheart' me. And you think *that's* why I'm asking?"

"Why else would it be?" Beau swings around to face me, his grin devastatingly beautiful and heartbreakingly broken. "You need the bonus. You need me to behave in order to *get* the bonus. What am I missing here?"

All of it. It's another quiet thought and it ripples down my spine. He doesn't get *any* of this, and I don't know where to begin: the part where Beau thinks collecting the twenty grand is as important as keeping him out of jail, or the part where he thinks he isn't worth saving?

"That's not why I'm asking," I manage at last.

"Isn't it?" More of that devastating grin. Beau eases toward me and my body pricks to attention. He stops when we're inches apart. Less. "Are you sure?"

I pull up my chin. "I think there has to be another way, and I'll help you find it, but..."

"But?"

"You have to trust me."

***

I sit at the kitchen table long after Beau's left. He didn't answer me, and most of me isn't surprised.

But there is the tiny, tiny part of me that's hurt. He doesn't trust me. *It's not like it's personal,* I tell myself. *Doubt he trusts anyone.*

And I get that. I don't want to, but I do. After my dad left, we took care of ourselves. No one else looked out for us, and now that Mom's taken a turn for the worse, I take care of her—and I do it alone because I can't rely on Dane.

I draw my knees under my chin and watch Beau through the kitchen window. He's walking to the paddock behind the cottage, the lines of his shoulders still tight. On the other side of the fence, the chestnut gelding is trotting closer, eager for pets and treats.

I smile. Horses and women just *love* this man.

Beau takes another step, falters, and my heart catches in my throat. He's limping. Really limping. After two or three more agonizing steps, Beau stops and looks at his feet, face screwed up in pain.

My bare feet hit the tile floor. Do I need to go out there? Does he need help?

But then Beau presses himself on. He reaches the fence and leans heavily against the top rail. Then, after a moment, he glances around.

Like he's checking to see if anyone's watching, I realize, easing away from the window as his gaze sweeps in my direction. *He hasn't healed right, and he hasn't told anyone.*

For a second, I don't know if I want to cry for him or yell at him. Everything seems to fall into place with dizzying quickness: *this* is why he makes excuses about riding, *this* is why he's gone off the deep end, *this* is the reason for his obsession with Mr. Landers and Parish.

I frown. Well, it's part of the reason. Beau isn't riding because he's taking a break. He isn't riding because he *can't*.

That accident took everything from him: his horse, his livelihood, his identity.

I slouch, wrapping both arms around my torso and feeling like someone's leaked all the air from me. How horrible for him. Riding is Beau's world—something else I understand because I love design the same way he loves horses. Even though I'm thousands of miles from New York, I can still do what I love—within reason. Maybe it's the 'within reason' Beau needs to find.

And just like that, I get an idea. Ellie's speaking at an international course designer's workshop tomorrow. She's there as a consulting rider, someone the apprentice designers can learn from. What if I took Beau to watch? Few people know showjumping like he does. What if he started designing courses instead of jumping them?

My heartbeat speeds up. The thought tastes like hope and excitement, like *possibilities*. Now I just need to convince him to try it, and—

My cell rings. I glance at the screen. It's Scott.

My stomach does a funny flip. Maybe he's right. Maybe I should just go to New York and have faith I'll find a position. But as I watch Beau, I feel pasted to the spot.

I pick up. "Hey."

"You call this 'work?'" Scott bellows at someone on the other end. "It looks like an acid trip."

"Hey," I repeat, trying to bring him back to me.

No response. Scott continues to yell and now whoever is being yelled at is yelling back.

"Stop being an ass," I tell him, knowing damn well he's listening to me even if he is throwing a hissy. "Take a step back and *breathe*."

"I can't! They're sucking my soul, Holls! They're sucking my soul straight through my chest and eating it!"

"Okay, now you're just being disgusting."

He grumbles something I don't catch and I'm glad. I'd probably have to hang up on him to make a point and then he would call back and I would have to ignore him and—

"Have you thought anymore about what I said?" he asks.

"The part about how I'll die alone and cats will eat me?"

"The part about having something for yourself."

"Yeah. I have."

"Good because I just found two investors and we're a go. I'm starting my own line. I want you to join me."

Everything in me goes still. "Are you serious?"

"Deadly. I have a contract for you and everything. Come home."

Home. The word ripples through me. Where is my home anyway? Here in Atlanta? Up in New York? I can't tell anymore. "Can you email me the contract?" I ask.

"Of course, I can. I'm not living with cows and rednecks."

"You know I'm going to have my own requirements to add to it."

"Like what?" Scott's tone turns sullen. "My balls in your handbag? I think they're already there. I've been begging you to come back for months."

I grin. "As charming as that would be to pull out at cocktail parties, no. I don't want your balls. I do want you to do some anger management classes and you have to agree to stop abusing the staff."

"I am an artiste—"

"You're an asshole, Scott. You want me? You have to change." I pause. "Think of it as a transformation."

There's a pause that's so long I'm pretty sure Scott's considering it something else entirely, but I bite my lip and say nothing. I want this, but I want it on terms I can live with.

"I'll send it to you tonight," he says at last. "And the anger management...it might not be a bad idea. Trev says it would help."

"Trev the yoga instructor?"

"Yeah."

Huh. I don't know Trev, but I like him already—and I almost can't believe Scott's entertaining the idea of anger management counseling.

"He's really changed me," Scott adds like he can read my thoughts. "Love can make you do amazing things."

I smile. "Probably the best thing about it."

He snorts. "If you think that you're doing it wrong. I gotta go, okay? I'll email you tonight."

I hang up, brain spinning. If he agrees...if I can be brave...if I can *do* this...my hands begin to shake. It feels like everything I've wanted is right here for the taking. So why am I so scared? And why am I suddenly wondering if maybe it isn't exactly what I want anymore?

Because if I do this and fail, I'm really done, I think. *When I left New York last time, it was because of someone else's failure. If I go back and can't make it...*

The cottage's back door scrapes open and Beau appears. I clutch my cell phone with one hand, watching as he walks slowly across the living room and drops to the couch.

If I hadn't seen him limping earlier, I would think it was just his way of moving: deliberate, precise. He'll never say anything to me about what's really happening. Then again, can I blame him? It's not like I tell him my secrets or my worries.

So why do I want to go to him now?

Comfort, my brain flashes. It's practically in neon lights. If I closed my eyes, I'd still see the glow.

No, no way, I tell myself. Beau is distraction. Beau is an endorphin rush.

Beau is what I want right now.

Who I want.

And I'm moving before I even realize it. I walk across the kitchen, tugging loose my hair. I shrug my cardigan off my shoulders, letting it fall to the floor. I peel my cami up, revealing the lacy bra underneath. I stride right up to Beau until I'm standing between his spread legs.

"Distract me," I say.

His eyes darken. "Gladly."

CHAPTER 25 | Beau

I pull Holly down on top of me, tugging her close until her knees are wedged tight around my waist and her perfect breasts are shoved against my chest. For a moment, the dull ache in my hip and leg are gone. My whole world becomes Holly. I'm not sure what drove her to strip and come for me, but I'm sure as *hell* not going to argue.

I palm her ass with both hands and she moans. I grip harder and she grins. "Yes," she whispers.

And, just like that, I'm shattered.

"Holly Holly Holly," I murmur against her neck, kissing the soft skin higher and higher until my mouth is on hers, and my hands are buried in her hair.

She pulls back a little, looks me in the eyes. "Harder," she whispers and I tighten my grip in her hair. She smiles, going soft against me. It's my favorite invitation, and I realize I could play this out, take my time, but I can't.

I flip her onto her back, wrestle one handed with my belt until it loosens. Her hands scrabble at my lower back, my hips. Her hot palm slides around my dick and I hiss.

"Christ," I groan, "you do that again, and we're—"

She does it again, grinning wickedly. "Condom. Now."

I paw for one, leaning across her to the remaining stash from last night. She palms me again and I nearly drop everything. I don't think I've ever been this hard.

It's her, I realize slowly. She unravels me.

"Here." Holly tears open the package and smooths on the condom, pumping me once and again, and then pulling me close. Her gorgeous legs spread even wider, urging me on, but I can't stop staring at her. She's so fucking perfect like this.

She rolls her hips, and my dick throbs. "Now," she begs. "I need you now!"

I couldn't stop if I tried. I enter her with a firm thrust and those long legs snake tight around my hips. Tighter. My eyes nearly roll back into my head. Pain rides up my spine and it's almost like it's happening to someone else. Right now, everything is Holly—wet, hot, *soft* Holly.

"*Never* get enough of you," I manage, thrusting again. She gasps, eyes closing, fingers tightening. I circle my hips, grinding on her clit until she moans.

Close, I think, dick going even harder at the sound. *She's* so *close*.

So am I. Looking at her like this? Christ. I'm going to come. This isn't slowing. I grind against her clit and she screams, arching her back and urging me on. The harder I use her, the more faraway everything feels.

Everything but Holly.

Suddenly, her breaths are my breaths. Her heartbeats are my heartbeats. *Everything* is made up of her. I press my palm to her cheek and her eyes fly open, meeting mine.

"Beau?" she whispers.

It threatens to crack me open.

I snake my hand between us, finding that tiny sensitive part of her I know so well now. I rub and she moans.

"Beau," she breathes, eyes sliding shut.

I tap her and she gasps. "Look at me," I command, and when she does, I'm gone. I rub her once, firmly, and she comes in a screaming rush, never looking away and sending me over the edge. I thrust until I'm spent, until we're both shivering with aftershocks.

Holly bites my shoulder gently, bringing me back. When I look down, she looks up at me with a dreamy expression.

Or is it? Because her gaze pins me to the spot. I see through you, Beau Kent, she'd said. Right now, I feel like she absolutely does.

She blows a strand of hair out of her eyes and gives me a heart stopping grin. It's afterglow or flirting or whatever you want to call it, but it's also something else. There's something about the moment that feels...different.

It's not the first time Holly's looked at me like I'm more than I am, but it's the first time I actually want to believe it.

***

Hours later, Holly's asleep and I'm coming out of my skin. Part of me wants to wake her up, take her from behind or pull her down on top of me.

Or tell her how you're flying apart, I think. I'm sitting up in our bed, but I feel like I'm flying a thousand feet above us. It's Landers and Parish and Arch, and hell, it's everything.

Then Holly murmurs in her sleep and rolls over, one arm sliding across my lap. There's the most relaxing heat radiating off her. It makes my heartbeats slow.

Wake her up, I think, and then immediately after: *You're an asshole if you do.*

I used her hard. Of course, she used me too and the memory almost makes me smile. Too bad it can't make me sleep. I ease out from under her arm, taking two limping steps before finding my stride. I barely make it to the bedroom door before wanting to return to her.

What the hell is wrong with me? A couple of nice comments and a few lingering smiles and now I'm...I don't even know what this is. I can identify how my chest is squeezing tight at the sight of her, how I want to climb back in bed next to her, but I also know it's not me.

Distract me, she'd said, and I had—thoroughly, I might add—but she's distracted me too. If I keep looking at her, I'll start looking past what happened. I'll be out of the moment and looking at the future and everything that happened will be nothing.

And I'm already nothing. Without riding, there's nothing left.

I reach for the bedroom door, and for the first time, I notice the box sitting on the chair by Holly's bed. Chills climb my skin. I know that box. I packed it and put it away...

And Holly found it, I realize, chills *and* nausea now sweeping over me. Even so, I can't resist taking it. It feels like someone else's hands lifting the box into my arms, but I can't stop. I carry it into the living room and leave it on the couch, telling myself to leave it.

I pace in loops around the house, every step making my hip twinge. Night has turned my windows into darkened mirrors. Every time I turn, I see my shadow self: thinner, shaggier, *wrong*.

And the box is still waiting.

What the hell? I figure, and open it. I try not to focus on the framed pictures and end up on a set of DVDs in clear plastic cases. I slide one out. The cover says: Spruce Meadows. My second to last competition before Arch died.

Put it back, I think. *You don't want to look at any of that.*

Except I kind of do. Let's take a look at what I used to be. Why not? I turn on the television and slide the DVD into the player, not noticing that the auto-play is on until I'm suddenly inches from my own grinning-like-a-jackass face.

The British announcer stiffly calls my name, number, and horse's name as I wait for the bell to begin. For a second, I can't breathe.

Then I force myself back a step—and another. I drop onto the couch and watch as I ride around a mini-prix with a mare we've long since sold. The videographer cut all my rides to run together in one long montage. I think I had four or five horses going at that show, looking at it now it feels like more.

Another one of our sales horses—a big, gray this time—sails past the camera, jumping beautifully over the outside course. It's like a stab to the gut. This is who I used to be. That was my life.

I'd thought it would be mine forever.

My stomach squeezes like I'm going to be sick, and I swallow it down, forcing myself to finish. The Grand Prix is the last clip and the videographer catches Arch and me just as we're coming through the in-gate.

Arch is acting like a fool, trying but not really trying to buck me off. He shakes his head and dances toward the crowd. Even at a distance, you can see my grin. I loved how he loved his job.

Then the bell rang and we both turned serious. The course was twisty. Hard. My head still remembers the last turn, but my body does too. The way Arch sat down and spun for it, the power of him coming up from underneath me. It felt like flying.

It felt like we could do anything.

I rewind it back and watch it again.

And again. I watch how I used to ride and how I used to move. I watch it over and over until I fall asleep, and then it gives me night-mares.

CHAPTER 26 | Holly

When I wake up, the other side of my bed is cold. I could've sworn Beau had fallen asleep next to me last night. We'd moved from the couch to the floor to my bedroom wall and then, well, my bed. I sit up, raking my fingers through my tangled hair.

Maybe he went back to his bed, I think, kicking the covers off. Early morning sunlight dapples my room, turning the soft gray walls even paler. *That would be normal for this sort of thing, right?*

This sort of thing. I nearly laugh. Like there are rules and whatever going on between Beau and me is something that happens to everyone. We're in weird waters—and that's why I shouldn't feel bad about the twinge of disappointment I felt when my hand reached for him, and he wasn't there.

I shower, dress, and there's still no sign of Beau. *Just as well,* I tell myself. *You can get some work done. Maybe it'll clear your mind and you'll think of another angle on Landers and Parish.*

It's not an entirely bad idea. Work does that for me sometimes. I'm so focused on the fall of a skirt or the placement of a sleeve, my subconscious wanders to other stuff. Only as soon as I open my bedroom door, I know work is pretty much going to be impossible.

Beau's lying on the couch, dead to the world, and the television's still on. Some horse show video is on repeat, the sound turned low. As I get closer, I can hear the announcer's voice: And now, number two-eighty-three, Beau Kent riding Arch."

My stomach goes cold and oily. I'd forgotten to put the box of videos away, and he'd found it. I can't believe he didn't wake me up, yell at me for invading his privacy. Instead, he...I look from the television to Beau's startlingly pale face to the almost finished bottle of vodka on the coffee table. It's left sticky, clear rings on the wood.

Instead, he tortured himself, I think, swallowing. This has to stop. Not because he's Beau Kent Olympian, or Beau Kent gorgeous and great in bed. It needs to stop because he's a person, and sometimes I think everyone forgets that.

Carefully, I pick up around him, collecting all the DVDs he's pulled out and shutting down the television. In the silence, I can hear his breathing: too light and too fast. His brows draw together and mouth goes tight. Nightmares? It seems like it.

I take the box back to the closet and creep out of the cottage, heading for the Bronco. I need Ellie. I'd asked for Beau to trust me. I can't let him down, but I need her help.

I glance at the clock on my phone. By now, she'll be down at the stables. Maybe I can catch her between horses.

It's another chilly morning promising to turn into a warm afternoon. My breath rises in puffs ahead of me and the Bronco's cab feels like a meat locker. After a minute of coaxing, the engine roars to life and I floor it up the farm road, spotting Ellie's truck as I swing through the entrance gate.

She's gotta be around here somewhere, I think, parking under the stable's wide shadow. I hop out and walk inside. The place is a flurry of activity with horses being fed or taken out and stalls being cleaned. It's pretty much chaos, and I nearly miss Ellie carrying a saddle toward the tack room. She sees me and waves. "Hey!"

"Hey!" I run down the stable aisle, following her into the blessedly warm tack room. Thanks to the heater and probably twenty carefully oiled saddles, the whole place smells deliciously of leather.

Ellie grins at me as she hangs up her saddle. "What are you doing down here so early?"

"I wanted to see you."

"Yeah? What's up?"

I take a deep breath and try to school my voice so it sounds casual. "You're speaking at that course designer program today, aren't you?"

It's pretty good, but Ellie still catches me. She cocks her head, dark braid sliding over one shoulder. "Yeah. Why?"

"Do you think I could bring Beau to watch?"

"Sure." She shrugs. "They'd be thrilled to have him. I mean, he's *Beau Kent*."

I smile because I'm supposed to, but inside I cringe a little. It isn't the first time I've heard someone say that, but it's the first time it hits me low in the stomach. This is another reason Beau acts like Beau. He's living around his legend. If he comes out and tells everyone he can't ride anymore, his past will be the only thing he has left.

Ellie props one foot on one of the glossy wood tack trunks and unzips her riding boot. "Why so interested?"

"I think it would be good for him."

Her brows rise as she tugs the boot off. "You used to think a swift kick in the ass would be good for him too. What's changed?"

I open my mouth and then close it. I don't know what to say. That my mind changed when I saw how Arch's death shattered him? That my mind changed when I learned he was hiding his pain?

That *everything* changed when I realized he was drowning?

But none of that is mine to say. It would be giving away his secrets.

"You can't save him," Ellie says softly. She straightens and curls one arm around my shoulders, pulling me close. She smells faintly of dust and horses and crisp, cool air. "You can't save everyone."

"I know."

"So...why are you trying? He's had every opportunity to get back on track and he's thrown it back in everyone's faces."

I nod. It's true. He has. But he's also hiding the real reason—his injuries—because he's scared everyone will turn on him once they realize he can't ride anymore. Again, these are secrets I can't share, and I'm praying Ellie will go along with me even though I can't make her understand.

"I think he needs one more shot," I say. "Please?"

She blinks, surprised. Emotions from curiosity to suspicion to plain confusion flit through her expression. "Why course design?" she asks at last, turning her attention back to her boots.

"Because he needs something else besides riding." Which is the truth even if I'm not disclosing everything. I've been lucky enough to be given a second shot at my dream. Beau hasn't been so fortunate. He has to find something else. Maybe this will be it? I know you can't save people, but you can give them another chance.

Ellie still doesn't look convinced though. She studies me with growing suspicion.

"You don't need water to drown," I tell her. "We both know that. I think this might be a lifeline for him. I can't explain it, but I hope you'll go along with it?"

Her eyes snap up, meeting mine. "Of course, I'll go along with it. I'm just curious...and worried. About you. Not him."

"Why are we worrying about Holly?" a deep male voice asks.

Ellie and I turn. Ellie's boyfriend, Caleb, is slouched in the tack room doorway, looking gorgeous and moody. Ellie swears he's a lot of fun, but the only time I ever see him genuinely smile is when he looks at her.

"Because she has terrible taste in men," Ellie says, flashing me a smile. "Just like I do."

"And thank God for that," Caleb says, a smile tipping up one corner of his mouth. "We're going to breakfast before the course designer seminar, you want to come, Holls?"

"Please?" Ellie tugs my sleeve, eyes bright. "Let Beau come on his own and you come with us. When's the last time you were off the farm for fun? You have to get out more."

"Says the world's worst workaholic."

She grins. Before Caleb, Ellie was notorious for fourteen hour days and a complete inability to talk about anything but horses. Now that

Caleb's in the picture, she still works crazy hours and talks only about horses, but she's more inclined to go out than she used to be.

She's also really, *really* happy. It wasn't like Ellie hated her life before Caleb. She didn't. She loves her job, but I think Caleb was the icing on the cake. Would she have been happy without him? Absolutely. But being with him makes everything even better.

I want that, I think, and I want it so much it nearly drags me to my knees. I clear my throat. "I can't. Work stuff."

Ellie taps one finger to her chin. "Huh. I seem to remember you telling me I need to get out more."

"What can I say? I was right." I can't stop my grin. "And look what happens when you listen to me."

We both cut our eyes at Caleb who's waiting patiently and pretending he has no idea what we're talking about.

Ellie blows out a sigh. "Okay. If you're sure."

"Positive. Y'all have fun. I'll see you later today."

She turns for Caleb and he gives her a slow grin filled with promise.

No way *they're making it to breakfast*, I think, ignoring the pang of jealousy squeezing my heart. I want a guy who looks at me the way Caleb looks at Ellie. I want missing dinner reservations because we can't keep our hands off each other, lying in bed talking for hours because we love the way each other's minds work, *depending* on each other.

I want someone I can lean on when I can't go on.

I don't admit that to myself very often, but I'm admitting it now. It's what I want. It's also a great reminder of why Beau isn't that guy—will *never* be that guy. This thing we're playing at? It's only going to break my heart.

CHAPTER 27 | Beau

It's almost nine when I finally roll over. Everything smells like bacon, and the radio's playing some sort of Top 40 love song crap. Holly. She must have been up for ages already.

Blearily, I run one hand over my face. My skin feels tingly, and I'm fucking exhausted even though I must've gotten six or seven hours of sleep. I haul myself into a sitting position and glance around for Holly. She's at the stove, humming and shifting from foot to foot.

She doesn't realize I'm up, and I take a moment to enjoy her. There's a grace to Holly's movements I haven't noticed until now. She's smooth. The way her hips swing? It makes my fingers itch to dig into them. I like how practiced her cooking is, how easy. It's...relaxing to watch, like she uncurls something in me I didn't even know was knotted.

I haven't moved, but Holly stops, head cocking to one side like she's heard something. She turns, and smiles at me. "Come eat."

I nod, convinced if I say anything my voice will crack like a loser's. This living together thing has messed with my head. It's like we're playing husband and wife and it's making me...like it.

Holy shit, that'll get you going. I push to my feet, looking around for the DVD cases I'd left out last night. They're gone. I look for the packing box, but it's gone too.

My stomach settles on its side. Holly must've found everything and put it away. I study her from the corner of my eye, trying to decide if she's looking at me any differently, but she's not looking at me at all. She's turned back to the stove, one bare foot reaching up to rub against her other calf.

I can't stop staring at it. The nightmares have left me feeling fuzzy and gritty and faraway. Looking at her? I feel centered.

And also cross as hell.

"You coming, or what?" she asks without turning around.

"Yeah." I clear my throat and ease my way into the kitchen, needing ten or so steps before my hip and back loosen. Holly slides an overfilled plate of eggs, toast, bacon, and fruit across the table and returns to the stove.

All my favorites, I think, sitting down and staring the food. *What's the deal? Does she feel sorry for me?* The idea spikes sour points in the back of my mouth.

"What's with the Susie Homemaker shit?" I ask.

"I told you: some of us like to eat real food." She pauses, spatula hovering. "Why? Do you think there's a special reason?" The questions are so light they sound like flirting. In fact, if I didn't know she knew about the DVDs, I'd think it *was* flirting, but I do know.

And she knows.

And I'll be damned if we're going to talk about how sorry she is my career is over. Scrambled eggs and fruit aren't going to cut it, and I damn sure don't want her pity.

"Nothing?" she presses.

I don't answer. I can't.

"Beau?"

I look up. Swear to God, the way the sunlight catches in her pale hair makes her look angelic and sexy and my dick begins to stir. It's like the universe is conspiring against me. Every time I try to get a handle on this, I...don't.

"*Beau*," she repeats.

I blink, coming back to myself. "Yeah?"

"Did you know I used to ride?"

I frown. Where is this going? "Yeah, you and Ellie used to ride together."

"With Parker, our other best friend."

I'm still searching for the angle on this and I'm not finding it. "Okay."

"My point is," she continues, smiling broadly, "I used to ride and I preferred mares, which means you don't scare me. If I can convince eleven hundred pounds of hormonal beastie to jump around a four foot course, I can handle you growling at me. M'kay?"

I stare at her. She stares at me. I clear my throat, shifting in my seat because even this is getting me hard. "Point taken."

"Good. I have a few things I need to do today," she says. "Come with me?"

Three little words. They're throwaways, but my heart swings hard anyway.

***

As we leave Twelve Oaks, a moving truck rumbles past us, pointed toward Adele's home. They're probably coming in to prep for the party. Depending on the theme, the complications, and the sheer number of people, these things can take days to set up.

"Is there a theme this year?" Holly asks, maneuvering the Bronco out of the truck's way.

"Always. It's..." My stomach sinks a little. I have no idea, and it's not that I care about themes or decorations or who's invited, but I care that Adele used to tell me that stuff. Key words: used to. We've drifted, and when this Arch thing goes pear shaped, we'll be done and I will have lost everything.

"The theme is something," I say at last. "I forget what she picked. Four more days until your freedom," I add. It's more for me than for her. I need another reminder Holly's only here for a little while longer, this thing between us depends on

"'Something,'" Holly echoes, smiling. "Such precision."

"What're we doing anyway?" I ask as she merges the Bronco onto the Interstate.

"I have this idea," Holly says.

I perk up. "Really?"

"Not that kind of idea." She grins, one handing it through a turn. Someone behind us honks and she waves like they're old friends. "Don't you ever get...tired or whatever?"

Not of you, I think, and send up a silent prayer of gratitude the thought didn't come out my mouth. Instead, I grin right back at her, dragging my eyes over and over her until her cheeks go bright pink. "Want to pull over and we can find out?" I ask.

Holly shakes her head, a haze of blond hair falling across her forehead. Usually, she wears her hair in a loose braid, but today she's knotted it on top of her head in some complicated twist I want to dig my fingers into. There's still the sexy silk cami, the slouchy sweater, and the form fitted jeans slid into those battered boots.

"I thought future fashion mavens would wear more complicated stuff." I skim one finger under her sweater's edge, feeling the soft heat of her skin beneath.

"For me, fashion is about being myself."

It's a good answer—even if it is a little breathy. I smirk, skimming my finger lower. Right on cue, her breath hitches.

"Beau?"

"Yeah?"

"Stop it before I run us off the road."

Heaving a huge sigh, I slouch back in my seat as she zips us across town, driving like a crazy person. Either I'm getting used to it or my blue balls have taken all the blood from my head because I'm not that bothered. This is actually...nice. We're not talking, but I still feel like I'm getting to enjoy her. I don't know what that means, but I'm smart enough not to pick it apart.

Then Holly gets off at the Conyers Horse Park exit.

And then she takes the highway deep into the countryside.

This is the way I used to take to Fairfield, a private farm that concentrates on French and German bloodstock. I always visited their latest foal crop to see if anything caught my eye. Sometimes, it did, and over the years, Adele has bought three or four weanlings off my recommendation. I haven't been back since well before Arch died though, and I'm not sure I'm ready to do it now.

Actually, I'm damn sure I'm not ready to do it now.

"Why are we here?" I ask, craning my head to get a better look at the farm sign as we pass. They've updated it since the last time I was here, exchanging the sun-burned army green background for something closer to emerald. The letters have been touched up in white and gold paint. The horse is now a deep, chocolate-y brown.

"I wanted you to see something," Holly says. She sounds light and normal, but her hands have tightened around the steering wheel. Her knuckles stand up white.

"What are you up to?" But she doesn't need to answer because we swing around the bend toward the barn and I see my answer: it's a course designer meet. Almost a dozen men and women are crowded around a single speaker who's yelling about the evils of modern show jumping design.

Not that I'm surprised. Andrew Davies-Whitley is especially evocative when half in the bag and since it's—I check my cell—after ten in the morning, I'd say he's well on his way.

"The fuck are we doing here?" I ask as Holly angles the Bronco in between a pair of sleek sedans. She puts it in park and turns to me, blue eyes huge and worried.

"Ellie told me about it—she's one of the consulting riders. It's part of the course designer certification—the one you need for international competitions."

"And?"

"And I think you'd be really good at it."

It's like my brain stalls out. I blink at her. I blink at the crowd surrounding Andrew. I end up looking at my hands. They ache. The longer I look at them, the more they suddenly hurt.

"I know I sprang it on you, but I thought..." That expressive mouth of hers screws up. She doesn't know what to say either. It's sort of comforting.

Sort of.

"You do realize that guy called me a monkey in riding boots?"

"Yeah." She nods, a little pale. "And you were the only person who jumped his Olympic course without dropping any rails and then called *him* a joke so, you know, there's that, right?"

I'd be lying if I said the memory wasn't rather pleasant, but now is *really* not the time. I glare at Andrew until Holly plucks at my arm.

"Beau." Her cardigan slips, baring one smooth-skinned shoulder. "I'm serious. I *really* think you'd be good at this."

Part of me thinks she's right. The rest of me wants to run, and it's that part that pisses me off. I glare at her. "What is this? Now I'm your charity case? A project boyfriend or something?"

Holly lets out a winding sigh. "Just...try it. Please?" She pauses. "For me?"

We both go quiet. I can't believe she's asking, and judging by the look on her face, she can't believe it either. I don't know what to do. She's asking me to trust her. She's asking for a favor.

She's doing you *the favor, dipshit,* I think, and it's true. I would never have signed up for this. It wouldn't even have *occurred* to me.

But it did to Holly.

I've had women who have cheered for me from the sidelines, women who have fussed over me, complimented me. I've never been with a woman who knew me—maybe even knows me better than I know myself because I had never considered looking into course design.

And realizing it makes my chest squeeze tight.

"Fine," I manage, gritting my teeth and hurling myself out of the Bronco. "But you owe me."

"Sounds like fun," Holly says behind me. I can hear the smile in her voice. It rises through me like steam.

CHAPTER 28 | Beau

Fairfield is a smaller farm—they prefer the term 'boutique'—and they've had to make use of every inch. The paddocks are electric green from heavy fertilizing and careful maintenance, and the riding arenas bump right up to the property's edges. The barn is monstrous though. Designed in a horseshoe shape, the horse stalls and tack rooms surround a courtyard studded with flowering trees. Andrew's set up his whiteboard and ego smack in the middle. There are probably ten or fifteen people crowded around him, perched on fold-up chairs and furiously taking notes on striding calculations as Holly and I approach.

Briefly, Andrew looks our direction. With his thin, stooped shoulders and penchant for tweed blazers with elbow patches, he's always reminded me of a college professor. We've never liked each other, and when he recognizes me, his face screws up like he's tasted something sour. To his credit though he waves me closer, a little flick of his hand that makes it look like I'm being summoned.

God, he annoys me.

"Children," Andrew announces, his upper class British accent turning the word arch and condescending, "I'm sure you've all heard of Beau Kent. He'll be joining us for the remainder of the day."

The children—none of whom is younger than thirty—murmur their hellos and I nod in return.

"Glad to be here," I tell Andrew, and he puffs up, pleased.

"Take a seat," he tells me as Holly retreats to one of the courtyard's wrought iron benches. She slouches in the sun, looking half boneless and entirely relaxed—except for her tapping foot. She watches me like she can't look away.

She's worried.

She shouldn't be. Just because I don't usually keep my mouth shut doesn't mean I *can't* keep my mouth shut, and I spend the next two hours doing just that. Andrew finishes his lecture on striding—basically how a horse moves, how long each stride is, how it can be manipulated to be shorter or longer—and, then gives the floor to another international course designer, Michael Benson.

Rode one of his courses in Tryon, I think. *Or was it at Devon?* Either way, I have the vague memory of tough showjumping course with lots of questions and options for riders to puzzle through. I look over the small crowd, watching for anyone else's reactions, and all I see are people snatching glances at me. My skin starts to crawl, and I cut my eyes toward Holly again. She smiles.

"I'd like to thank all of you for coming," Michael begins, resting one hand on the back of a folding chair. He's a slightly built guy, like a jockey or a gymnast. "I'd like to begin by discussing new safety measures in course building."

It's not a bad way to spend a few hours. Figuring out better ways to keep horses and riders safe over enormous jumps? I'm in, and it's refreshing to see everyone else being just as enthusiastic. Or it is until the conversation begin to derail.

"What did you think about the last Olympic course?" a guy to my left asks me. His wraparound sunglasses shield his eyes, preventing me from gauging his expression, but there's a dark undertow to his tone. He has a point to make, and he wants me to help him.

"Well," I say carefully, "it was Andrew's course."

"We know. I'm asking what you thought of it—from a rider's perspective. There was a lot of negative feedback from the teams on that course. What did you think?"

I sneak a glance at Andrew. The muscles in his jaw are jumping. Just by being here, I'm disrupting things, and we both see it. I open my mouth, but Andrew cuts me off with another pompous wave.

"What a good idea," he says, nostrils flaring a little. "Let's here from someone who's been in the game—well, not for a while, right, Beau? You haven't been on the international stage in ages."

I force myself to go still, but I can't stop myself from rising to the bait. "A year."

"Ah, that's right. Not so long, but your world ranking is *so* low now." Andrew gives me a savage smile. "But no matter, I'm sure you have some insights. Do stand up and tell us."

I pause, everything in me leaning toward the Bronco. I want out, but I pull myself straight. Slowly, I stand. "Yeah, fine, let's talk. How about we start with your cross country course? You had four rotational falls last year alone on your courses, Andrew. You created these massive obstacles and, hey, that's fine, but you put them in such a technical order and required such a high rate of speed, you sacrificed the animals. You weeded out the winners by punishing the horses."

A few gasps ripple through the crowd and the other course designer is nodding. Andrew on the other hand looks like his head might twist off. So much for winning him over.

Not that I cared.

"You have to decide, are you testing the horse?" I'm picking up speed now, opinions flooding to my surface. Actually, it feels like more than 'opinions,' it feels more like belief and bone mixed together. "Or are you testing the rider? The best courses challenge each, but I think it's our duty to challenge the riders more than the horses. Can the riders make smart decisions? Can they personalize their approach to a course to better support their particular horse's strengths? If they can't, punish *them* not the horse."

I shove my hands into my pockets and realize I have a hole—make that two holes—in them. Might be time to retire these shorts. "Just my two cents."

I sit down—not that it matters, everyone is still staring at me. Andrew's gone pale, but Michael's nodding. "I agree with you," he says, "and that's what makes course design so hard, people. It's also what makes it great."

I shrug. I'm not sure if I feel the same, but I want to stick around and find out. The next few hours pass in a merry-go-round whirl. I'm not usually someone who likes to sit still, but it moves remarkably quickly even for me. I like the technical aspects of course design—do you want four strides or five strides on this combination? How would that play out with the next jumps? How does that flow with the previous jumps? What am I asking the horse to know?

It's the last bit that really works for me. Every competition level has certain training requirements. By using certain jump combinations, you can reveal training holes and challenge the riders—and if you do it right, you can reveal those training holes in a way that everyone goes home safe at night. The horses' welfare can come first.

Michael and Andrew break the session off around four, giving everyone time to go back to their hotel rooms for a bit before dinner. Everyone crowds around, comparing notes, but I search out Holly, eventually finding her inside the stable's lounge, answering emails.

"Hey."

She looks up, her blond braid swinging forward. Her sudden grin makes me grin. "You did good, Kent."

I stand over her, searching for the sarcasm or edge or dig. There isn't one. Once again, Holly looks at me like she really does see me.

And she likes what she sees.

I wait for the familiar sense of panic to tighten my chest or clog my throat and it...doesn't happen. I lean down, taking her face between my hands, and kiss her. Her mouth opens on a puff of surprise and I take full advantage: touching my tongue to her lower lip, skimming my fingers along the nape of her neck, teasing her in the way that always leaves her wanting more. When I finally break away, she's panting.

"What was that for?" Holly whispers.

"Everything." Because for the first time in months and months, my whole body feels light. Not necessarily pain free, but...light.

It's been so long since I've felt like this, I almost don't recognize the feeling. It's hope.

CHAPTER 29 | Holly

During the drive back, I expected Beau to be quiet, or at least a bit tired, but he's wired for sound, talking almost nonstop. By the time I park my Bronco next to his truck, I've learned that Andrew Davies-Whitley was probably born a pain in the ass, and the possibility of being a course designer makes Beau seem like another person.

He didn't tell me that last part, obviously, but it's easy to see.

He's *happy*, and it makes me smile like an idiot. Then I catch *him* smiling at *me* and heat curls through me. Every time I look in his direction, he's studying me like I'm someone else, and I can't really blame him, he seems like someone else to me too.

"I've never seen you so...passionate," I say as we turn off the Interstate, catching the winding highway that will lead us back to Twelve Oaks. It isn't exactly true. I've seen Beau get plenty passionate enough with his groupies or a nice bottle of Scotch, but it wasn't anything like I saw from him today.

"It's been a long time," he says after a moment. "Really long time."

Usually, we would start some sort of bickering, but he stays quiet and I stay quiet and the next forty or so minutes pass easily by. At home, the lights are still on in the stable, casting glowing orange squares across the darkening paddocks, and you can still spot grooms running back and forth, finishing up for the evening. I park next to Beau's truck and get out. It's colder than when we left Fairfield and I pull my cardigan closer as I follow Beau up the steps and into the cottage.

Inside, we trail to the kitchen and I survey the fridge's contents, trying to decide what to do for dinner. It shouldn't be a hard decision—thanks to my grocery shopping we have plenty—but Beau's behind me now. His warm breath ghosts across the back of my neck. "What do you want?" I ask.

"Would be better if I showed you."

He swoops in, picking me up and kissing my neck until I'm screech-ing and laughing like a maniac. "No!" I pant. "I mean dinner!"

Beau pulls back to give me a sharp, predatory smile. "You sure that's what you meant?" He kisses my neck harder, nipping the tender skin. "Because I'll give you anything you want."

It gives me chills, and it shouldn't. We're flirting. It's nothing, but I can't ignore the promise that seems to shimmer in the air, the feeling that this could be more.

***

In the end, we do a stir-fry thing with vegetables and good wine. It's fun. I get why Beau always has people around him. It's not *just* about his fame. He's funny. He has great stories.

He's unbelievably sexy.

You are such a groupie, I tell myself, dumping my dirty dishes into the sink. I turn on the hot water and reach for the soap, but Beau nudges me to the side. "You cooked," he says. "I got this."

I open my mouth to tease him about being shocked he knows how to clean up, but honestly? He's been this considerate since I moved in.

Is this what you're really like? I wonder, leaning against the counter and finishing my wine. *If it is, I could get used to it.*

Really used to it, if I'm being honest. There's something relaxing about being with him, like I've stopped to rest after a lifetime of run-ning.

Which, if I'm still being honest, is stupid because I love my life. I'm working toward what I want. I have goals, *friends*.

Would make him the icing on the cake, I think, suddenly remember-ing I've thought the same thing about Caleb and Ellie. The realization prickles at the back of my neck, a hair-raising charge.

"Wine on the porch?" Beau asks, wiping his hands on a dish towel.

I nod.

"Open another bottle?"

I nod again, and he brushes past, flashing me a toe-curling grin. I take a bottle of red from the cabinet, and focus on popping the cork and refilling our glasses. Outside, orange light suddenly dances on the window glass.

He must've started the fire pit, I think, padding across the kitchen and nudging the French doors open. *Perfect.*

It's chilly out on the porch, the temps falling fast now that the sun has gone down. Beau's slouched in one of the teak chaise lounges, staring up at the stable. It's dark now. All the horses are bedded down for the night, and presumably, all the grooms off to find dinner for themselves.

"For you," I say, passing him a glass. Beau takes it, and me, hooking one arm around my waist and pulling me into his lap. Normally, this would result in some pretty frantic groping and I would be dragging him back inside, but tonight it feels so good to just rest next to him.

Somewhere, one horse neighs and another answers. It's so peaceful. I find myself taking deeper and deeper breaths.

"You okay?" Beau asks.

"Yeah. Just...just a long day."

The dark is velvety and verging on cold. I wriggle closer and Beau tightens his grip on my waist, his forearm lying on top of mine. The firelight catches on his tattoos and I can't stop myself: I slide my fingers up the inside of his wrist, tracing the letters as I go.

His horses:

Black Label.

Only.

Arch.

His successes:

Washington.

Devon.

Harrisburg.

So many victories laid out in small, dark lines. It suddenly seems sad, like he needed each one to remind himself he still existed. "Why?" I ask, still tracing.

Beau pauses. "Would you have preferred 'Mom' or 'I love Gina?'"

"You don't know any Ginas."

He grins. "That you know of."

I keep tracing the lines and he takes my hand in his, holds it carefully. "It's a reminder of how far I've come," he tells me. "The legacy I have to live up to. It's everything I've ever wanted. I had it...and now it's gone."

I stay still. This is the closest Beau's ever come to telling me what's really going on. Before, I wanted to know. Now, I'm almost scared.

"What do you mean?" I ask carefully.

"I'm not coming back from the fall, Holls. I can ride, but I'll never ride as well again."

And there it is. The sheer, awful honesty leaves me breathless, and for some reason, it's worse than when he told me, one way or another, he would make Dell Landers and Parish pay. For a few seconds, I don't understand how that could be and then I know: Beau's showing me who he really is. The revenge is a part of him, yes, but *this?* This is almost his everything.

"Is that what your doctor says?" I ask at last.

"It's what I know."

I brace my hands against his chest and push myself up, facing him. In the firelight, his hair and eyes look even darker, like most of him has burned away. "You're not a doctor."

"I did the exercises, the physical therapy. It isn't working."

"Then you need a new doctor."

"Or I need to get real."

I pause, turning the words over and over in my head, listening for the edge of panic I'd expect...and it isn't there. He sounds resigned, not enraged. "Is that what you want?" I ask at last.

"No, of course not. I wish it had never happened. But after today…" He hooks a strand of loosened hair behind my ear and cups my cheek with his warm palm. "Maybe there's something still out there for me after all."

My heart trip-trips. He said that like a promise—no, more like a hope, a *wish*. I'm chilled, but something inside me warms with the possibility. There could be so much more for Beau's future.

There could be so much more for our *future*, I realize. It's another one of those funny, secret thoughts. It ambushes me and suddenly I can't put it aside. I'd like to see what the future would hold for Beau and me. I really would.

Except…except…there is no future as long as he wants to destroy Dell Landers and Parish. I don't know what a shared future with Beau would be like, but I *do* know where the revenge will lead him: destruction.

I can't watch that.

I clear my throat, clear it again. "Does that mean you're going to let Dell Landers and Parish go?"

Beau goes still, eyes shining in a way that makes my skin go even colder. "Why would I do that?"

"Because." I sound small and so very faraway. "Because you're going to be more than they ever will be."

"And what kind of person is that? What kind of person would I be if I let them get away?"

Someone who would still be in one piece, I think. *Someone who won't kill his own integrity because it's the last resort.* But of course, I can't manage any of that. It's like my voice has died under Beau's glittering stare.

"Is that what this was about?" he asks. "Getting me to that seminar today? You trying to turn me into a good boy? Or just distract me?"

"No." I force a teasing smile. The energy between us has shifted and it's ridiculous of me, but I feel like I've lost something. Something I really want even I can't name it. "Well…not entirely."

He leans closer, our lips brush. "Until I finish them, it's never going to be over."

CHAPTER 30 | Holly

I wake up to sunlight hitting me in the face, and my cell phone frantically buzzing under my pillow. I roll over, peering at the screen. Ellie. In spite of being less than half awake, I smile.

"Hey," I say, pawing hair out of my eyes. "What's up?"

"Parker!" she shrieks. "Parker called! She's on her way to Twelve Oaks!"

I blink. My brain's too slow to fully understand and then suddenly I get it and sit up straight. "Are you serious?"

"Deadly. She called me while she was on her way. Can we come to Camp Cargo Shorts?"

I start to say yes and stop. After last night, I don't know where Beau and I stand—actually, that's not quite true. We're standing somewhere between Not Good and Holly Is An Idiot For Thinking Beau Will Change His Mind. "No," I say at last, twisting out of bed. "Pick me up and let's go to breakfast. Do you have time?"

"Sure." Ellie's tone has lowered. "You okay?"

"Totally. This is the best day ever if Parker's coming home." It's true too. I didn't realize how much missing her had been a constant, low level ache until now. Beau can suck it. I have my best friends. I grab a pair of jeans from my dresser and tug them on. "Does she seem okay?"

Ellie makes me a funny noise, something between uncertainty and worry. "She said she was sorry for being AWOL and she'd explain everything. But she didn't sound that great, to be honest."

My stomach squeezes. I *knew* something was going on. There's no way Parker would ditch us like that. "How far out are you?"

"Maybe fifteen?"

"I'll be ready before that. Let me meet you at the barn and we can go get breakfast together."

157

"Perfect! See you soon!" Ellie kisses loudly into the phone and hangs up. I spend another minute getting dressed, tossing on a cami and sweater and hopping around as I stuff my feet into socks.

The cottage is deserted and silent, no sign of Beau anywhere. *Probably at the barn*, I realize and wonder if I'm up for running into him. *Of course, you are*, I tell myself. *Stop being stupid when it comes to him.*

"Stupider," I mutter, rummaging through my bag for my keys. "Always at the freakin' bottom." It isn't helping that my hands are shaky. The prospect of seeing Parker after more than a year makes me want to jump up and down, but something cold still runs down my spine. Why is she here now? And why so suddenly?

I hop in the Bronco and drive up to the barn. The usual work trucks are parked outside, but a tiny rental car has pulled in next to them and when I see the silky brown ponytail twitch over a woman's shoulder, I know it's Parker.

She's not alone either. A massive brown dog takes up the entire back seat. He lunges from side to side, making the whole car shake. I wave as I swing the Bronco into a parking spot and she waves back. The dog barks, spraying the window with spittle.

"Hey!" I cry, launching myself out of the driver's seat.

Parker gives me a thin smile. She has an overnight bag slung onto one shoulder, and as she reaches for the rear passenger seat door, the huge, shaggy dog jumps between the two front seats. He gets stuck, wiggles madly, and finally bursts free with a yelp

Parker swears. "Wookie! Behave!"

Wookie's whole body wags as he looks up at his mistress. I can't tell if that's behaving, but it makes me smile.

"Parker!" I run to her and we hug. Hard. She still smells like Clinique Happy and the cinnamon lattes she loves. "It's been way too long."

"I know, right?"

I push back, holding both her upper arms in my hands. She feels slighter than usual and her large brown eyes are smudged with shadows. "You look like hell," I blurt. "What happened?"

For a second or two, she looks like she's going to laugh it off, and then her expression shutters. "Matthew happened."

My stomach sinks. Matthew is Parker's husband. He inherited a successful remodeling business in Seattle, and they moved to be close to the business right after they married. She'd seemed so happy.

I start to ask what happened, but Ellie floors it up Twelve Oaks' drive. She parks next to me, hurls herself out of the truck, and straight into Parker.

"Parks! Oh my God! It's so good to see you!"

"And you! Oof, Ellie, you're squeezing me to death!"

Ellie pulls back. "Because there's nothing left to squeeze. Are you okay?"

Parker takes a shaky breath. "No." She pauses. "Matthew and I are getting a divorce. I need somewhere to crash. I know I haven't been a great friend, but...can I stay with one of you?"

"Of course, you can!" Ellie hauls Parker into her arms again, eyeing me from over our friend's shoulder. I shrug, unable to find anything to say. *There are more fish in the sea? His loss?* It all seems incredibly trite. Probably because it is when you're faced with the reality.

Ellie faces Parker, a plan already making her eyes glint. "Caleb and I are staying at his family's place. There must be a dozen bedrooms. You can have your pick. Of course, we'll need to stash your stuff somewhere..." Ellie's eyes trail over the rental car. It's way too small to be hiding anything. All three of us look down at Wookie and then Parker's overnight bag.

"This is all I have," she says, and it's so soft I almost miss it. "This and Wookie."

Hearing his name the dog/pony pricks his ears and starts dancing around us. Ellie scratches his massive head. "What on earth do you feed him, Parks? Children?"

Parker's laugh is short and strangled. "He slept with one of our real estate agents. He wants to marry her."

I close my hand around hers. It's not that cold outside, but her fingers are icy and there are tears in her eyes. "I gave up everything for him. I gave up you two and now look..."

I ease my arm around her too thin shoulders and pull her close. "Yeah, look, you're back with us."

"I'm so sorry," Parker whispers.

"Nothing to be sorry about," Ellie says, stroking her back. Our eyes meet again. Ellie's are flashing dangerously. I give her my serious face, the one that means whatever she's thinking she better quit. I love her, but Ellie has a history of bad decision in the name of righteousness.

"I lost everything," Parker continues. She isn't crying, but tears still snake underneath her words. "I guess I should say I *gave* him everything. I couldn't get out of there fast enough." She takes a gulping breath of air. "I'm broke. Like seriously broke."

Her cheeks are bright pink with embarrassment and her gaze is pinned to Wookie.

"I've been there," I tell her. "Kind of there now actually, but I can still take you to breakfast and we can still get you settled with Ellie and it will still work out. I promise."

"I feel terrible." Now Parker really is crying, the tears stream down her face. "I wasn't there for ages for either of you and now you're all I have. I'm sorry. I'm *so* sorry."

"Nothing to be sorry about." Ellie loops her arms around our shoulders, pulling us in for a tight, tight hug. For a moment, we aren't a pack of twenty-somethings. We're thirteen. Fifteen. Sixteen. We're on our way to prom. We're getting back from a horse show. We're graduating from high school.

It's the strangest thing. Everything really is falling apart around us, but when I hug them, I feel like it can still be fixed, like whatever happens I can handle it because we're together.

CHAPTER 31 | Beau

It's been two days since our argument, and Holly hasn't touched me. It's like we slid backward. No, that's not quite right. Sliding backward implies that we were going somewhere to begin with. Now, we're just back to where we were.

Where we belong, I remind myself. It's true, but my chest twists anyway. After I told her I would never let Landers and Parish slide, it was like all the light in her went out. She almost looked like she might cry, like she pitied me and was afraid for me and that's bullshit.

Just thinking about it makes my hands fist around my truck's steering wheel, this isn't about revenge. It's about justice. It's also about prevention. Getting away with killing horses for money will only make Landers and Parish bolder. It isn't a question of *if* they'll do it again. It's a question of *when* they'll do it again. Someone has to stop that.

If Holly can't understand why that someone has to be me then whatever. Screw her. She doesn't get it, and there's only so many times I can explain it. I turn into the stable's parking area and park my truck down at the end.

She doesn't get it, I think again, and put like that, I should be at peace with my decision to keep going, but I'm not. I'm pissed. Holly sees the truth behind everything. How can she not see this?

I'm still gripping the steering wheel with both hands—ten and four like some rattled, newbie driver—and that's when it hits me:

You respect her, I realize, my stomach swooping down around my feet. *You want her to understand this. You want her approval.*

What. The. Hell?

"So not going to happen," I announce to the empty, chilled truck cab. In fact, the idea's almost comical. Ever since that night, we've been at each other's throats. I keep digging at her. She keeps riding my ass.

This morning, we argued about tonight's meet and greet at Caleb Reese's family farm, Jacks or Better. It's a fundraiser for the next Olympic team and I'm supposed to go, shake hands, and stand for pictures, but I hadn't RSVP'd and Holly had to smooth things over with some donors. She was irritated. I was irritated. I ended up walking out of the house and driving around to stables.

Like a freaking teenager, I think, frowning. I lean back into my seat and watch two grooms lead two of the horses out. Ace is on the right, but one of Ellie's new, young jumpers is on the left and bouncing around like an idiot. Most likely, they're going to be turned out together in the hopes Ace will have a calming influence. Judging by the young horse's dancing, it's a nice thought, but probably won't work.

I grin. Moments like these make me love horses even more. They're feisty and rowdy and have more energy than they sometimes know what to do with. As riders, we're supposed to channel it, turn it into brilliance, but we also have to protect it whenever we can. They do a remarkable job of hurting themselves. We don't need to help.

I turn, opening the truck door, and my back twinges hard. No way am I up to tonight's party. I ache already, my temper is on edge, and I don't want to be ponied out in front of donors.

I also don't want to admit any of this to Holly.

Inside the stable, it's a bit warmer and I feel myself begin to loosen. It's good to be back. The rhythm of the barn hasn't changed. In some ways, it's exactly like stepping back in time. This could be a year ago. Two years ago.

Deep in my coat pocket, my cell rings. I fish it out and I glance the screen. Local number, but I don't recognize it. I hit the answer button anyway. "This is Beau."

Nothing from the other end. Maybe the faintest whoosh of wind in the distance.

"This is Beau," I repeat, but there's still no response. Wrong number? Bad connection? I start to hang up and someone squeaks.

"Beau? This is Kat."

She sounds close to tears, and chills run up my arms. "Hey." I pause, stepping to the side to avoid being run over by one of the guy's dragging the feed cart through. "Are you okay? You don't sound good."

"I'm not. I'm so not." She sniffles, and then takes a deep breath. The inhale barrels down the line. "Can I come to Twelve Oaks? I have something you need to see."

***

In barn clothes, Kat looks even younger than she did at The Hole in the Wall. Her black hair is scraped into a ponytail, her cheeks are exhaustion pale, and there's a smudge of something green on her jacket. Horse slobber if I had to guess. I used to wear it all the time too.

She's parked out by the work trucks, but hasn't come in. She stands next to her little Civic, glancing over her shoulder like she's scared someone's going to spot her.

"Hey," I say, crunching across the gravel toward her.

"Hey," she whispers. Her eyes are glazed over with tears, and I hesitate. I'm so not good with crying.

"C'mon," I say, ignoring the twinges riding up my leg. "Let's take a walk. I'll introduce you to Black Label and Only."

In spite of her misery, Kat's expression brightens at the offer to meet my Olympic horses. She hurries alongside me, her arm brushing mine as we walk down the tree-lined path toward the paddocks. Neither of us says a word. In fact, with every step Kat seems to shrink deeper and deeper into her jacket.

Then suddenly, she pulls her chin up and faces me. "Did you hear about what happened at Chatt Hills last night?" she asks.

I stumble for a step and right myself. "No."

"Another horse died. Sudden heart attack."

"Yeah? That's terrible."

Kat nods, eyes pinned to Black Label. The rangy German-bred stallion spotted us coming down the path and has trotted to the gate, eager for cookies or pets or anything else we might be willing to give him. For a horse who was aggressive enough to jump five-foot-plus fences, he acts like a Golden Retriever at home.

"I saw George Parish coming out of his stall." Kat's voice goes tight, one hand plunging into her jacket pocket. "I followed him, and he threw this into the garbage."

She pulls her hand back out, showing me a syringe inside a plastic sandwich bag.

My blood goes cold. "Kat," I manage, trying for gentle, but knowing I'm missing it by miles. I'm way, way too pissed. I make her name sound like a curse.

Damn Parish, I think. *Damn him straight to hell*. I grit my teeth, take a deep breath, and try again: "Why are you bringing this to me? You need to contact the police and the competition organizers."

"Because it'll blacklist me for sure!" Tears glaze her eyes again. She stuffs the plastic bag and both hands back into her jacket pockets, hunching into herself. "You understand that, right? I mean, you have to. You've made your whole life about horses. You have to understand why I want to make mine the same way."

"Yeah." My throat's gone dry. Above us, a breeze rushes through the red and gold-leafed trees making the branches shiver. "I do."

"So you can take this to them. The police."

The temptation hits me like a drug. For a heartbeat, I'm euphoric—and then I crash back into reality. "Kat...people think I'm on a witch hunt. If I come forward with this, it's going to look awfully convenient."

"If someone doesn't come forward, he'll get away with it again."

My throat tightens. She's right, of course. We reach Only's paddock fence and I reach across to give him a scratch. He leans into my fingers, eyes rolling back in his head. Such a goof. Normally, I would laugh, but my stomach's gone cold, oily. "That someone has to be you, Kat. Honestly? I wish it could be me. It would make me look less unhinged, but it can't be. *You* saw it. You have to come forward."

She doesn't respond and I don't push her. We spend a couple minutes quietly scratching Only. I can't tell what Kat's thinking, but her eyes have cleared. She no longer looks seconds away from tears.

"Want to meet Black Label? She's right over there." I bump my head toward the next paddock where a bright bay mare watches us with interest. I can't tell whether she'll come up for pets or run around to show off. Honestly, I never know what Black Label's going to do. I've always considered it part of her charm.

Kat nods and follows me to the mare's paddock. "She's beautiful," she says as we watch Black Label decide to show us—or maybe Only—her moves. She gallops across the grass looking every bit like the million bucks she is.

I miss that gallop, I think and it's like getting the wind knocked out of me. I'll probably never ride it again. I shake myself and face Kat. "Who owned the horse?"

"Guess."

I don't need to. My blood is already boiling. "Was Landers the sole owner?"

"No, the horse was owned in syndicate with the Monaham family. The daughter was showing him and he wasn't doing so well."

"Let me guess, refusals during competitions? Or just not fast enough to win anymore?"

"I don't know exactly. I think he was for sale, but the offers were coming in low—or that's the rumor at least. You know how people whisper."

"No kidding."

Kat leans her forearms against the paddock's top rail. "When I started riding...I never thought it would be like this and now...now I can't un-see it. I feel like everything's ruined."

"Maybe it's time for a change of pace? Different barn, different discipline."

"Why? It's the same all over. The things people do to animals." She shakes her head, looking ill. "I'm just a groom, Beau. In the horse world, I'm nobody. The changes that need to be made for the welfare of our animals have to come from people like you. People will listen if you say it. You're our best, our brightest."

The compliment makes my skin crawl. I'm the farthest thing from best or bright these days. Another breeze sets the trees to whispering and Black Label explodes, racing off in the other direction, bucking.

"Like it or not," Kat continues, turning to meet my gaze, "owners and riders look up to you. I can be buried, but you can't. If I have to come forward..." She takes a deep breath and pulls her chin higher. "Then you have to come with me."

She sticks her hand in her jacket again and then holds out the sandwich bag. After a moment, I take it.

CHAPTER 32 | Beau

I walk Kat back to her car and make sure she's well on her way before I climb into my truck. Somewhere around the farm road's second bend, my hip begins to protest all the walking, but I can barely feel it. I can't pull my thoughts away from Kat and Arch and Parish.

And now a new horse.

I could've stopped that.

At home, I struggle a bit on the porch steps, pain from my back and hip making my teeth grind. I let myself inside, and it takes my eyes a minute to adjust to the dim light.

Then I see Holly.

She's grinning and for a second, it swings my heart right into my throat. Most of me is still thinking about Parish.

The tiny bit that's left wonders how she can still make me feel lighter. Even when the whole world has gone dark.

"Good to talk to you," she says, and briefly, I'm confused, and then I realize she's on the phone. Probably with someone I've pissed off—not that you can tell from her voice. She sounds light and breezy and like she's talking to her favorite person ever. I watch her wander in circles as she chats, looking sexy as hell.

She's piled a slouchy, soft sweater on top of some frilly white dress. It's super short, perfect to show off her legs in a pair of gray suede over the knee boots. Her blond hair's loose and she keeps touching the ends, twisting them around her fingers.

Just watching her makes my hands curl.

"See you soon," Holly says and hangs up. She tosses her cell onto the coffee table, eyes on me. "You're on for tonight. No excuses." A pause. "Beau? Are you okay?"

"Another horse died." Just saying it leaks all the air from me, and I'm half shocked I'm still standing. "Happened last night. Kat saw George Parish go into his stall, and when he left, she followed him. He threw this is into the trash." I toss the plastic bag to her, and she catches it. We both go quiet.

Holly swallows, and then swallows again. "What are you going to do?" she finally asks.

"Don't know. Get it dusted for fingerprints and then...?" I look at her and she looks at me and the silence stretches out between us, fragile as glass. We're acting like strangers. "Maybe we can get some of the contents tested. I guess it's possible some of the chemical could still remain."

"Do you think it would stand up in court? Don't we need chain of evidence or something?"

And now we're being polite—super polite actually—and I don't know what to do with that either. Holly's eyes keep going from me to the baggie with the syringe. She watches me like I'm some sort of wild animal that might attack.

That's how she sees this, I think. We're only a few feet apart, but it might as well be miles. "I don't think it will stand up in any court, but if Kat comes forward as a witness and we confirm Parish's fingerprints on the syringe, maybe it'll be enough for an investigation."

"But not a conviction."

I take a deep breath. "Exactly—and that's the problem. An investigation could find them not guilty, and we know they are."

See? I want to say. *That's why it won't work to do this on the up and up. That's why I have to take care of them myself.*

But there's no point. Deep down, Holly's noble, and I'm...not.

"But Kat..." she trails off. "If she'll come forward that has to help. *Will* she really come forward?"

"Not happily, but yeah." I rub both hands over my face. God, I'm suddenly so tired. I limp toward the couch, catch myself, and start to move right again. I don't know why I bother—she knows—but letting her see it now feels wrong. I don't look at her and she doesn't say anything. Maybe it'll be like it never happened.

Except I want to touch her. I want to pull her into my lap and press my face into her hair and breathe until the knot in my chest is gone. Touching Holly does that for me.

Or it used to.

Screw that, I'm sure it still would, but it doesn't matter anymore. She's going to want me to do the honorable thing here, and I'm willing to try, but if no one opens an investigation and no one pursues this—red creeps into my vision and I force myself to breathe.

I drop heavily onto the couch and look up at Holly. Sunlight from the nearby windows catches in her hair and glides along the curve of her cheek. "Kat knows it's the right thing to do, but she's terrified it will end her career. She wants me to come forward with her. Kid actually thinks it'll help."

"It would."

I jerk back like she's slapped me. "The sole witness teams up with the guy who's been telling everyone it's fraud and animal abuse? You don't think that's a touch convenient?"

Tentatively, she eases closer and perches on the couch's armrest, hands clutched so tightly the knuckles go gray. "If she needs you to help her be brave, then I'd say screw how it looks."

"'Screw how it looks?'" I echo. "This coming from the designer."

"Don't be an ass." Her whole body's gone tight. She's almost vibrating. "Kat needs you to help her come forward. She looks up to you. You may not like that, but it's the truth."

"I won't be any help."

"You will be to her."

I don't respond. I can't. Holly's looking at me like I'm someone else, someone *better*.

Like I'm some sort of hero.

***

I'm not of course. There's nothing heroic about me. And when I drive up to Adele's to tell her what's happened, I feel even worse. I'm not sure how she's going to react and I'm damn unsure how I'll react to that reaction.

I drive my truck around the back of the house, and park by the family vehicles. For years and years, I *was* family. I'm not sure how much of that will survive after this. Probably not much.

Even so, Adele deserves to know. I have the syringe in my jacket pocket and the names of two fingerprinting labs that could rush the results. I don't want her broadsided. After our last talk, I feel like she'll be willing to listen.

But even if she's not, I'm still going through with the fingerprinting and I'll still take Kat to meet with competition officials.

I've just gotten out of the truck when Martie opens the door, grinning at me and pulling her wrap tight against the chill. I wave. Even though we're at the back of the house, it's no less opulent: sculpted hedges jutting out of ornate planters, bluestone pavers laid in a herringbone pattern across the drive, and of course, the house itself.

The whole place is quiet and filled with sunshine. The mid-morning light catches on the huge windows, turning them white, and the custom copper weathervane twists in the breeze. The slate roof and shingle siding make me feel like I've been transported to Nantucket, but the huge porch and daybed swings are unmistakably southern.

I step through the graceful arched doorway, and Martie surges forward to give me a hug. "This is unexpected," she says, pulling me into the kitchen. Everything smells like warm bread and something's cooking on the stove. "You here for some breakfast?"

"No. Thank you though." I hesitate, the familiarity of the house winding around me. "Is Adele here?"

"About to leave for the first day of the board meeting. You better hurry."

"Study?"

She nods, and I take the short hallway through the butler's pantry into the main house. Adele's study is in the east wing. She doesn't use it as much as the barn office, but we've done a bunch of farm reviews here, even looked at some sales videos for overseas horses so I know where I'm going. I knock twice at the dark-stained wooden door, and I almost think I've already missed her when I hear,

"Come in!"

I do, catching Adele in the middle of stuffing a briefcase with papers. She's wearing a fitted, long-sleeved black dress with pearls and black heels. Her hair is escaping its chignon, and when she looks up, a dark strand cuts across her eyes.

"Beau?" Her face creases into a smile. "It's so nice to see you. Did you need something?"

"We need to talk. I know you're about to leave, but..." Another horse has died, and it's our fault? I've been proven right?

Or how about, I'm about to rip your business partner a new one?

Technically, they're all true, and none of them feels like the complete reason anymore. I pull out the baggie and flip it onto Adele's desk. It lands with a soft thud, and her eyes widen. "Is that...?"

"Yeah," I say, and give her the latest update. I tell her about what Kat saw and the new horse that's been killed and I start to tell her we're responsible for this, this is our fault because we didn't stop Parish and Landers before, but the words die when I look up and see Adele's expression. She's gone gray around the edges. When she sits down in her desk chair, she doesn't look like she'll be able to get back up.

"You said you had some labs that can do the fingerprinting?" she asks me at last.

"Yeah." I slide the note with their names and numbers toward her, and she picks up the paper with a shaking hand.

"How long until we can get the results?" she asks.

"They've promised a week."

"If they confirm the suspicions, we'll need to contact Ritch...and Don, of course."

I nod. Ritch being the president of the United States Hunter Jumper Association, and Don being the president of the Federation Equestrian International. Both organizations were involved in hosting the competitions where the horses died.

"And Melanie," I add, reminding her of our insurance agent. She approved the multi-million payout for Arch. She'll need to know as much as anyone.

"I've had her over for dinner more times than I can count," Adele says softly, eyes shining and faraway. "It's never going to be the same again, is it? Everyone will believe I killed my horse for money."

"No one who knows you would ever believe it," I say and the truth of it turns the words into a rush. They spill out. One look at Adele though and I can tell she doesn't believe me. She picks up the phone, bravery and determination schooling her features into something smooth, calm. She knows she's walking into a shit show and she's still doing it. I really admire that.

After dialing, she sits back, reaches into her desk, and pulls out a bottle of whisky. "To truth," she says, and takes a quick swallow. She grins and passes it to me.

I take it. "To truth," I say, and now we're both grinning.

CHAPTER 33 | Holly

I have design block. Or creativity block. Or whatever you call it when you can't concentrate on your real future because you're too mired in your present.

And mostly you can't stop thinking about Beau Kent.

I stare down at the sketch I've been agonizing over for the past three hours. It's still not right. It's supposed to be a punk-influenced ball gown and it just looks...messy. I need to take away a few elements or maybe combine them more effectively.

Or maybe just give up, I think, flinging myself back against the kitchen chair and glaring at the ceiling. One of the biggest things I've struggled with in design has been my utter inability to make what I see in my head turn out on the dress. It morphs. It changes. It eludes me.

This isn't to say I don't like how most of my designs turn out. Eventually, I do. It's the getting there that kills me—kills *all* creative types, if I'm being realistic about the process.

Which, of course, at this moment I don't feel like being.

"Embrace the journey," I mutter, but I stuff the ball gown sketch under two magazines anyway. I never like embracing the journey. I like embracing the destination. It's my favorite.

Buried under patterned silk swatches, my cell vibrates with an incoming call. My heart leaps. Beau?

I paw through the fabric and find the handset. Not Beau. Scott.

I scowl at the little swoop of disappointment. *There is something seriously wrong with you,* I tell myself, and answer, "Hello?"

"How're the sketches coming?"

I pass one hand across my face. "Like I'm drilling thumbtacks into my gums."

"That's a visual I didn't need."

"But now you have it. You're welcome."

Scott gives me a derisive snort. "So it's not going well?"

"I'm distracted." I frown. Is that *all* this is? Well, it's all I'm going to admit. I shift around in my seat, trying to get comfortable. "I just need to work through it."

"You should change locations," Scott says. "Always helps me."

"Or you could distract me." I rub one hand over my face. "What's up?"

"Everything," he says and I can hear the grin in his voice. We spend the next hour talking about our first moves—what kind of workspace we'll need, what kind of help we can afford, and when I can start. I'm a little vague on that last one since so much depends on getting Beau through the board meeting and finalizing things with my mom, but Scott doesn't push me and by the time we hang up, our respective to-do lists are about a thousand times longer, but it's good.

Great, I tell myself. *This is going to be great.*

Or it will be if I can get these sketches down. I slide them back out and frown. Nothing's coming to me.

Maybe I should *change locations*, I think, staring out the window for the millionth time. There's no sign of Beau's truck up at the farm. Everything looks peaceful as ever. Maybe I'd feel better sitting outside? It's warm enough today. I could go down to the young horses' paddocks and try to relax.

That'll work, I think, gathering up the sketches and fabric swatches. I head for the Bronco, arms so overfull I don't even notice when I leave my cell behind.

CHAPTER 34 | Beau

When I get back, the Bronco's nowhere in sight and the cottage is cold. I walk through the living room, circle through the kitchen, and check out back. Definitely no Holly.

I scrub one hand through my hair, annoyed and annoyed that I'm annoyed. I wish she were here. I want to talk to her. Apologize for being such an ass. She saved me from tanking my career—and hurting Adele. I would've broken things I would never have been able to mend.

I owe her for protecting me.

The realization is small and squirming and uncomfortable as hell. Would I have looked out for her the same way? I honestly don't know. I've been such an ass lately.

Or always, I guess, depending on who you ask.

Something buzzes, interrupting my thoughts. A cell? I check my pocket. Not mine, I think, glancing around and spotting the small white iPhone peeking out from under some notebook pages.

It's Holly's. She must have left it when she went tearing out of here. I glance at the screen just before the call rolls to voicemail. It isn't a saved number so I figure it's not a big deal until the caller dials again. And again.

Probably important, I think. Important enough for me to answer it? I waffle, letting the number kick over to voicemail again—and then it calls back.

I pick up the cell, thumbing the answer button. "Hello?"

"Is Ms. Benson there?" It's a woman on the other end, voice tight with urgency and worry.

"Uh, no, she isn't. Can I take a message?"

"Are you *Mr.* Benson?"

I hesitate, curiosity swirling through me. "Yeah."

"Oh, thank goodness!" The woman looses a winding sigh of relief. "My name is Nurse Lawrence. Your mother-in-law had a fall. You need to come down to the Piedmont emergency room."

I feel my eyes bug, images of Holly being terrified flashing through my brain. "I—I—*what?*"

"Your mother-in-law had a fall. You need to get down here." She pauses. "Go get something to write with. I'll wait."

"Uh...okay." Later, I'll be super grateful she knew I was reeling. Right now, I'm just grateful she's telling me what to do. I don't even know the right questions to ask, but she walks me through everything and I spend several moments scribbling down directions and information.

"I'll see you soon," Nurse Lawrence tells me, and hangs up before I can respond. I blink at the phone in my hand. Holy shit. I need to find Holly, but to start? Twelve Oaks is almost a thousand acres. She could be anywhere.

"Please be down at the barn giving someone hell," I mutter, using my cell to call the stable. It rings and rings and eventually Charlie picks up and grunts that he hasn't seen her. "Thanks," I say and hang up. I try Ellie next.

"Holly with you?" I ask her.

"No. Why?"

"Her mom had a fall." I go to the front windows, checking to see if Holly happens to be driving up. She isn't. Where could she be? "She's at the hospital and Holly needs to meet her."

"Oh God." Ellie sounds sick. Or maybe it's just me. My stomach's gone sour. "I'll find her," she adds. "She has to be around here somewhere."

"Thanks. I have her cell. Can you get her to call me? I've got all the information."

A slight hesitation. "Sure."

We disconnect, and I realize I'm pacing in circles around our small foyer. *Chill out*, I think, but I can't. There's no way. This is Holly's *mom*. "Fuck me," I mutter, and head for my truck.

*****

The hospital is about thirty minutes away, but it feels closer to hours. When I finally get there, I keep checking and rechecking both cells in case Holly's called. She hasn't.

Where are you? I wonder, and my stomach does another uncomfortable squeeze. I don't think she's hurt, but I know she'll freak when she finds out she left her phone and this happened. Holly doesn't take well to being unprepared or out of control. I need to get a handle on it.

I park and wind my way to the emergency room's front desk. The line is four or five people deep, and the receptionists look harried. By the time I get to them, it takes a few minutes to find out where Mrs. Benson is and what's going on.

"She's already upstairs," one of them tells me at last, eyes pinned to her computer screen. She looks up and points to my right. "Room three-oh-three. Take the elevators."

I nod, not really trusting myself to talk past the tightness in my chest. This isn't the same hospital they life-flighted me to, but it smells the same—a tang of disinfectant alongside recycled air—and it brings back memories I thought I'd successfully lost. I'd drifted in and out of consciousness for two days because of the pain meds. The nightmares were awful, but waking up was worse.

I had to have another surgery before leaving, and then two more after that. Everyone was convinced I'd never ride again. I didn't bother arguing because I thought I knew better. What a fucking joke. The only thing that kept me going was knowing I *would* ride again.

And promising myself I would take down Landers and Parish.

I reach room 303 just as a young woman in scrubs steps out. She's writing on a clipboard, her dark braids swinging around her shoulders.

When she looks up her brown eyes widen and then narrow. "Can I help you?"

"Here to see my mother-in-law." I'm almost surprised how easy the lie comes. Even to me, it sounds natural. "She was taken in with a broken hip."

"Oh, I'm Nurse Lawrence. We spoke on the phone." She opens the heavy door behind her and leans in. "Mrs. Benson? He's here."

"Who's here?" Mrs. Benson is lying down and hooked up to a half a dozen machines, but she still manages to wiggle around to look at me. "Who's he?"

"Ha ha, Mrs. Benson," I say, trying to look innocent as I slip into the room. "She thinks she's funny."

Nurse Lawrence shakes her head. "More like she's loaded with pain meds. I'll give you two a minute. Doctor Ramirez is currently with another patient so it may be a while before you see her."

I give her my widest grin. "No problem."

In fact, I think, *the longer the doctor takes the better*. It will give Holly more time to get here. I mean, *surely*, Ellie's found her by now. I feel vaguely shitty about lying my way in here, but I would feel worse if I didn't, like I would be letting Holly down somehow.

Nurse Lawrence closes the door behind her, and I take a seat as far away from Mrs. Benson's bed as I can. Now that I'm here, I'm not exactly sure what I should be doing. Small talk? Pep talk? No talk? I have zero clue. Her mom's tiny with perfect posture and the wildest head of white hair I've ever seen, but somehow it's still like looking at Holly. It's probably the blue eyes.

Or maybe it's the gleam in those blue eyes. The old lady looks like she's plotting something and it makes the hair on the back of my neck stand up. Whenever Holly looks at me like that, I know I'm not going to like whatever she's thinking. Speaking of Holly...

C'mon, I think, glancing at her cell and then mine. *Where* are *you?*

"So who are you really?" Mrs. Benson asks, fingers smoothing over her paper thin hospital blanket. "Friend? Boyfriend? Random stranger?

We look at each other while I debate my options—all none of them. What the hell I guess. She seems awfully lucid for someone who has to be in a lot of pain and on medications. Maybe I can reason with her.

"Okay," I begin, shifting in my seat, "please don't be upset, I know we haven't met. I'm Holly's...friend. My name's Beau. Beau Kent. She's on her way, but I know she wouldn't want you to be alone."

"That's very thoughtful of you."

I frown. I'm not used to be called thoughtful. Actually, I don't think I've *ever* been called thoughtful. I glance at the door again, praying Holly will appear. She doesn't, of course, and when I look back, Mrs. Benson is studying me. This close, I swear to God her hair looks spray starched. It's huge.

"Are you feeling okay?" I ask, rubbing both hands on my knees. "Can I get you anything?"

"No, I'm fine—or as fine as I can be. Fell in the shower," Mrs. Benson explains. She takes an InTouch magazine from her bedside table and begins flipping through it. "I was trying to give myself a lightning bolt *down there* and I slipped."

I pause. I can't get my brain past lightning bolts and *down there.* "Oh," I manage at last, eyes still bugging. "Well, ah, happens to the best of us. That's a tricky...move."

She nods. "That's exactly what I told the paramedics. They acted like they had no idea. Maybe they don't? Now what kind of friend are you to my daughter? Friend friend? Or friend with benefits?"

It shouldn't be possible, but my eyes bug even more. I'd almost rather talk about her pubic hair getting shaved into lightning bolts. No, actually, I'm *sure* I'd rather talk about her pubic hair getting shaved into lightning bolts than talk about what I am to Holly. I stare at Mrs. Benson, trying to think of how to answer and she nods wisely.

"Ah," she says with satisfaction. "Friend with benefits."

"Do you know what friends with benefits means?"

"Of course." She pauses, one bony hand hovering over her magazine. "Do *you* know what it is? Because if you don't, I can explain it."

Holly's cell rings. *Thank God*, I think, sagging in relief, but when I look at the screen, it says Dane. Who the fuck is that?

Can't be any worse than this, I think, thumbing the answer button. "Holly's phone."

"Who are you?" The voice definitely belongs to a Dane. It's male and indignant and probably belongs to a guy who wears khaki shorts embroidered with little whales or pineapples.

I glance nervously at Mrs. Benson. "I'm Holly's...friend."

Mrs. Benson cracks up.

"Oh for Christ's sake," Dane fumes, some sort of clacking sound coming from his end of the phone. I assume he's typing, but it sounds like he's trying to beat his keyboard half to death.

"Put Holly on," he orders. "I had to pop up to Atlanta for a meeting and now I have a voicemail from the hospital saying I need to call them. I do *not* have time for this. I need her to handle it."

The arrogant tone instantly spikes my temper. I switch the phone to my other ear and take a deep breath. "And you are?"

"Holly's brother—now put her on the phone."

I grind my teeth before saying, "Can't. She isn't here right now. That's why I'm answering her phone. And whatever you're doing? You need to stop and get down to Piedmont. Your mom had a fall. She's going to be fine, but I'm sure she'll want to see you."

"Is that Dane?" Mrs. Benson asks, looking up from her magazine. "Don't invite him down. He'll only be tiresome."

"Did she just call me tiresome?" Dane sounds like he's about to reach through the phone. "I am not tiresome. I'm busy."

Oh, for the love of—"You're breaking up," I tell him.

"What? I am not. I have full signal."

"Can't hear you, man. There's—" I blow into the speaker, making the line crackle "—some sort—can't." I hang up.

Mrs. Benson pans both hands apart and says, "See? Tiresome. It isn't his fault. It's a hereditary problem—not mine, obviously—but his father's. George was very tiresome."

"Yeah?" I consider her. "What other faults does Dane have?"

But she never gets to answer because the door swings open and Holly spills through.

CHAPTER 35 | Beau

Holly's breathing hard, blond hair falling in her face and cheeks gone pink. She must've sprinted to the room. I jump to my feet, but she doesn't even see me. She rushes straight to Mrs. Benson's side.

"Mom! I'm so sorry! I came as quickly as I could!"

"Oh, you shouldn't have. I just had a little slip" Her mother's smile is positively angelic. She taps her rolled-up magazine against her blanket and then points it at me. "Your friend here has been keeping me company."

"Friend?" Holly turns and spots me. Her eyes widen. "What...?"

Well, this is awkward, I think. Holly's staring at me like I've sprouted two heads, or worse, like I'm the reason her mother ended up here, and I'm staring at her like...I don't even know what.

"Hey," I manage at last.

"Hey." She pauses. Her face is still deathly pale, but she gives me the perky Everything Is Handled Smile I've come to know and hate. "We're good. I've got this."

"Yeah, totally. I'll just...wait outside. It was nice to meet you, Mrs. Benson."

"And you, dear." The old lady's eyes are practically glowing with mayhem.

I turn, trying to leave the room with as much dignity as I can. I don't want to know what she says to Holly once I'm gone.

Actually, I do. I've kind of always wanted a filter-less grandmother or grandfather. Old people can get away with saying way worse shit than I do. For once, I'd be the good influence.

Across from 303, there's a bench and I collapse onto it, watching the nurses and doctors walk by. A few of them eye me, probably wondering what I'm doing. Honestly, I'm wondering too. Should I stay? Leave?

I should probably leave, but I can't bring myself to do it. I can't tell if Holly's actually okay, or pretending to be okay. That moment when she said they were good? I call bullshit. She looked seconds away from vomiting or crying.

A few minutes later, 303's door open again, and Holly joins me. We sit knee to knee in silence, and I have the overwhelming urge to take her hand, but I don't move. She's almost vibrating with nervous energy. I feel like if I touch her, she'll shatter.

"I was working on that project for Scott," she says finally, gathering her cardigan close.

Like she does when she's stressed, I realize, and then wonder when I learned that. Was it over these past two weeks? Or was it even before that? Back when I wanted her for the conquest.

As opposed to how you want her now? I think, and my skin goes cold.

"I didn't mean to leave my phone," she adds, pulling me back to the moment.

I clear my throat. "Okay."

We go quiet, and it takes me a full three seconds to realize she feels guilty and is trying to explain herself. To *me*. Of all freaking people.

"People forget stuff," I say. "It happens. Don't worry about it."

"How can I not? She fell. She broke her *hip*." Holly falls silent, staring at the hospital room's door and looking close to tears. "This is my fault," she whispers. "If I'd been there, it wouldn't have happened."

"Holls." It's only the second time I've called her that, but the nickname feels right. It rolls off my tongue like I've used it forever. "She fell in the *shower*. You couldn't have stopped it."

"I could've—"

"Honey, unless you and your mother have a much closer relationship than I thought, you wouldn't have been there. It still would've happened."

Her eyes are huge and shining when they lift to mine, I know she knows I'm right. She doesn't want to admit it, but I can tell she knows. Her shoulders straighten the tiniest bit, her chin lifts.

For a moment, we study each other, and it curls something nameless through my chest.

Or maybe not so nameless because I want to hold her.

I look away, clearing my throat. "I talked to your brother. Is he always such a dick?"

Holly snort-cough-laughs. "Only on days that end in y."

I grin and then catch myself. "Wait," I say, thinking this over and suddenly seeing why Holly is, well, Holly. "Is *he* the only help you have with your mom?"

"Well, yeah—but it's not like she's a burden. She's great."

She's hell on wheels, I think. "But now she's going to need more help. You can't leave her."

"No."

"So how're you going to get your business running?" My timing is shit. As soon as I ask, I wish I hadn't. Holly hunches into herself. She doesn't answer, but it's not like it matters. I already know the answer: she won't. Knowing she was away from Mrs. Benson and this happened? Worse, knowing she was away from Mrs. Benson while working on her designs and this happened? There's no way Holly will continue. She'll give up her dream. She'll give it up so her mom can have a better life and Dane can continue with his and...

And I know what it feels like to lose what you've always wanted, I think. But I *don't* know what it's like to lose it because you're putting someone else first. I've never been that selfless. She's a better person than I am. Way better. Honestly? I'm in awe.

"I'll work something out," she says finally, and it takes everything I have not to call her out for lying to herself. I lean back against the bench and feel the cold laminate bite through my thin T-shirt. I have no idea what to say. I want to comfort her and I don't know how.

"Why did you come?" she whispers.

I pause. There are so many things I could say here, but I go for honesty: "Because you needed me to come."

Holly goes still. "Since when do you play hero?"

"Since always. I can wear spandex pants like nobody's business."

She laughs, throwing her head back so her silky ponytail falls like a ribbon. I grin. It wasn't that funny. She's just *that* stressed, and when she finally goes quiet I can tell worry has sucked her back under.

I nudge my elbow into her side. "You're thinking about me in spandex pants, aren't you? It's okay. I'll give you a minute to compose yourself."

"Ms. Benson?" Another woman in scrubs—Doctor Ramirez, I assume—walks our direction. She's a curvy, Latina woman, probably in her late thirties. "You're Ms. Benson's daughter, right?"

"Yes!" Holly pops to her feet and they shake hands.

"I'm going to check your mother now," Doctor Ramirez says. "Would you like to sit in?"

"Definitely." Holly leans down to grab her bag, and hauls the brown monstrosity onto one shoulder. "Just one minute," she tells the doctor before turning to me. "Thank you."

This is the part where I'm supposed to say 'you're welcome' or 'no big deal,' and I even open my mouth to say it.

Only as soon as I look at Holly, I can't look away. She's putting on that mask again, the one where everything's fine and she's on top of it and would never, ever need help.

She's had to be like that, I realize. *She takes care of everyone else. There's no one around to take care of her.*

"Is there anything I can do to help?" I ask at last.

She shakes her head. "No, I got it. It's fine."

Then she plasters on a smile and walks away.

CHAPTER 36 | Holly

She's going to be okay, I remind myself. *She's fine—or as find as she can be with a broken hip*. Part of me is still in full blown panic mode, and I spend a long time holding Mom's hand even after she's fallen asleep. Dane calls once more, but I barely have the energy to tell him more than I'll call him tomorrow.

"Fine," he says. "And who was that anyway? The guy who was with you?"

"Friend."

"He's an ass."

Out of habit, I start to agree...and stop. Today wasn't like the past couple months. In fact, the past week and a half hasn't been anything like I've seen from Beau. I'd always known he loves his horses, but he also sticks up for low level employees, and apparently, waits with old ladies in case they get scared.

He's also consumed with revenge, I remind myself.

"I hope you're not getting involved with him," Dane says, pulling me back to the moment. "You can do better."

Can I? It's a weird, wild thought and I push it away. "I gotta go," I tell my brother, and disconnect. Mom's asleep so I kiss her cheek one last time and collect all my stuff, making a mental note of all the things she'll need me to bring back.

Clothes, toothbrush, toothpaste, I think. There's more, of course, but that's a start. I'm so tired I could fall down, but I drag myself to my car, and as soon as I'm behind the wheel, I call Ellie. She picks up after one ring and I say, "He went to the hospital."

"I'm sorry...*what?*"

"Beau. He went to the hospital. He stayed with my mom until I could get there."

187

Ellie whistles low and long. There's a rustling, like she's getting out of bed, and for the first time I realize the time. Oh my God, it's late.

"I'm so sorry," I say. "I should've looked at a clock."

"Oh, please. I would've been mad if you hadn't called. Hang on." Ellie murmurs something and a low voice answers her. Caleb. "Okay, I'm back," she says. "He stayed at the hospital? That's really nice of him."

"I know." I rub one hand over my face. My whole body feels tingly with exhaustion. I can't keep doing this. I can't be in all these different places at once. The realization makes me want to start crying all over again. "I like him, El—and the fact that he did this? It makes me like him even more."

"And this is a bad thing...why?"

"Because he isn't a good thing for me. He's going to pursue the Arch situation until someone goes down for it—him or Landers. He's in a ton of pain and he's hiding it from everyone."

"And yet he still showed up for you."

I sigh. "Exactly."

"Honey." There's an unwilling note to Ellie's voice that makes me tense. Whatever she's about to say worries her. "You take care of everyone. You're good for everyone. I want you to be with someone who's good for you."

"You think Beau is?"

"I'm not sure. I'll just say...the jury's out on him. He has moments of greatness. The fact that he showed up for you? That means the world to me. I couldn't be there, but he was and you didn't have to handle this alone. I like him more now too."

I pick at my steering wheel, unable to find anything to say. I don't want to read too much into this. Depending on Beau Kent is like asking an arsonist to hold your matches.

Or is that just what I thought was true?

The inside of the Bronco is chilly and pull my coat a little closer, watching people drift toward the cars.

"You there?" Ellie asks.

"Yeah."

"Tell me about your mom. Is there anything I can do?"

I smile through sudden tears. Ellie is the only person who ever asks me that. Well, until Beau did tonight. I shove the thought away. I shouldn't have just walked off like that, but I didn't know what to say or do or...ugh.

I rub my eyes until colors explode behind the lids. "Thank you, but no. There isn't anything at the moment. I have to get my head around the whole thing. She'll be in the hospital for another few days then we have to move her to a rehab center and then she can come home. I don't know. There are all these details and I can't seem to get a handle on them."

"You need sleep."

"Yeah."

"You need help."

I don't say anything. I can't ask Ellie to handle this. I could ask Dane, but I don't want the guilt trip, and I don't want to feel indebted, and more than anything, I want everything to be okay. It's a little kid wish, but it's also one I can't shake.

"You know I love you, right?"

"I love you too. I'll figure it out. Don't worry."

"Too late," I whisper after we hang up. The chill is starting to nudge under my clothes and I turn the Bronco's ignition. It rumbles to life. I turn the heaters on full blast and turn toward my house.

Clothes, toothbrush, toothpaste, I think, looping everything we'll need over and over again so I don't have to think about tomorrow and I definitely don't have to think about Beau Kent.

CHAPTER 37 | Beau

Holly doesn't come home that night. Makes sense, of course. I don't know why I'm vaguely disappointed. She probably spent the night at the hospital.

I'm annoyed though—no, not annoyed. Uneasy. I spend most of the small hours of the morning limping around and around my place, eventually ending up on the back deck so I can watch the sunrise.

Twelve Oaks always looks especially perfect in the morning—pink light, shadows stretched under the trees—and usually it's soothing as hell for me, but today it doesn't work.

I fix a pot of coffee and turn my attention to my schedule for the day, but I can't focus for shit and my mind keeps wandering back to Holly. She's alone, and I'm not sure which part I hate more: that she is alone, or that I now know she is. I can't look at Holly and see the same woman. She's not less now.

She's more.

I always knew she was strong—hell the woman busted my balls without breaking a sweat—but I never thought about where that strength came from.

Or worse, the grief she's carrying around in her private life while handling everything else. I don't have that kind of grace or ability or whatever. Holly's mom is slipping away and she's carrying on. I'd be three-quarters of a bottle in. Permanently.

I sip my coffee, remembering how fake that smile looked as she turned away from me. She needed help. I should've stayed. But staying seems like something that Ellie or a boyfriend would do, not the guy she's banging for fun.

Furthermore, I shouldn't have *wanted* to stay and I did. I'm not sure what that means.

A car door slams and I tense. Holly. Has to be. I'm moving before I realize it, every hurried stride spiking pain into my hip, but I barely feel it. I come through the back door as she comes through the front. We both stop. Stare.

"You're up," she says, tugging her ponytail loose. Blond hair cascades around her shoulders. She's wearing fresh clothes—a menswear button up shirt knotted at her waist and one of her micro-mini skirts—but there are deep shadows beneath her eyes. "I would've thought you'd be exhausted."

I shrug. She drops her purse to the floor, kicks off her shoes, and walks toward me. A tingle climbs my spine.

"Tired?" I ask.

Now she shrugs. "Not nearly enough." Her hands have gone to her blouse's buttons. She undoes them one by one as my mouth goes dry.

"I could help with that," I say. "I'd love to wear you out."

She slips out of the shirt, revealing creamy skin and a hot pink, lace bra. "I'm counting on it."

I grin. I can't help it. Barefoot, she's eyelevel with my collarbone and I have an excellent view of her too perfect cleavage. She takes another step, and we're toe to toe. It takes everything I have not crush her to me. In this game, I wait.

She looks up at me from underneath a fringe of blond hair. A half smile curls her mouth. "Wear me out?" she whispers.

"Gladly." I push both hands into her hair, tilting her head back so I can kiss her. She gives in so fucking sweetly, opening her mouth and relaxing against me. I have to bite back a moan. I kiss across her cheek and suck the tender skin of her neck until she sags against me. "Make me forget," she whispers.

I hesitate, hands pressing against her back, hips pressing into her stomach. Three little words and it feels like they're loaded.

But then she whispers please again, and it's like something in me cracks. Suddenly, I can't touch her enough. I want to be everywhere.

I lift her up and she wraps both legs around my waist. "I can do that," I whisper.

"Do it faster."

I laugh, pulling her close and nipping her neck. She arches into me, grinding against my already throbbing cock. "Like that is it?" I ask. "Hard and fast?"

She whimpers and I toss her to the couch, all the fantasies I had before rushing back to me. I straighten, pulling off my clothes and pulling on a condom. "Lose the panties."

She reaches under her back, fumbling for her skirt's zipper and I drop my jeans to the floor. I kneel over her, tugging her panties off with a quick jerk and settling myself between her legs. "Later," I say, pushing her skirt above her hips. I yank her bra down, going even harder when I watch her perfect nipples peak. She loves our little games.

We both do.

"Beau?"

I glance up. Her face is pinched with worry and exhaustion and *hunger*. I feel it too. I enter her hard, one quick sweep of my hips that leaves her gasping.

"Hard and fast, right?" I whisper into her ear and she moans. It's fucking perfect. She's fucking perfect.

"Hard and fast," she says, and holds onto me like I'm something more.

CHAPTER 38 | Holly

With every stroke, my legs fall farther open. I'm going boneless. Weightless. I feel like I could float away except for Beau's body pressed against me, holding me down.

His mouth finds mine, kissing me hard before he begins to work his way down my jaw...my neck...

He finds my breasts, instantly lightning his touch. His tongue circles my nipples and it's too light and too teasing and I'm coming out of my skin. I push into him and he pulls away. I moan and he lightens even more.

"Now, please, now," I beg.

And he does.

He licks me and I shiver, arching up for more. He draws one nipple into his mouth, sucking hard. Electricity rushes across my skin and everything falls away—or maybe my world has just shrunk. It's just Beau now.

My head lolls back as I enjoy him.

He strokes me again, grinding on my clit until I'm desperate to come. I dig both hands into his hips, urging him on and he stills.

"Ah ah," he murmurs, pulling out and pushing back in. "Wait for it."

It should bring everything back—all my worries, all my thoughts, everything that has to be done—but it doesn't. If anything, my focus shrinks even more. I can only take what he's going to give me.

He nibbles my neck, pinning my wrists behind me with one hand while tugging me higher onto his hips with the other. "Stay," he murmurs, nipping the skin between my neck and shoulders before placing both hands on my hips. He lifts me, filling me so slowly I want to claw him. He grins like he knows it too.

"Frustrated, honey?" His thumb brushes my clit as he pushes into me again. It sparks pleasure through me. Even my toes clench. "Ready?"

Another rub. Another spark. I whimper, head tossing from side to side. I want to grind on him and I can't. I want to come and he won't let me.

"Say it."

I open my eyes, look at him, and smile, startling both of us. He looks down at me and I look up at him and I can't stop smiling.

"Please."

His thumb circles my clit, pressing firmer...firmer. His eyes hold mine. "Come for me. Now."

One more touch and I'm gone, clenching and clenching around him, screaming as I arch back. His fingers dig into my hips, holding me against him as he begins to stroke me firmer, harder. The delicious friction pushes me over again and again. He snarls something against my neck, bucking once. Twice. He comes in a rush as I clench again and again around him.

"Holy fuck." Arms shaking, he looks down at me, spent.

"Again?" I whisper.

His head tips back as he laughs. One second I'm underneath him and then he's flipped us, pinning me between the couch cushions and his chest. "Just give me a couple minutes. I'm not tired, of course, but you are. I can tell."

Now I'm laughing. *I enjoy you*, I think, closing my eyes. When did that happen anyway? It should feel new, but it doesn't. Everything in me warms to him. It's like we fit.

"You have Mrs. Mar's party tonight," I murmur. It's morning now, and Beau has things to do. As his assistant/keeper, I need to make sure he does them.

"Sssshhhhh," he whispers. "Later."

"You can't forget."

"I won't." He angles me closer, and my bones go heavy. The world outside his cottage is threatening to break me, but right now? It feels like I'll handle it. Somehow.

With him.

The idea makes my eyes fly open. I stare up at Beau and he smiles at me, smoothing one hand over my hair. "We'll go to Adele's party after we visit your mom, okay?"

I hesitate, not trusting my voice not to break, not trusting my words to be enough. "Why would you do that?"

"Because I want to, and...because you shouldn't have to be alone. Not when I can be with you."

I tremble. Earlier, I'd had a little kid wish that everything would be okay, and right now, it really feels like it just might be. My world might be reeling, but it's going to work out because Beau's there.

You're in love with him, I think, waiting for my stomach to sink or my skin to go cold. It...doesn't happen.

Instead, I feel like I will figure things out. Maybe that's love? It isn't about everything being perfect, but the feeling that everything will work out as long as you're with him. The world can be burning down around you, but you know the two of you can handle it.

Or maybe I'm just exhausted because before I can puzzle it out, I'm asleep.

CHAPTER 39 | Beau

I wake up a couple hours later, but Holly's still sleeping hard. She's paler than usual and her fists are clenched by her chest, the veins on her hands standing up. Tense. Hardly a surprise with everything going on.

I ease off the couch and tuck a blanket around Holly, careful not to disturb her while I tug my clothes back on. If I want to take her back to the hospital for a visit, I need to get a few things done first. I'm supposed to review some vet reports for Adele plus follow up with the lab about the syringe, but I'd like to get down to the stable first.

I'm feeling more and more like that these days. Back before the accident, I was always there by seven. Always. I liked the calm before the day's chaos, having quiet time with the horses before everything began. After the accident, I couldn't bear doing it anymore. Some of that had to do with some spectacular hangovers. The rest? I just couldn't look at them without seeing who I used to be—and who I wasn't any longer.

But thanks to Holly, I'm feeling closer and closer to who I used to be, and even more importantly, closer and closer to who I *could* be. There's still a future for me. I'm stupidly grateful for it too.

I pull on my jacket, watching her sleep, and realize I owe her far more than I can repay. She gave me back my life. I've never been one to dance around and sing about how the hills are alive with music, but I'm pretty damn close.

When she wakes up, we need to talk, plan. Her mom's accident can't derail her New York dreams. With the bonus money from Adele, Holly will finally be able to get her fashion line going—gotta be honest, I'm not really sure what's involved in that, but we can work it out.

God, I think, stomach suddenly dropping. *I hope she* wants *to work it out.* One of the amazing things about Holly is how much she has going on. She doesn't need me. She can handle herself. Just because I want her doesn't mean she's going to want me.

I pause, resisting the urge to wake her up now and insist I'm the one for her. *You don't need to*, I remind myself. *You can win her over. She's almost there anyway.*

Used to be, the thought that a woman was falling in love with me would make me panicky or bored or restless. Now, I feel centered. *Holly* makes me feel centered. Now I just have to be the same thing for her.

I shove my feet into work boots and step outside as a sleek, burgundy SUV speeds up the farm road. It swings into my driveway and skids into park, bits of gravel flying. The door swings open, and a slight, dark-haired man hurls himself out. Parish.

"You fucker," he spits.

A pulse runs through me, like the jolt before starting a course, the adrenaline pump that accompanies as fast gallop. I should probably be scared. Instead, I'm fucking delighted.

I stomp down the stairs, barely aware of how my hip throbs with each stride. There's a sharpness to the air this morning. Fall is almost gone and winter is definitely here. It sets my blood humming.

Or maybe it's just the sight of Parish. My hands have already curled into fists. "Good to see you, Parish," I say.

"I want it."

I grin, thinking about telling him it's too late, that I've already sent the syringe for testing. It's the truth, and the best way to handle this. Parish is trespassing. He's looking for a fight. I should take the high road.

But when has that ever been fun?

"Want what?" I ask.

"Don't play games." He takes a step toward me, fury purpling his face. The faint whiff of alcohol hits me. "I know that girl went through the trash and found my syringe. I also know she went straight here afterward."

"*Very* impressive. What else do you know?"

"*Give me* the syringe."

My grin widens. "Come and take it."

CHAPTER 40 | Holly

A door slams, waking me. I roll over on Beau's couch and sunlight hits me full in the face. I blink. I can't believe it's morning already.

Worse, I can't believe I'm still this tired. I need to get going. I have a ton to do before heading to the hospital. I sit up, a light cotton blanket slipping from my shoulders and pooling in my lap. I finger the fabric. I know I didn't pull this over me.

Which means Beau did.

So he's thoughtful and *gorgeous*, I think. Great. Like anyone can resist that.

Like I'd even been trying.

I shake myself. Now is *so* not the time to be stupid and gooey. I have stuff to do, people to take care of, a life to get back on track. Just because Beau is occasionally thoughtful doesn't mean he isn't also damaged and complicated and...pretty much amazing.

I frown. It has to be the exhaustion talking, but our moment at the hospital felt, well, like another one of our *moments*. And messing around this morning? It felt like something more than messing around.

And it can't be.

Can it?

I mean just because I'm in love with him, doesn't mean he's in love with me. My frown deepens. Is Beau Kent even capable of falling in love anyway? Two weeks ago, I would've laughed myself silly at the very thought, but now I think about how he looks at me, how he cared about my mom being scared...

How he cared enough to show up for you, I realize. You don't do that for just anyone. Of all people, I know that.

I push to my feet, wrapping the blanket around me and heading for the bathroom. After the longest, hottest shower of my life, I shuffle into

my bedroom and get dressed. I pull my softest, slouchiest sweater over
a lacy bralette and grab my boots from the closet. Tonight, I'll need a
dress and makeup, but right now I'm going for comfort.

Back in the living room, I collect my scattered clothes, glancing up
again and again because Beau should be back any minute now and—

And I hear a shout from outside.

Unease tiptoes down my spine, and I tell myself I'm being stupid.
It could be one of the working students riding by or some of the farm
workers goofing around. I ease toward the windows and see the Bronco
out front...Beau's work truck next to it...and a shiny, burgundy SUV
parked crooked in our driveway.

My heart thumps *hard*. That's George Parish's vehicle, I realize.

Then I see Beau and Parish. There's blood on Beau's shirt and fists,
blood on Parish's face. Parish grabs Beau by the throat and Beau heaves
him away. I wrench the door open and stumble out. In the distance, a
siren whines.

"Hit me," Beau taunts. Both men are squared to each other now.
Parish's face is already bruising, and when he jams his finger into Beau's
chest, I half expect Beau to grab the other man's finger and break it in
half.

Actually, I fully expect him to break Parish's finger, but Beau
doesn't. He *laughs*.

"Scared, Parish?" he asks, voice mocking. "You fucking should be."

Two more cars surge up the farm road, dust billowing behind them.
The first is Mrs. Mar's Range Rover. The second is a police car. My
blood goes cold.

"Beau?" I manage. He turns, and for a heartbeat, I don't recognize
him. His eyes are wild, glassy—and his smile? It's chilling. It's a thing
made for war.

Mrs. Mar and the police officer yank their vehicle into the driveway, screeching to a stop. The officer is out first, ordering Beau and
Parish to step away from each other.

"Right now," he yells.

To my shock, Beau actually does. He steps back, brushing off Parish's grip. The other man's gone utterly still, but there's hatred radiating off him. This isn't over—for either of them because Beau's smile is still fixed in place. It says "gotcha" and "want some more?" and "give me a reason" all at the same time.

The police officer pulls Parish to one side. "You stay over there," he tells Beau. Mrs. Mar joins Parish and the officer. Even from here, I can see she's shaking.

"Holls." Beau strolls to me, long, easy strides that never hitch. Even once. He's hiding everything really well right now.

He pulls me to him and gives me a toe-*curling* kiss. I come up breathless, my nipples already aching. "Damn," he whispers, holding me tight. "The things I'm going to do to you tonight."

"What's going on?"

"Parish figured out I had the syringe. He wanted it back." A devastating and bloody grin. "So I told him to come and take it."

"*What?*" I sound like an idiot, but maybe that's because I am. Instead of just telling Parish to leave or telling him we'd already sent the syringe away for testing, Beau went for something showy. Then I glimpse Parish's bloodied face as the police officer leads him to the cruiser.

He went for something violent, I think. An icy wind wraps around us and I shiver. Beau's triumphant expression turns concerned and he tucks me closer. There's blood on his shirt, but he's careful to keep it away from me.

"Hey," he whispers, turning toward me, but not before I see Mrs. Mar glance our direction. Her eyes narrow. "You need to go back in? I'll get this taken care of—Parish came after me. He's trespassing and drunk. After I'm done, we'll go up to the hospital, see your mom, go for some food." A smile turns up one corner of his mouth. "Apparently, there's a party we're supposed to go to tonight. I've gotten a reminder or ten about it."

For a couple seconds, I can barely breathe. It's that smile. It does amazing and indecent things to me. Just looking at him, I can feel myself warming, leaning closer, wanting more.

I could let this thing with Parish go. I could look the other way.

At the very idea, my fingers tighten on Beau's sleeve.

But I would always know he would never be someone I could depend on. Beau is the kind of person who will destroy himself to make a point. He values revenge over integrity. He welcomed Parish's attack because it allowed him to hit back, hit Parish like he'd wanted to hit him all along.

Sure, *this* turned out in Beau's favor, but how long until he turns his sights on Landers? The need for revenge will consume him again, and he's already admitted he's willing to do whatever it takes to bring the man down.

Even if it's the cost of his own soul.

I pull away. "I can't do this."

"What?"

I try to swallow and can't. There's a sudden thickness in my throat. "I quit. All of it. I'm done with Twelve Oaks, and I'm done with you."

And I walk away without looking back. I can't. If I do, I know I'll cry.

CHAPTER 41 | Beau

Two weeks later...

The knock at the door sets my heart thumping. My first thought? *It's Holly*. My second thought? *You're a dumbass*.

I drop the books I've been organizing and ease to my feet. It's been two weeks since Parish was arrested and Holly left. She won't take my phone calls. She won't answer the door. She won't even let Ellie talk to me.

Actually, I'm pretty sure the last one is Ellie's idea. Every time I'm around the other woman, I catch her staring at me like she's making plans for where to hide my body.

Regardless, I still don't understand why Holly left. If I did, I could fix it. I know I could. We belong together. I'm the one for her—even if she doesn't want to admit it.

As I step into the foyer, I spot Adele through the front door's glass. She's casually dressed in dark jeans and a white button up, but her hair is smoothed into one of her complicated twist and she has pearls at her ears and throat.

I open the door, and she smiles. "Can I come in?" she asks.

"Of course." I back up to let her through and immediately begin to notice how feral the place looks. I've unpacked my boxes of trophies and pictures, but I haven't put anything up. They're just strewn about the living room. And the laundry situation? That's everywhere too. It looks like my dryer threw up. "Uh. Tea?" I ask.

"That would be delightful. Thank you." Adele sweeps a bunch of my T-shirts into a pile while I heat up water in the kitchen. By the time I come back, she's looking at my pictures, taking several moments with each. I pass her a mug of tea and she sets it down on the coffee table. "Thank you. I had forgotten about the Saugerties win. That was an amazing weekend."

"It was." The mare I'd been riding had sold soon after. Last I heard, she was doing beautifully with her young rider. They were coming up through the highly competitive junior ranks.

Adele sets the picture aside and folds her hands, studying her rings for a moment. "I owe you an apology."

"No, you don't."

"I do. I should have believed you." She looks up at me, tears shining in her eyes. It makes my stomach go sour. "I didn't want to think Dell was capable of something like that."

"No one does. It's...horrific."

She nods. "I saw Holly today. I asked her to come by for her bonus check."

I tense, half hoping she'll tell me more and half dreading that she will. "Yeah?"

"'Yeah,'" she mocks, dropping her voice so it's deeper and turns the word casual. "She wasn't going to accept it, but I insisted. She's the only assistant we've ever had that could keep you on track. I told her to consider it combat pay." Adele pauses, watching me. "Are you really going to do this? Pretend you don't care that she's gone?"

"I don't—I mean, I do. I'm glad she's moving on. We both knew this position wasn't forever. It was just a stop gap to what she really wants."

"And there wasn't more to it? I saw you in the driveway. I didn't say anything at the time—I was a little busy with the police—but your expression was plain as day. You love that girl."

I open my mouth, and then close it. I don't know what to say. Honestly, I'm not sure I trust myself to say anything. She's right.

Adele sighs. "Beau, you are like a son to me. I am incredibly proud to have watched you grow into the man you are."

"Two gold medals tend to do that to people," I say. The fondness in her voice makes me squeamish. Adele and I are close, but even we don't talk like this.

"Stop it," she tell me. "Even if you hadn't won a thing, I would still be proud of you. You're an amazing rider and an even better horseman. This industry changes people—often for the worse. I think it's made you better, but Beau?"

I look at her and she looks at me and the silence stretches out between us. "If you let that girl go because you can't be brave enough to admit your feelings, you're a fool and a coward."

"Tell me how you really feel Adele."

"I always do." She smiles at me, and after a beat, I smile back.

"It isn't that simple. I've done something wrong and she won't tell me what it is."

"So? I think it *is* that simple. If you want to be with her, you'll either figure it out or make her tell you. Anything else is wasting time. You know I would give anything to have my Harrison back." She pauses and I shift from foot to foot, unsure of what to say. She rarely talks about her dead husband. He was her everything, and years later, she still mourns him.

Adele inhales hard, blinking back tears. "We don't get forever so we have to make the most of the time we do have—and right now, Beau? You're wasting time *missing* Holly when you could *be* with her."

My stomach freefalls. She's right. Holy *shit* is she ever right. "Why are you always so good to me?" I ask. "I've never deserved any of it."

"Because we're family by choice. We stay with each other when it's hard. We push each other when it's even harder." Her smile is so sad I know she's talking about ARCH and Landers and Parish. We've been through a lot together. It hasn't always been easy.

"Beau?" Adele prompts. "Why are you still standing here?"

I grin, leaning forward to kiss her cheek. "Hell if I know. I'll see you around," I say, and run for the door.

***

The Twelve Oaks' stable is quiet. Most of the horses are out in their paddocks and the morning chores have been long finished. As I walk through, I spot a couple of the grooms heading for their cars. Midday errands probably.

Someone's banging around in one of the stalls, and quicken my pace. I hope it's Ellie. She should be here. I round the corner and spot a faded brown cap crammed onto a head of rabbit-white hair.

"Sam?" I ask.

"Yeah?"

I pause. Sam is the only man I know who can make 'Yeah' sound like 'Fuck you.' I never know if he's pissed at me, pissed at the world, or if pissed is his default setting. He came to Twelve Oaks with Ellie. He's been her family's head groom since forever and does an amazing job keeping the horses in top condition.

I'm also fairly certain he doesn't like me.

"Ellie around?" I ask, leaning into the stall. The old man looks up from the colt he's grooming and gives me the evil eye. I smile like I'm oblivious. *Make that* definitely *certain he doesn't like me*, I think.

"Why?" Sam asks.

"Because I want to ask how the Flexible filly is settling in." In reality, I already know the filly is settling in, but Sam's watching me like I might have my sights set on Ellie's virtue.

"Oh," he says at last, still with the evil eye. "She's out back."

"Thanks."

The old man either grunts or groans. I'm not sure. Either way, he goes back to work and I head out to find Ellie. It takes a couple minutes, but I eventually spot her down by the lower riding arena, setting exercise poles.

"Hey," I call.

Ellie straightens, bracing one hand against the sunlight's glare, and when she sees me, her hand drops. "What?" she demands.

I hesitate. This might be a mistake. Ellie's stare is just as frigid as Sam's, but without the bushy eyebrows. "Look," I begin, "I know I fucked up."

"No, Cargo Shorts." She stomps past me, slamming her shoulder into mine as she heads for the barn. "You don't know."

"Cargo—? Never mind." I jog ahead, cutting her off. "How can I make it up to her?"

"I'm not helping you."

"Ellie, please."

"No." She darts around me and I have to catch back up, jarring my hip in the process. I hiss a curse and she actually stops. "Please," I tell her, straightening. "I'm not above begging."

"You're not above a lot of things."

"Fair point. Probably best just to give into me then isn't it?"

Ellie sighs, and when she finally looks up at me, her eyes are beyond sad. "If you were serious about her, you'd already know how to make it up to her." She takes a hesitant step, and when I don't move to stop her, continues back to the barn. I watch her go, feeling like my last hope is going with her.

And then I realize she's right. I do know. I know *exactly* what I have to do.

CHAPTER 42 | Holly

I must've hung up with Scott twenty minutes ago, and I'm still staring at the phone, wondering what the hell I'm going to do. After Mrs. Mar—*Adele*, I remind myself. She insisted I start calling her by her given name—wrote my bonus check, I didn't know what to do with it. I have the money for New York now, but Mom's about to come home from the hospital. I want to be with her, but I want to take that job offer from Scott.

You want too much, I tell myself, and carry my coffee cup to the dishwasher, spending way more time than necessary arranging and rearranging the dirty dishes inside. After the neat orderliness of Beau's, the house I share with Mom feels almost chaotic—the cluttered kitchen with its chipped cabinets, the furniture that overfills the rooms, and the tangled rear gardens. The back of our house runs up against the local polo fields, and during nice weather, Ellie and I like to sit outside and watch the matches. And get giggly on mimosas and carbs.

I could really use an afternoon like that, but it's not going to happen any time soon. Winter's arrived in the south, and it may not have snow, but it's plenty cold enough to keep me inside and the polo ponies down in Florida.

Not to mention, I should be working, not goofing off.

I glance at my sketchbook. Punk rock ball gowns are mixed in with banded-colored swimsuits and wide-brimmed straw hats. Scott had *freaked* when I emailed him a few of the images. He'd been so excited. We'd talked for almost two hours, and I'd sounded so breezy on the phone, like I was on top of everything, and everything was fine, and la la la no panic attacks here.

Ugh. I don't know what to do. Dane and I have gone around and around and the only solution is for me to stay put and take care of Mom.

"I can't leave right now," he'd explained last night at dinner. "I'm right on the verge of a promotion. You don't even know if your designs will do anything."

"Thanks," I said, rolling my eyes.

"You know what I mean. Give me another year—two years tops—I can take care of her and you can go back. *If* that's what you really want," he'd added.

I'd started to argue and then gave up. It's not the timeline that necessarily bothers me. Although honestly, it *does* bother me quite a bit because I don't have another two years. Scott isn't going to wait.

What really upsets me is the way Dane always dismisses my career as some sort of passing phase. He rarely asks me about it, and when he does, it's always in the most generic terms. It isn't like other people's questions.

Correction, I tell myself, frowning. *It isn't how* Beau *asks questions.* That's the real problem here, isn't it? I feel my frown deepen. Of course it is. I'm still not over him. It's taking everything I have to hold back from answering when he calls, or to stay out of sight when he knocks on my door. His last voicemail said he didn't understand why I'd left.

But he does. We'd talked and talked about it. He knew my stance on revenge and paybacks—and I knew his. How could we possibly work?

Bottom line, we can't, and yeah, I'm taking the coward's way out by going silent, but this is what I need to survive losing him.

And more importantly, losing what we could have had. Every time I close my eyes, that future wells to the surface: course design and dress design, laughing together and kissing by the fire.

Feeling *safe*. That's what I'll miss the most. Beau made me feel safe and like everything would turn out okay, but he's actually more danger-ous to my future than anything else right now.

My cell rings and check the screen, half-hoping and half-dreading it's Beau. It isn't. Ellie's picture flashes up at me. She's changed it to a goofy shot of her duck-facing for the camera.

"Hey!" I say brightly.

"Hey yourself, stop making yourself sound happy when you're not." With anyone else, I would probably bristle, but this is Ellie, and more importantly, she's right.

Not that it isn't annoying, I think. "Is this better?" I ask, dropping into a normal tone again.

"Not really." She sighs. "If I hit Beau with my truck, would it make you feel better? Because you know I'd do it for you. Happily."

"I'll help!" Parker calls from the background. She's been helping out Ellie for the past few days, and I won't say she's better, but she's get-ting there.

I curl up on the kitchen's window seat. Outside, the wind blows dried leaves across the patio and I can feel the chill through the glass. "What's up?"

"Beau's on his way to you—at least I think he's on his way to you. He took off out of here with this look in his eyes and I wanted to call you, but then some buyers showed up early and Parker had to occupy them and then we both got stuck."

My mouth goes dry. "Why's he coming over?"

"Why else? To beg you to forgive him."

I rub a shaky hand over my hair. "How long ago did he leave?"

"Twenty minutes?"

"Sounds about right," Parker adds.

"That would mean—"

Bingbingbingbing! My doorbell chirps frantically as some-one—Beau—holds down the button. Ellie sighs. "That would mean he just got there. Look, Holls, hear him out, okay?"

"Why would I do that?"

"Because when he's not obnoxious, he makes you happy, and because everyone deserves a second chance. I don't think he'll screw it up again."

"And you know this *how?*"

Bingbingbingbing!

"I don't," Ellie says over the noise, "but I know you and I know he's crazy for you and...I don't know." Her voice drops. "Everyone screws up, and lots of people apologize, but not a lot of people mean it. I think Beau means it. I think, for you, he'll change."

The doorbell stops ringing and Beau starts knocking. He isn't going away this time. The pounding is damn near relentless.

"And it's the *change* that makes me think he's different," Ellie adds.

"I gotta go," I tell her.

"Good luck!"

I'm going to need it, I think. *It's the change that makes me think he's different.* She's right. It does make him different. It means he wants to do better and that means...

I take a deep breath, toss my hair back, and go to meet Beau.

CHAPTER 43 | Holly

She's not going to answer. I know she's home. Her rolling death trap Bronco is parked out front, but she isn't answering the door. I take a step back, considering her front door's sunny yellow color and wonder at what point do I cross from Desperate To Apologize into Stalker territory.

Because this is feeling pretty close.

"Holly?" I call and ring the doorbell again. "I know you're home!"

There's a rustle of leaves to my right as one of her neighbors peers over a manicured hedge, eyeing me.

Getting closer to stalker by the minute, I think. This isn't working. Clearly, I'm going to need to switch tactics. Maybe flowers. No, screw that. Sky-writing? Too dramatic. Plus, I'd have to make sure she was outside and that would probably involve kidnapping and—

The sunny yellow door swings open and Holly appears, scowling. I gape. I can't help it. It's only been two weeks, but my body rushes to attention like it's been two years.

She looks...perfect. Her blond hair is tumbling out of its braid and there's the faintest smudge of ink on her jaw. She must've been sketching—

"What. Are you. Doing, Kent?"

"Giving the neighbors something to talk about?" The tiniest glimmer of a smile and my heart leaps. "We have to talk."

Holly makes a scoffing sound and leans against the door frame, arms crossing over her chest. She's wearing my favorite slouchy sweater again—the one that's super soft and always slipping down her shoulder. Everything in me screams to touch her, but I know I have to give this space.

I know I have to be honest.

"I was wrong," I tell her, clenching both fists at my side so I don't reach for her. "I thought I wanted revenge more than anything. I thought I wanted my old life back. I thought...I thought it was better the way it was before—that *I* was better the way I was before—but it wasn't. I'm not. Because you're not there."

I pause, praying she'll say something, but she doesn't. Holls watches me like I'm breaking her heart, like I'm killing her.

You're doing it wrong! I think, briefly considering throwing myself at her feet. It won't work though. I know that. *Stick to the plan,* I tell myself. *Keep going with the truth.* She turns to go back inside and I catch her wrist, feel her pulse tap against my fingers.

"When you're around," I add, feeling that pulse climb, "I feel like I can do anything."

"You won two gold medals before me. Pretty sure you were doing just fine on your own."

"But I wasn't. Not really." Climbing and climbing, her pulse is frantic as a butterfly's wings. "You were right: I was lonely. And I was so used to being lonely I didn't even recognize it anymore. I don't want to go back to that."

This should be Holly's opportunity to crow about how she was right and she doesn't. If anything she looks even sadder. It sends a cold chill down my spine. Did I realize what she means too late? Are we really over?

She glances away, staring at something in her neighbor's yard. "You went after Parish when you didn't have to. You could've been seriously hurt. He could've had a knife, a gun." She swallows and shifts. "You could've died."

I pause. There's a lot I could say here, but I need the *right* thing. I tighten my grip around her wrist, feeling her heartbeat in my hand, and suddenly the right thing comes to me: "I shouldn't have," I tell her. "I know that now. I *should've* known it then, but I was...angry. I wanted them to pay."

I pause, knowing what I'm about to say is the biggest truth I owe Holly, but it still might not be enough to save us: "You need someone you can depend on, and in that moment? It wasn't me. You've been let down by people giving into their emotions and running off the rails and leaving you to pick up the pieces your whole damn life and I want that to stop. I want it to stop with me. I want to be the person you can depend on. I want to help you do New York on your terms—or if you don't want to do New York, we'll figure out how to make your line launch from here. Whatever it takes, I'll do it."

Her breath hitches and I can't tell what that means. Are we better? Are we worse?

I ease forward, tucking one arm around her and pulling her close. She lets me.

Holy shit. I nearly yell at the top of my lunges I'm so relieved. I hug her hard and feel her hug me back even harder. "You make me a better person, Holly. You make me *want* to be better. For you. For us."

I lean in for a kiss and she stops me, mouth hovering over mine. "I'm going to hold you to that, Beau Kent."

I grin. She grins. I crush her to me before saying, "I know you will."

EPILOGUE | Holly

Three months later...

The clock ticks over to five, and I drop my sketchpad like it's on fire, kicking both of my feet to the battered wooden floor of our warehouse space. "See ya!"

"*What?*" Scott looks up from the work table where we've scattered every fabric scrap we own, and glares at me. "You can't leave! I'm surrounded by idiots! I'll never make it!"

I level him a Stop Being Dramatic Stare, and when that doesn't work, I grin. I can't help it. Only another hour—maybe two—before *he's* here.

"It's *Friday,*" I remind Scott, working my fingers through the tangles in my hair and rebraiding it. "Call it quits and start the weekend."

"I can't quit. I'm in the middle of a breakthrough and I'm surrounded by idiots!"

"Then keep going." The interns gasp at my flippancy, and I have to resist an eye roll. I've been this flippant since they got here. It's not changing. Scott and I are partners now—the bonus money made sure of it.

Besides, it's impossible to please him when he gets like this. Our first show is still four months away, but he's already reached panicked levels, agonizing over each and every detail. I get it—I'm just as bad—but I also have something else on my mind.

Someone else on my mind.

"You'll be fine," I reassure Scott, "and they're *not* idiots. They're amazing."

The amazing idiots nod defensively. In reality, they aren't idiots, but they're not exactly amazing either. We have a collection of recent fash-

215

ion school grads and a few interns helping us. They're learning. It's to be expected that they will make mistakes.

I just wish some of those mistakes did not include ordering the wrong fabrics, getting fitting times confused, and in one horrible case, hot gluing my boots to the floor. I still don't know how they managed that one and I'm not sure I want to know.

"I can't believe you're taking time off," Scott complains, flicking down a swatch of stunning magenta velvet. I'm using it on one of the ball gowns. "I only have you for another month."

Now I really do roll my eyes. "And then I'll be in Atlanta. We'll Skype and I'll still be working. Everything will still be moving forward."

"Until your cats—"

"Ah ah." I press one finger across his lips, silencing him. "If you say one more thing about my dead body being eaten by cats, I will burn all your Betty Gable wigs."

The amazing idiots and Scott all gasp. One amazing idiot actually clutches his throat. "You wouldn't!" Scott says.

"You know perfectly well I would." I nod cheerfully and kiss him on his cheek. "I'll see you Monday morning."

Late afternoon sunlight dapples the floorboards as I get my trench and bag out of the antique armoire we're currently using for storage. Thanks to Scott's boyfriend, our new work space is fantastic: lots of natural light and ridiculously high ceilings. Who knew yogis could be so very well connected?

I slip my arms into my coat and glance up at the sign I've hung above the door. It says, "Teamwork makes the dream work."

Scott thinks it's cheesy as hell and he's right, but it's probably one of the truest things about me right now. I'm here in New York again because I have an incredible family that's helping me be here.

Ellie's keeping Parker busy, and checking in on my mom pretty much every day. Though se almost doesn't need to because Beau's over there all the time. He's even learning to cook so they can have dinner together.

"Wait....*what?*" I managed when she told me.

"Yep. Macaroni and cheese *and* he brought wine. Your brother thinks he's trouble. I say you should keep him—unless you don't want him, in which case I'll keep him." She pauses. "I'm so proud of you, you know that?"

Hot tears had stung my eyes. "Really? I was worried..."

"That I would miss you? Of *course*, I miss you—I even miss your brother when he's gone—but I want you to go for this. I know you can do it."

And I'd been hanging onto those words ever since.

I'm really lucky, I think as I step outside our building. A cold breeze noses under my clothes and I tug my trench coat closer, preparing to walk the few blocks to my hotel.

As promised, Scott's letting me stay with him, but since Beau's flying in for the weekend, I wanted us to have some privacy—and for Scott to have a bit of a break. I can't imagine it's been easy having a non-stop house guest.

I wave to the front desk clerk as I run for the elevators. If I hurry, I have time for a shower before Beau gets here. He said he would catch an Uber at the airport and meet me here. If his flight hasn't been delayed and traffic hasn't been too terrible...I glance at the time on my phone. Yeesh. I need to hurry.

Inside my room, I toss my shoes in the closet and hop around, pulling off my clothes. The hotel's nice: gorgeous view of the skyline, luxurious bathroom, *huge* bed.

That might actually be my favorite part.

I crank the water as hot as it'll go and hop in the shower, careful not to soak my hair as I scrub off city grit. I so did not miss the dirt, but it feels wonderful to be working in the city again. At the end of the day, I'm tired in all the right ways—physically *and* mentally—but I'm happy too.

I get out of the shower, drying off, and slipping on one of the dresses I designed for next summer. Yeah, it's skimpy in all the right places, but if I layer it up, I won't freeze while we walk to dinner. I watch my reflection as I wiggle around, trying to zip up the back.

There, I think, finally getting the zipper to close—just in time for someone to knock at the door.

My breath catches. We've been seeing each other for three months now, and he still makes my stomach do summersaults. I rush out of the bathroom and fling open the door, grinning.

Beau braces both hands on the doorframe, leaning in to kiss me. I throw my arms around him, pressing all of me to all of him and it's still not close enough.

"Grab. Me," I pant and feel his mouth curve into a grin.

He's teasing me already and the realization sends a delicious chill zinging up my spine. I step back, breathing hard.

Beau's eyes are all over me. "Fantastic dress," he says. "Now take it off."

Want More?

Sign up[1] for a FREE prequel novella and get notified about Emma Ashe book releases, cover reveals, and bonus material!

...

Get the next book: **emmaashe.com/books**[2]

...

Read on for an excerpt from *Deeper Than Temptation*, Book #4 in the Deeper Than Love Series

---

1. http://www.emmaashe.com/signup-book

2. http://www.emmaashe.com/books/deeper

TEASER CHAPTER 1 | Aiden

And now she knows I'm jealous, I realize, staring Parker down because I'm furious, but also because I can't help myself. It seems like when it comes to Parks, all I do is stare. I haven't been able to look away from her since the moment she became my twins' nanny. Right now though? I want to argue.

And undress her. Honestly, the reminder just pisses me off even more, but my anger is nothing in comparison to hers, and I can't really blame her. Minutes ago, my jealous inner fourteen-year-old escaped and I insulted her professionalism. It was a dick move.

Parker lifts her chin, dark eyes flashing. "You told me you needed me to 'handle things' because you didn't have time. Well, I'm handling them—and how *dare* you imply I was flirting with that guy!"

It's not funny, but I force myself to laugh anyway. 'That guy' is another kid's dad. He came by to watch Parker give a riding lesson to the twins because he wants to enroll his own kid in lessons, and after laying eyes on Parker, he wants her too. She has no idea how he was looking at her, how attracted he was.

But I do.

"You really don't know how he was looking at you, do you?" I ask.

She gapes at me. "Nothing was going on between Brandon and me. If you saw something, you're inventing it." She pauses, looking half a second away from tears, and it nearly rips me in half. "No one looks at me like that."

"I do." It's so quick it probably sounds like a line, but it's the truth—probably the biggest truth we've ever shared because I can't *ever* take my eyes from her. Call it instant attraction or lust at first sight or whatever, but I've wanted Parker since day one. It's totally out of line. I'm her boss. She's the twins' nanny.

And yet we can't seem to keep our hands off each other.

"In fact," I continue, "I look at you like that all the time, and you know it." Her breath quickens, and it pools heat in my gut. "And furthermore, I know you look at me the same way."

I also know it knocks the breath out of me every time.

Parks nods, and catches herself, eyes narrowing at me in annoyance. "Fine," she says at last. "I like looking at you. What of it? We have...a thing."

"We do," I whisper.

"Doesn't mean anything."

"Nope."

"Because it can't," she adds.

"Right."

"Exactly." We talk to each other like we're on the same page, and everything's fine. But my already small apartment kitchen suddenly feels even smaller. Everything is filled with Parker. She's doing that absent nod thing, blinking those doe-eyes the way she always does when she wants me, and I can't stop walking toward her. I can't stop until we're toe-to-toe, until she has to look up to meet my gaze. It makes her lick her lips, and I have to hold myself back from touching her.

"See?" I whisper, and she shivers. "You're doing it again: looking at me like you want me to kiss you."

"Maybe I do."

Shouldn't be possible, but I go even harder. My dick strains against my jeans, but I stay still. I'm never going to be the asshole who forces himself on a woman—let alone the asshole who forces himself on an employee. If she wants me, she's going to have to say it.

And without me uttering a word, the realization dawns in her eyes. She licks her lips again.

"So kiss me," she says, and my mouth goes dry. "Because I'm wondering if it's worth it."

A challenge. Christ, I love that. I love how she gives as good as she gets—and she's about to get everything from me. I bend to her, hands taking her face, fingertips brushing her hairline. For a heartbeat, I hold my lips millimeters from hers, and then I fit myself to her. She feels just as good as I imagined she would. Parker's all heat, all softness, and it nearly takes me to my knees.

I tease her—hell, tease both of us—by keeping the kiss deliberately light. I want her to want this as much as I do, and she's almost there. Her hands are all over my chest—exploring me, *learning* me—and I hiss against the corner her mouth. She doesn't feel as good as I imagined. She feels *better*.

And just as she's about to melt into me, I pull back an inch, feel her ragged breathing. "Worth it?"

"Maybe."

I laugh, wrapping my hand into her hair and tugging her head back for a harder kiss. She gives into me so sweetly, but it makes me want more. I deepen our kiss, my tongue sweeping her mouth and setting our rhythm. It makes her sag into me, turns her softness even softer and her heat even hotter. She enjoys me taking the lead.

Which is exactly how I like it. The realization jerks me out of the kiss. I pull away, grabbing the hem of her T-shirt.

"This doesn't count," she pants, helping me yank it over her head.

Doesn't count? Briefly, I'm confused, and then I realize she's talking about last month's decision to keep our hands off each other. That was some ridiculous bullshit on our parts. That was back when I thought I could keep my hands off her, back when I thought this was just attraction.

Back when I thought I could keep my feelings in check.

I lift her, wrapping her legs around my waist. "Doesn't count."

"Means it won't happen again."

Even through her jeans, I can feel the heat of her pressing into my dick, and my head spins. I tighten my grip. "Then I better do everything I've been wanting to."

And I grind once against her, watching her expression as I slide over that sensitive place between her legs. It makes her gasp. I rub her again, and she moans.

"I like that," I tell her, unable to stop my grin. I've wanted that moan for weeks. I've *dreamed* of that moan. "Do it again."

But I don't give her the choice to deny me. I thrust once more, and her head falls back, breasts lifting up and begging for attention. I lick my lips. I'm ready.

I put her down, and she staggers, eyes fluttering open in confusion. "What's"—she swallows—"Is something wrong?"

"God, no. I'm just trying to decide where to start." I run my fingers along the band of her sports bra. "Take it off."

Shyness creeps into her expression. She reaches for me, but I step back. "Ah ah. Take it off."

Color flares in her cheeks. Parks *is* shy. She had an asshole husband who did a number on her self-esteem, but I've seen moments of the real Parker—the woman who's confident and self-assured. The woman who can put me on my knees with a look. She has no idea what she does to me, and I want to show her.

Still blushing, Parker pulls the sports bra over her head, revealing small, but perfect breasts. The nipples are already hardened, and it makes my mouth water.

All the things I'm going to do to you, I think, taking her in both of my hands and rolling the tightened peaks between my fingers. Squeezing. Pinching. Torturing both of us until—

"Please," she whispers, and I'm undone.

I flip her around, pressing her ass into my shaft as my hands go to her jeans' button. I tug it loose, and shove everything—panties, jeans—past her knees. She gasps.

And I bend her over the kitchen table.

I slide my hand down her bare spine and over her bare ass, finding that tender spot where cheek meets thigh. I stroke her for a moment, watching goosebumps climb up her arms. "I've been thinking about this for ages," I say, squeezing her with both hands, spreading her until she's pinned.

She whimpers, making my dick throb. Hard. "Thinking about what?" she whispers.

I laugh. God I love how she plays. "I think you know," I say, fanning my thumbs across her ass. I can't decide if I want to kiss her or spank her. "I think you just want me to tell you."

And saying it out loud makes me realize how much it's true—and how much I want it. I *want* her to talk to me. I *want* her to tell me all the dirty things she needs from me.

So I can give them to her.

I wrap my hands around the backs of her thighs and listen to her hiss. "Tell me," I say lightly.

"Tell you what?"

There's a teasing lilt to the question and it makes me laugh again. I can't help it. Forget the kissing, I give her an open-handed slap across her ass and she jerks, struggling against the table's edge. No good though. She's pinned and I can do what I want—and when I push her forward another inch, she goes still like she's suddenly realized that.

Is that going to be okay? I wonder and lean over her, pressing my chest into her back. "Is this what you want? Because I can stop—"

"Don't you dare."

And just when I think my raging hard-on can't get any worse. Three little words and she's nearly bent me in half. I shift my weight, enjoying her heat as my dick brushes against her. She's slick already, and it takes every ounce of self-control I have to keep from thrusting into her.

"Tell me," I whisper, and feel her shiver underneath me. "Tell me you want to hear how I've been fantasizing about you."

Her breath catches. "Have you?"

"Every damn day."

"Fantasizing about what?"

"You're soon to see."

TEASER CHAPTER 2 | Aiden

I pull back, running my hands down her shoulders and across her arms. I flatten her to the table, and then curl her fingers around the edge, squeezing them for a heartbeat so she understands she's to stay put.

I've wanted her like this for ages, and I want to enjoy every damn minute of it. I straighten and pull off my clothes. Parker fidgets, and I know I should say something, but the sight of her—bare for me, on her tip-toes, bent over, *pinned*—has left me damn near speechless. I have fantasized about her for months now. I have imagined her in every way possible, and she still leaves me in awe.

She trembles and lifts her head, starting to look around for me.

"Ah, ah," I say, hearing how my Irish accent has grown thicker, harder. It always does for her. "This is for me."

I drag my fingers through her wet folds, and my eyes nearly roll back into my head. She feels fucking fantastic. "I could look at you like this all damn day, do you know that?"

She inhales like she wants to answer and I caress her again, rendering whatever response she had into mindless whimpering. I grin. I like that. I'm going to have to do it again.

"Waiting on me with your perfect ass in the air," I continue, sliding my fingers back and forth, "getting wetter and wetter as I play with you."

And she is. Dirty talk turns Parker even wetter. She's getting frantic against my hand, needing more pressure, but it feels like I've waited forever for this and I want it to last.

"Please?" she manages. She tries to push back and slips. *Beauty of this position*, I think, not stopping. She can't get purchase—she's up on her toes, and her arms are too far ahead. All she can do is enjoy, and I want to give it *all* to her.

Up and down. Up and down. I find her clit with one knuckle and rub her over and over until she's moaning.

"I love how you melt for me," I whisper, backing off before she can come. I slide my knuckle to her entrance and begin to play again. It makes my brain scramble. "You give so sweetly," I manage.

She growls. "I'm not going to be sweet if you keep playing with me like this."

"Aren't you?" I push in one finger, and she gasps. I push in another, and she squirms, making small noises of delight. I stroke her, setting a rhythm that I know will madden her. It already makes my eyes want to roll back in my head. "Because I think this is exactly what you need."

"I *need* an orgasm," she mutters, sounding irritated—or rather trying to sound irritated. She's melting for me again, relaxing into me and letting me take the lead. *Damn*, I love that.

"Oh, you'll be getting your orgasm." I scoop my fingers, and she cries out, growing wetter in a rush. She enjoys our games, and knowing she enjoys them nearly makes me come on the spot. "But right now, you need this."

"I don't—"

I stroke her again, reminding her who's in charge and she gives to me. She sinks into the table, letting me have her until she's close. Too close. I want to take my time with this. I want to enjoy every *second*.

I nudge her legs farther apart, and she lets me take them wide. "Christ, yes," I whisper, pulling out my fingers and replacing them with my thumb. I find her clit with my fingertips and she arches hard against me, giving me the perfect opportunity to slide my free hand under her.

I cup one breast and then the other, playing her nipples like I did before: twisting them, pulling them. I play until she cries out, going wet and hot against my hand. She's desperate for this.

We both are.

Doesn't take away from this being wrong—we both know it—but I'll deal with that later. Working for me might have been what brought us together, but the attraction between us is bigger and *better* than any-thing I've experienced. Up until now, we've denied ourselves. I want to show Parks why that's such a bad idea. I want to prove to her this could be more than just complicated.

"I love how sensitive you are," I tell her, still playing with her breasts. I run my thumb over and over the hardened peak, enjoying how she squirms helplessly under me. "Would you like my mouth on them?"

She whimpers, and I smile.

"Good," I say. "Because I want my mouth on them too. I'll be en-joying that later as well."

"Enjoy it now," she moans.

"No. I'm enjoying this."

"Aiden?" Lust and worry snake underneath my name. I go still as she peeks over her shoulder, eyes wide. "Why are you doing this?"

The question could mean so much—*why do I want her, why am I taking her*—but somehow, I know it's *why am I teasing her?*

I grin. I can't help it. "Because it's the only time I ever see you soft, and I know it's *because* of me. It's *only* for me."

And then I slide my fingers to her clit, and pinch.

Her mouth falls open in shock and pleasure. She screams, arching her back. Her eyes are wide and pinned to me. Now *she* can't look away, and I have to will myself not to spill all over her.

"Again," I whisper, and my fingers stroke her twice as my thumb slides forward, tapping that hidden place inside her that I know will shatter her and it does. She falls forward, bucking against my hand as her orgasm takes her in wave after wave.

"Mmmm," I breathe, pulling her off the kitchen table. She fits beau-tifully against my chest as I settle both of us in the closest chair: her back to my chest, her legs draped on either side of mine. It's another position I've fantasized about, and now I get to have her.

I run both hands down Parker's sides and tug her knees wider apart. She shivers. My dick has pushed up between us, and I can feel her scalding heat. It makes my breath catch.

"Christ, I don't think I've ever been this hard," I mutter, keeping one hand on her hip while I pull on a condom with the other. "Are you ready?"

She goes still, and I can't tell what she's thinking. I don't like that. At all.

"Parks?" I whisper, lifting my hips so my dick skims across her clit. "Are you okay?"

"Don't you *dare* stop."

It's even more frantic than before, and I catch myself grinning against the back of her neck. *Hells yes*, I think, and lift her, the head of my dick prodding her slick entrance. "Yes, what?" I ask.

"Yes, *please*."

And I pull her down, feeling her gasp as she stretches around me. I pump her once and hold her tight, a stream of curses escaping me. "You are fucking *perfect*."

She is too. Hot, wet, and sweet as hell. Parker stays tight against me, but her shoulders have gone rigid. I get it. To be open and exposed like this for me, it has to be intense for her. It's what makes it so good for me.

But more than anything it has to be good for *her*.

I give her a gentle pump, and find her breasts, teasing her nipples and kissing her neck. "Stay with me."

A tiny moan escapes her, and my hands tighten. I spread my knees wider, taking her legs even farther apart. Her skin goes hot, but I can tell her brain is working overtime. "Stay with me," I add, "or I'll bend you over the table again."

She gasps, eyes flying open to meet mine. I don't look away. I hold her gaze until her focus narrows just to me. Only to me.

"Stay with me," I whisper, "and I'll do this for you."

And I pump her once, feel her pussy clench around me. Pleasure makes her whole body slacken, relax. It feels so good, I nearly come. I *knew* she'd be like this. I *knew* it would be this good. Her head falls back, dark hair tangling around me. This is what she needed.

What we've both needed.

"That's right," I tell her. "Just enjoy." I lift her and then slide her down my cock, lift and slide. She feels fucking amazing. She's perfect like this. I could take her all night.

"More," she moans, and my fingers clench around her hips. I should make her wait. I should make her *beg*. But I'm already lifting her, already increasing our pace because she needs it and I can't help but obey.

I bounce her harder, and she gasps, going softer and softer in my arms. "Yesyesyes, like that," she whispers, head whipping back and forth as I drive her toward another release.

"Again." I grip her ass, pumping her up and down as I slide my other hand around, finding her clit. She jerks against me.

Sensitive, I realize. *So sensitive she probably doesn't think she can come again.*

I'll need to show her otherwise.

"Come for me, Parks."

She squirms, shaking her head as tension begins to climb her spine. *Losing her*, I think and grab a handful of that dark hair, pulling her backward until she's arched over me, impaled and trembling and *needing* because by my taking control like this, she's gone even hotter. She's burning alive for me.

And I'm burning for her.

I thumb her clit once, twice. "Come for me, Parker. Come for me *now*."

She does. She comes hard, seizing my forearm and biting down until it smothers scream after scream. It works. She *is* quieter, but I can still hear my name on her lips. It rolls through me like honey and lights me up like gasoline.

TEASER CHAPTER 3 | Parker

He barely lets me catch my breath before he pushing me for another release, another wave of pleasure. I knew Aiden would be demanding, and I knew I'd enjoy it. I just didn't realize how much. My body responds to him like it was made for him.

Like he owns it.

The realization spikes pleasure through me again, and Aiden tightens his grip. I'm pinned to him, but I feel like I'm flying. Soaring. The chair squeaks under our combined weight and he pumps me hard.

It drives a gasp from me. I love it. Love. It. All that teasing, all that soft *soft* play, and it's only made him as wild as it made me. My pussy clenches around his hard length, and now *he* gasps. His breath coasts along the back of my neck, the skin of my spine. I feel him everywhere and it makes me moan.

"Never going to get tired of hearing that," he mutters, fingers flexing against my hips. "Never."

And I love hearing him say that. It turns me frantic, hungry. I ride his shaft, letting it satisfy me in a way that his fingers and thumb never will. I thrust my hips back and he hisses. I grind down...

And he comes.

He swears under his breath. The words are quiet, but I still catch a few—things like *you're perfect* and *beautiful, so beautiful*—and it makes me feel triumphant. I don't remember the last time I felt perfect, let alone beautiful, but right now Aiden makes me feel that way.

He also makes me feel incredibly sexy. Which is kind of hilarious since we're still in his kitchen and I'm still straddling his lap, legs apart and back arched. Before, my head kept wanting me to think about how exposed this position left me—every dip and curve on me was on display—but now, I love it. I'm spent, relaxed. We might be in his apartment, but I feel a thousand miles away.

Aiden is a mini-vacation, I think, and nearly giggle.

He shifts underneath me, and carefully, withdraws. I start to sit up, expecting him to put me away, but he pulls me back, keeping me tight against his chest. It makes our breathing match. In and out, in and out, and ever so slowly I come back to myself.

Reality leaks in: the refrigerator's hum, the moonlight stretching across the floor. Somewhere outside, a horse neighs and I can hear the faint pounding of hoofbeats as they play in the night. It all comes back—and then I feel Aiden. He's *trembling*.

I did that to him, I think. It would make me smile, but suddenly I realize I'm shaky too. Our chemistry is like nothing I've ever experienced. The power nearly knocks me breathless.

"Are you okay?" I whisper.

He rubs his warm hands up my arms. "I'm fucking fantastic."

The force behind the words startles me. It's so raw, so...honest. I glance over my shoulder, taking in Aiden again. The shadowy kitchen light throws his usually blue eyes into darkness, but his blond hair looks almost white. After two months of taking care of the twins, I'm used to beautiful Aiden, smiling Aiden, the man who pretty much looks like sunlight incarnate.

But the Aiden I'm looking at now is nothing like those Aidens. He's straight out of every indecent fantasy I've ever had. The shadows turn his already sharp cheekbones sharper and throw his already hard jawline into something razor-edged. He looks like something I could cut myself on, and then he smiles and his whole expression turns relaxed. He's almost boyish looking as he studies me, smiling at me like everything is perfect.

Gotta admit it certainly feels pretty perfect. I've never come like that before.

"Parks?" He palms my hips, and in spite of the fact that we've used him hard, I can feel his shaft stir. "You okay?"

He's grinning at me like he can't stop, and that makes *me* grin. How did we go from something so intense to something so...light-hearted? I laugh because the whole thing feels ridiculous, but the laugh comes out all shaky. "Yeah, it was fun."

"Only fun? Is that a challenge?"

Heat swirls through me, and I go still. He's teasing, but my body responds like it's been beckoned.

The power he has over you, I think, searching for any pang of nervousness or unease at this realization and...not finding any. That's kinda crazy.

Or maybe it isn't.

When I divorced my ex, it broke me. I'd been so in love with him. I'd followed him clear across the country, leaving my family and friends behind. And he'd taken advantage of that. I'm not the same person anymore. Maybe enjoying Aiden like this is something the New Parker does.

In fact, I want it to be.

I give him a slow smile, feeling how his body instantly tightens against me. *You can have this*, I remind myself. *You can have him.*

Then I say, "Definitely a challenge. Try again."

***

An hour later, I'm coming down again. This time, we're in Aiden's bed and it's probably the softest, best thing I've ever felt. I know that's the sex talking, but I'm struggling to keep my eyes open. Aiden's hard and warm next to me and I can practically feel the smug radiating off him. He's really pleased with himself. With other guys, it would be annoying, but this makes me smile. He loved satisfying me, focusing on me.

And you loved it too, I think, smiling wider. Maybe I should get back to our original argument, the one where he got jealous of Brandon talking to me, but I want to enjoy my bliss right now.

Might as well. After all, I just slept with my boss. There *are* consequences to this.

And just like that, *there's* my twinge of discomfort. I watch the shadows seep up the bare, white walls and tuck my pillow closer to me. We both know my job as nanny to his sister's kids isn't going to be forever. The twins have been living with Aiden ever since he moved to the States, and while they're amazing, they're also holy terrors who were recently thrown out of school for inciting a small riot during class.

That's where I came in. They needed stability. I needed a job. And Aiden? Aiden needed—and still needs—wins at international competitions, not a girlfriend. I frown. Wait. Strike that. I am not his girlfriend. I'm...whatever this is. I'm not sure.

And for a second—okay way more than a second—my body remembers his and it's entirely okay with 'whatever this is.' In fact, it would put up with a lot to have him again.

I shake myself. Get a grip. Aiden's in the U.S. for work, not for play. He rides jumpers for Caleb Reese, owner of Jacks or Better stables. They travel to all the major East Coast competitions, and even though he's only been here maybe six months, people are already whispering about how he's sure to take gold at the next Olympics.

He's getting his life on track, which I totally understand. I'm getting my own life back on track after marrying my boyfriend straight out of high school, moving across the country to help him with his business, and making him my world.

This is dangerous enough with normal people, but my ex was—*is*—a narcissist and I walked away with nothing just to get away from him.

And now you're sleeping with your boss, I think, listening as a horse neighs again in the distance. *Typical of you to make such bad decisions.*

Which unfortunately is the biggest truth about me: I made a terrible decision to marry Matthew, and now I don't trust myself not to make the same mistake again.

I've had these sorts of feelings before—well, almost. Sex with Matthew was never this good, but those butterfly stomach twirls I get when Aiden looks my way? How my heart double-thumps when Aiden gets closer? I know now those are warning signs. I like him too much. I let my feelings override everything.

Like when you rode him on the kitchen table, and then he took you *against the wall, and*—I mentally slap myself. The sex isn't the point. The point is I can't trust my feelings.

The idea makes me sigh, and suddenly Aiden's curving me closer to him. My back fits his chest, and for a moment, all I can think about is how perfect he feels against my shoulder blades. He holds me like he's trying to soothe me, and it threatens to lull me straight to sleep. I shouldn't. I should get up. I should go. But it feels so right to *stay*.

This is more than just lust and crazy attraction. Lying in his arms, I feel safe—and that's really saying something for someone like me. I feel like I've been walking on eggshells most of my adult life, but Aiden and I always talk freely. It's one of my favorite things about us.

There is *no us*, I remind myself, and as I drift off I promise myself there never will be. To protect myself, I need to keep him at arm's length, keep my heart firmly out of reach.

Even if I know I won't be able to resist having him again.

Want the Rest?

...

Get the full version from your favorite book sellers: **emmaashe.com/books**[1]

---

1. http://www.emmaashe.com/books/deeper

LEAVE A REVIEW

Thanks so much for reading! There are a lot of books out there to choose from, I appreciate you trying mine. Even if you completely hated it (really, really hoping you didn't!), I'm a big believer in the importance of reviews. If you could take a moment to **leave a review**[1] to let everyone know what you think, it would be so appreciated. Not only does it help other readers, but it also helps me become a better writer.

All the love,
Emma

---

1. http://www.emmaashe.com/books/deeper

ABOUT THE AUTHOR

Hi! I'm Emma and I hate writing about myself in the third person. I write fairly steamy contemporary romance. *Deeper Than Destiny* is the first book in my Deeper Than Love series. I'm having fun with these, and I hope you enjoy them too.

...

Deeper Than Love
Deeper Than Desire, Prequel[1]
Deeper Than Destiny, Book 1[2]
Deeper Than Lies, Book 2[3]
Deeper Than Secrets, Book 3[4]
Deeper Than Temptation, Book 4[5]

An Indecent Apposal
Something Real, Prequel[6]
Show Me Your Secrets, Book 1[7]
Claiming The Secretary, Book 2[8]
Second Chance Romance, Book 3[9]
All For Her, Book 4[10]

---

1. http://www.emmaashe.com/books/deeper

2. http://www.emmaashe.com/books/deeper

3. http://www.emmaashe.com/books/deeper

4. http://www.emmaashe.com/books/deeper

5. http://www.emmaashe.com/books/deeper

6. http://www.emmaashe.com/books/apposal

7. http://www.emmaashe.com/books/apposal

8. http://www.emmaashe.com/books/apposal

9. http://www.emmaashe.com/books/apposal

10. http://www.emmaashe.com/books/apposal

Better With You, Book 5[11]
Anyone But You, Book 6[12]

...

An Indecent Apposal Volume 1, Books 1-3[13]
An Indecent Apposal Volume 2, Books 4-6[14]

...

An Indecent Apposal Collection 1, Books 1-6[15]

Follow me at Emma Ashe Author on Instagram and Facebook or **sign up**[16] for book release announcements, cover reveals, and bonus content.

11. http://www.emmaashe.com/books/apposal

12. http://www.emmaashe.com/books/apposal

13. http://www.emmaashe.com/books/apposal-set

14. http://www.emmaashe.com/books/apposal-set

15. http://www.emmaashe.com/books/apposal-set

16. http://www.emmaashe.com/signup-book